UNDERSTANDING JANE

RUTHIE RAYBURN

BELL THE CAT BOOKS

For my favorite beta reader
and his fearless cat companion.

1

Somber grey clouds hung over the highway as Jane raced toward Seattle, driving her uncle's old sedan. It was a gloomy day in January, and she was late for work.

She was now only a mile from the Ballard Bridge. The bridge was her usual route into Seattle. She accelerated a little more, but the traffic around her was slowing down. With gritted teeth, she hit the brakes to keep from smashing into the car in front of her. As all the cars on the road crawled to a stop, she saw the two halves of the Ballard Bridge rise high in the air.

"Now?" she groaned. "A fucking yacht needs to go through the canal *now*?"

She ran a hand through her long-bobbed red hair, then turned on the mix CD in her car deck. She'd made it herself —a collection of her favorite '80s new wave and pop hits. Listening to '80s music was the only thing that made her daily commute to Seattle bearable. She felt practically vintage listening to music on a CD, but her car—a deep blue, early 2000s Volkswagen Passat that Uncle Chuck had left her after he'd died—was so old that it wasn't compatible with any of Jane's online playlists. So, she'd had to burn CDs for her commute.

Rain began to spatter the car's windshield. Jane rolled her eyes at the day's insistence on getting worse at every opportunity. She stretched her hand over to the passenger seat, attempting to open her purse, where she kept her cigarettes. She stopped just as her fingers brushed the small cardboard box.

"Not until the end of the day," she chided herself. "Save the lung damage for later."

When Jane entered the offices of the Hope Project Foundation, the non-profit organization where she worked, the reception area was still dark. There were employees in accounting and HR who showed up early and unlocked the main office door each morning. But, as the receptionist, it was Jane's job to turn on the lights.

Knowing her way in the relative darkness, she walked to the bank of light switches in the hall and flipped them on one by one. The fluorescent lights began to hum, and she jumped when they revealed a man sitting on one of the couches in the waiting area.

Who the hell would just sit alone in the dark before the office even opened? "Are you here to meet with someone? Can I help you?" she asked loudly, so anyone else on the floor could hear her.

The man looked up. He was comfortably middle-aged, and had unruly dark hair that was greying at the temples. He seemed perfectly relaxed, as if he were sitting on a couch in his own home. "I *am* here to meet someone. I'm a bit early," he apologized in a slight British accent.

"Do you know the name of the person you're meeting?" Jane's voice was wary. "Maybe I can find them for you?"

Now the man grinned, a quick flash of lips and teeth. "I'm here to speak with Caleb Williams. About the benefit this weekend?"

"Oh," Jane said, relaxing. "Of course, the benefit. Caleb's not usually in this early. Do you want coffee or anything? I have to make it first, but it's a fast machine."

The man waved his hand in the air, dismissing the idea. "Don't go to any trouble."

There was something familiar about him, she thought. He had a striking face, with high, prominent cheekbones, and his dark eyes were round and hooded. Unusual eyes. Maybe that was it. He looked like a person who ought to be remembered.

"It's my job to make coffee for the office," Jane told him, "so I wouldn't be doing it specifically for you."

His lips quirked upward, then quickly straightened, but she saw humor flicker in his eyes. "Well, in that case, yes." He nodded. "Black, please. No extras."

"You got it," she told him, then walked down the hall to the kitchenette.

While she was waiting for the coffee to finish brewing, she wiped down the countertops and straightened the small cubbies that held several varieties of tea. Cleaning the kitchenette was another part of her job. It was boring, mindless work, but after four years of sitting on her ass doing straight data entry, she'd developed a new appreciation for being on her feet. Since she'd only been in this new position for about a year, the novelty had not yet worn off.

When the coffee was finished, she poured some into a plain white mug, grabbed a cocktail napkin, and returned to the man in the waiting area. She set the napkin and steaming mug down in front of him on a glass-topped table, which was covered with glossy magazines featuring Seattle's hotspots—the Space Needle, a snow-capped Mount Rainier, and landscapes with Puget Sound and the Olympic Mountains in the background.

"There you go," Jane said. "Hopefully it tastes okay."

"Thank you." His smile was warm and appealing.

"I'm Jane," she offered. "I'm the receptionist here. So if you need anything, I'm just over there, at the front desk."

"Thank you, Jane." His eyes sparked. "I'm Liam. And I'll let you know."

She paused. "Do you want me to see if Caleb is in early? I can try his office."

Liam flashed a full grin now. "That won't be necessary. I'm certain he isn't in."

Jane left him to go to the reception desk and logged on to her computer. Once she was in the Foundation system, she glanced quickly through her email, making decisions about what to handle first, and what could wait until later.

Next, she checked the general office calendar, which included all of the CEO's meetings. Caleb liked both his assistant and Jane to be aware of his schedule. The first item on his calendar was blocked out for two hours, from 8:00 to 10:00 am: **Initial meeting with Liam Burns.**

Jane paused her scrolling. *Liam Burns?* Liam Burns, the spokesperson for the benefit? Liam Burns, the actor, star of PBS and BBC dramas, who would be human catnip as soon as all the women—and a number of the men—arrived at the office for the day?

She was not one of Burns' admirers, but she was mortified she hadn't recognized him. She was also embarrassed she hadn't given him a more enthusiastic reception. It was her job to welcome guests of the Foundation, and Liam Burns was the week's guest of honor.

Just then, the man himself appeared in front of her receptionist's counter. He set his coffee mug down and smiled at her. Up close, she noticed his dark eyes were tinged with green. He pointed to the mug. "Sorry to bother you. But do you know where I can get more of this?"

She started to stand. "I'll get it for you."

Liam held up his hand. "No, I'll get it myself. Need to stretch my legs. Just point me in the right direction."

Jane got up from her desk and gestured down the hall. "Just keep to your left until you see the room with the refrigerator and coffee machine in it."

He nodded at her, then disappeared down the hall. He'd only been gone for a couple minutes when the front door to the office opened wide, and Caleb called out her name.

"Jane! Is my eight o'clock here yet?"

Her boss's bright blue eyes darted around the lobby as he dropped an enormous black and silver travel mug on the counter with a bang. Caleb never drank the office coffee. He always filled his mug at one of the numerous local coffee shops.

"Yeah," Jane said. "He got here before you. He's...."

"So where is he?" Caleb interrupted her, sounding alarmed. "Did we lose him?"

Liam re-entered the room. "Caleb!" he called out. "Good to see you again."

"Oh, there he is." Caleb heaved a relieved sigh. He turned to Jane with a frustrated expression. "Why didn't you tell me he was here?"

She raised her eyebrows to her hairline.

Liam threw her a smile. "Jane's been fantastic. She

made coffee for me and got me all settled. I've no complaints. Shall we get started?"

"Can you come to my office first?" Caleb said to Liam. "I'm so sorry I wasn't in sooner, but the traffic was terrible."

"Just lead the way."

They started down the hall, in the opposite direction from the kitchenette, to Caleb's office.

"Jane!" Caleb yelled back over his shoulder. "What conference room are we meeting in?"

"South!" she called out.

She began responding to the emails she'd flagged as "urgent." When the scent of a floral perfume announced that Sasha, the Assistant HR Director, was approaching, Jane looked up. "Good morning," she smiled at Sasha.

"Well look at you," Sasha exclaimed. "Is that dress new?"

Jane nodded, smoothing her hands over her figure-hugging navy blue dress. The skirt fell below her knees and the dress had a modest neckline, so it was appropriate for work. Still, she knew she looked hot in it. She'd been blessed with voluptuous curves, and she thought she looked her best in dresses that showed them off. "I went thrifting this weekend," she said.

Sasha, who was willow thin, blond, and almost six feet tall, bent her head down and whispered, "So did you meet him?"

"Meet who?" Jane asked innocently.

"You know who!" Sasha accused. "I know you've got access to Caleb's calendar."

"Yeah," Jane grinned lazily. "I met him, and I made him coffee. We're getting married now."

"You don't even care, do you?" Sasha glared. "You're, like, oblivious. What's he like in person?"

"He's super hot," Jane reported, dutifully. "He also insisted on getting his own coffee refill. I was impressed."

Sasha groaned. "I hate that I'm in HR. There is absolutely no good reason for me to be in any of the meetings with him this week."

Jane shrugged. "So talk to him at the benefit."

"But it would be better if I established rapport first," Sasha fretted.

"First? Before what?"

Sasha rolled her eyes. "Don't make me say it out loud. I'm not supposed to be vulgar. I'm in HR."

"I thought he was married," Jane smirked. She was guessing. She had no idea whether Liam Burns was married or not.

But Sasha's eyes lit up, and she winked. "Not anymore. He's been divorced for a year."

The phone rang, and Jane picked it up as Sasha walked away from the reception desk.

"Good morning," she said, smoothly. "Hope Project Foundation, Jane Daniel speaking. How may I help you?"

2

At ten-thirty, Caleb burst into the reception area and banged his coffee mug on the counter. Again. When Jane looked up, Caleb's bright blue eyes were boring into her.

"Jane," he said, sounding serious.

"Caleb."

"We need sandwiches. For me, Liam, my assistant, and about five other people."

Jane grabbed a pad of paper and a pen. "Do you need me to take orders?"

Her boss waved his hands in the air. "No no no! Too much time. We have to get Liam out of here by one o'clock. He's been more than kind, staying past the end of our meeting. Just order a sandwich platter from somewhere good. Desserts, fruit, stuff like that. We need it by eleven-thirty. Pay extra if you have to."

Caleb drummed his hands on the counter as he started back toward the conference room. He was glowing, as if he, too, were vulnerable to their guest of honor's charm.

Jane called a local sandwich shop that she used for large

groups. While she was on hold, several staff members wandered into the hall near the entry way. Liam Burns was with them. As she gave the sandwich order over the phone, Jane watched Liam interact with Caleb; Caleb's assistant, Nancy; and a few other people on the Foundation's leadership team.

Liam was smooth, she concluded. He was the center of the staff's understated yet devoted attention, and he knew it. Even though everyone around him was buzzing with energy, he was at rest.

It made sense that someone who used his body as a medium for his art would be relaxed while surrounded by a group of overattentive people. Burns' composure was probably something to be admired. However, suddenly, he annoyed Jane. He was *too* smooth. She couldn't imagine him feeling self-conscious, or nervous, or even momentarily tongue-tied. But he must feel that way sometimes. He was human. She wondered if Liam's self-assurance was a mask he wore to conceal the real person underneath. It was possible. He was, after all, an actor.

When the sandwich platter arrived, Jane had one of the administrative assistants deliver it to the South conference room. The girl was glad to do it, to get a glimpse of Liam Burns. After she sent the assistant, Jane regretted not sending Sasha, instead. She knew Sasha would have done it. With pleasure.

Just before one p.m., Caleb walked out to the reception area with Liam, who turned and flashed a quick grin at Jane. "Nice meeting you."

"You too," she replied, politely.

She watched the two men through the glass doors of the entry while they waited for the elevator. They were in earnest conversation, though it looked like Caleb was doing most of the talking.

When Caleb came back inside, his own grin was wide. He banged on the reception counter as he went by. "This is going to be a great week!"

Jane stayed at work late, because Liam Burns' visit had generated extra projects, and she'd been asked to help with the overflow. By the time she left the office, it was after six. It took her longer than usual to get home, so she smoked two cigarettes instead of one. In theory, she was trying to quit. But the best she'd been able to do, so far, was limit her smoking to when she was driving. She'd given herself until she was thirty-five to quit for good. She was thirty-three now. So she figured she was doing relatively well in the cessation of bad habits department.

Once inside her condo, she shuffled to the kitchen to heat up a boxed frozen meal. While she waited for the microwave to finish cooking her dinner, she leaned against the counter and admired the cheerful oak cabinetry Uncle Chuck had installed. She loved her kitchen. Chuck had cooked a lot of meals for her there when he'd been alive. Hanging out in the kitchen made Jane feel close to him. He'd left his condo to her when he died. Even though Chuck was gone, every day in the condo was a reminder of his life.

When her frozen meal was done, she transferred it to a ceramic bowl, and ate standing up. Just as she was finishing, her phone started to ring.

It was her best friend, Bert. Even though he lived across the country, in New York City, he was her closest friend. They spoke to each other almost every day. Bert did most of his consulting work from home, accompanied by a large white Persian cat named Felix.

Jane picked up his call on her way to her bedroom to change. "Hey Bert." She put the phone on speaker, tossed it on the bed, and opened her closet.

"Are you okay?" he asked. "You've usually called to bitch about your day by now."

"Shut up," she said, automatically. She unzipped her dress. Then, because she knew it would drive Bert nuts, she added, "I met someone famous at work today."

"Who?"

"Guess." She dropped the dress to the floor. Then she pulled off her underwear, yanked her big, sky-blue terry robe off a hanger, and bundled herself into it. She scooped her dirty clothes off the floor and pitched them into the laundry hamper.

"The President," Bert guessed.

"Nope."

"Madonna?"

Jane took the phone off speaker, flopped down on her bed, and said, "Nope."

"Brian Williams?"

"You're into him?"

"Jane, will you just tell me who you met today?"

"Liam Burns."

"Oh my God," Bert said, after a moment of shocked silence. "You actually met *Mr. Masterpiece*?"

"Mr. Masterpiece?" Jane repeated. She traced her finger over the raised pattern on her handwoven bedspread.

"It's my nickname for him," he explained. "So. To rephrase: you actually met *Liam Burns*, the British actor. In the flesh? With those *eyes*? And that accent?"

"Most British actors have an accent," she teased. "Most

of them also have eyes."

"Jane. Don't be a bitch."

"Yeah," she relented. "I actually met him. Face to face."

"I think I'm jealous," Bert sighed. "He is so talented. And so fucking hot."

"Didn't he just do one of the Shakespeares for PBS?" Jane asked.

"*King Lear,*" he agreed promptly. "And he was superb. In my opinion, it's the best version of *Lear* PBS has ever done. OH MY GOD, you met Liam Burns! Why didn't you tell me? Why didn't you send a picture? Why didn't you text?!"

"Hey, chill out," she laughed. "I got him coffee, per my job description. After that he was in a conference room all morning. I hardly saw him."

"You could have at least sent me a text," Bert pouted over the phone.

Jane grinned. "I'm sorry."

"What's he like in person?"

Even though Bert could not see her, she shrugged. "He's good looking, I guess. He's not a jerk. Kind of slick, though."

"What do you mean, 'slick?'"

She flipped over on her stomach. "I don't know. A little too confident in his own skin?"

Bert laughed. "And that's a bad thing?"

"I like it when people are moderately nervous. It's endearing."

"Wait, why was Liam Burns even at your office?" he asked. "Is he helping with a benefit or something?"

"Uh huh," Jane confirmed. "We have a benefit this weekend. Work is going to suck all week. I might not even have time to call you and bitch about my day."

"But you have to," Bert insisted. "You have to keep me updated on Mr. Masterpiece."

"I'm not sure how much I'll see him around before the benefit on Saturday," she said. "But sure. I can send you updates."

"That would really make my day," he said solemnly. "So. How are *other* things?"

She played dumb. "What other things?" But she knew what he was driving at. He was prying into her personal life. Or rather, the lack of it.

"Any new acquaintances? Fuck buddies? Or —boyfriends?"

"Fuck buddies are best," she said, cheerfully. "No strings, no pain."

He sighed. "Janey. When are you going to go for something real again? You need something real. You deserve it."

"Hey," she protested. "I *have* real. My job is real. My bills are real. In fact my whole life is one hundred percent real, last time I checked."

"You know what I mean," Bert admonished.

Yes. She knew what he meant. He wanted to know when she would start dating again. Start trying to find "the one." But he also knew her history. He knew why it was hard for her to be in a serious relationship.

"I'll find somebody when I'm ready," she said. "Don't rush me."

"It's been nine years," he reminded her.

Before Jane could come up with a retort, a loud, drawn out meow sounded in the background.

"How's Felix?" she asked.

"He needs his dinner." Bert sighed again. "I should go feed him. Don't forget to text me when Mr. Masterpiece shows up! And take pictures if you can."

After promising to at least text, she hung up the call. She got in the shower, then bundled herself back into her robe, and sat cross legged on the bed with her back against the wall.

Boyfriends. Serious relationships. Jane shuddered. *No thanks*, she thought. Still, she knew her best friend meant well. He just wanted her to be happy.

She'd met Bert when she'd been getting out of a bad relationship. Her boyfriend, Carl, had been abusive, and Bert's friendship had helped her heal. He'd provided incredible emotional support. But he'd also been good at helping her with practical things, like getting a restraining order against Carl. He had taken her to a self defense course. He'd even brought her to a shooting range and taught her how to use a gun, though she'd ultimately decided against carrying one. Most of all, however, Bert had made her feel safe, when feeling safe was something she'd needed more than anything else. Maybe even more than love, she thought.

She yawned, loudly, and laughed at the sudden explosion of noise in the room. The moment of hilarity startled her out of her thoughts. She'd spent enough time traveling down a melancholy memory lane for one evening.

She wondered what Liam Burns was doing. Probably something boring, like watching television in his hotel room. Or maybe not. Maybe he was shagging someone from the Hope Project Foundation. It was definitely possible. He wouldn't have had trouble finding a willing participant.

"Or even several," Jane said, aloud, then grinned. It was going to be fun watching everyone fight over Liam Burns for the rest of the week. Especially because he wasn't her type. Then, she wondered what her type actually was. Once, she had thought Carl was her type. But she'd been wrong. She did not ever want to be wrong again.

3

Liam Burns was not on either Caleb's or the office's general schedule Tuesday. All day, however, the phones rang off the hook with final calls related to Saturday's benefit.

Jane hadn't been asked to help plan the event itself. She was relieved, because she disliked event planning even more than she disliked cooking. Both activities were items on a long list of things she felt women were expected to enjoy, but that she actually hated to do.

On Wednesday, Liam showed up mid-morning. As he and Caleb passed by her desk, they appeared to be deep in conversation. Neither of them acknowledged her. Still, Jane sent a dutiful text to Bert.

Mr. Masterpiece is in the building.

Bert immediately replied: *Pictures.*

Jane responded: *No. Am not your stalker by proxy.*

Bert shot back: *Bitch.*

Thursday morning, when Jane glanced through the schedule, she didn't see any meetings with Liam Burns, so she sent Bert a preemptive text.

No Masterpiece on the schedule today.

Then she began working on a data entry project she'd been putting off because of the crazy volume of phone calls. The project was easy, but tedious: transferring addresses from a spreadsheet to the Foundation's database. At least data entry wasn't the only thing she did for this job. She yawned, then stared back at the screen. Copy. Paste. Save record. Repeat.

"Well that's some face. Are you feeling ill? You look a bit green."

Jane glanced up. Liam Burns was standing at her receptionist's counter. He aimed one of his quick grins at her. Up close, his cheekbones were even more pronounced. He looked freshly shaved, and Jane caught a hint of cologne.

"Not sick," she said to Liam, "Just bored."

He patted one of his ears. "Couldn't you listen to something? Sitcoms? Symphonies?"

She looked pointedly at the phone. "I still have to hear the phone if it rings."

He nodded his head. "Good point."

She thought he would leave, then, but he stayed put. Did he expect something from her? Admiration? Fangirling? She couldn't praise him for any of his films or TV shows, because she'd never seen them. "Can I get something for you?" she asked. "Do you need sandwiches? Coffee?"

He shook his head. "No sandwiches. No coffee."

"All right." Jane returned to her screen. Copy. Paste. Save record. Repeat. After she had done several more records, she looked up again. Liam was still leaning against the reception counter. He was *still* watching her. It was unnerving, and he was making it difficult to do her job. She suspected he was angling for attention. Otherwise, he would have left her alone by now.

"Is there something else you need?" she asked, trying, but failing, to keep a note of exasperation out of her voice. "Someone I can page for you, maybe?"

Liam ignored her question. "If you *could* listen to something while you're working, what would it be?"

"'80s music," she replied, promptly. "Or maybe the Carol Burnett Show."

"Burnett is physical comedy," Liam objected. "You'd want to see that. Not just listen."

"Yeah I guess," Jane agreed. "So it would definitely be '80s music. Look, are you sure you don't need me to get Caleb for you?"

Liam's eyes glinted in a way that reminded her of his quick *smiles*, but his lips did not move. "I'm just making conversation," he said. "But yes. I mean no. I don't need you to get Caleb for me. In fact, I'm waiting for Caleb. We're going to lunch."

"Have you been here all morning?" she asked.

Liam nodded solemnly. "Yes. I've been here *all* morning." Then, leaning closer to Jane, he said, in a quiet, conspiratorial tone, "I'm finding Caleb a bit demanding. I've never met anyone quite like him. I wouldn't usually give this much time for—something like this."

Jane smirked in spite of herself. "That's very sweet of you. I'm sure he appreciates it."

Liam seemed to smirk back at her, then, but she wasn't sure. He could change his facial expressions so quickly. As he kept his eyes on her face, she was surprised to feel her pulse quicken, and a bit of color rush to her cheeks.

"Liam!" Caleb's voice rang from the hall.

Liam turned away from Jane to Caleb. "Ready to go?" he asked.

"Yes, finally," Caleb said. "I hope Jane's been treating you well."

"Indeed," Liam confirmed. "We were just discussing our mutual love of '80s music."

Jane raised her eyebrows, but remained silent.

Her boss pounded on the counter and Jane jumped involuntarily. Caleb had used more force than usual. "That reminds me," Caleb exclaimed to Jane. "Could you make a playlist for the benefit on Saturday?"

"A what?" she asked, not sure she'd heard him right.

"A playlist," Caleb was impatient. "My assistant told me you have encyclopedic musical knowledge."

"I do? She did?" She tried to recall a relevant conversation with Caleb's assistant. She interacted with Nancy often enough, but Jane couldn't think of any time she'd made an effort to demonstrate her knowledge of music—encyclopedic or otherwise—to Nancy.

"Yes!" Caleb's voice was becoming excited and somewhat high pitched. "I want to do something different with the music. We killed the live band idea weeks ago. We were going to use a satellite radio station, but how much better would it be to have a playlist specifically curated for our event, around some sort of theme?"

"A theme? What kind of a theme? Does it have to match the event decor?" Jane began to feel panicked. Was Caleb nuts? Two days before the benefit, and he wanted her to come up with a playlist based on a *theme*?

Liam half turned, so he could speak to Jane and Caleb at the same time. "You know," he mused, "It's amazing, but Jane and I were just talking about this. If you need a musical theme, Caleb, I think 'The '80s' would be a fantastic choice."

Caleb frowned. "Really? I was thinking more upbeat.

Like contemporary dance music. Something to make people get up and move around."

"'80s music is eminently danceable," Liam said. "I'm sure Jane would agree."

"I do." She looked from Liam, to Caleb, then back to Liam. "It's irresistible. '80s music. For dancing? People love dancing to '80s music."

"Maybe." Caleb seemed unconvinced.

"We *are* running out of time before the benefit," Liam pointed out. "I, for one, would get a huge kick out of an '80s dance party. I'd wager most of your guests would, too. People love nostalgia."

"All right," Caleb relented. "I guess I did spring this on everyone at the last minute. So. Jane. Can you do it? Will you do it?"

Both men watched her. Caleb was anxious, waiting for confirmation that his inspired last minute plans would be realized. Liam, Jane knew, thought the whole thing was hilarious.

"Sure," she said, trying to sound enthusiastic. "I'll do it."

"Great!" Caleb pounded on the counter again. "We'll need four hours of music, no duplicates. Oh, and you'll have to show up early with the playlist on a device, or make it accessible online. Probably both, just to be safe. Liam, let's go. I'm starving!"

As they started out the door, Liam looked back over his shoulder, and winked at Jane.

On her lunch hour, she sought out Caleb's assistant. She found Nancy in her cubicle, stuffing letters into envelopes.

Jane leaned over Nancy's cubicle wall. "Can I talk to you for a minute?"

"Sure," Nancy said. "This week is crazy, isn't it?"

"Definitely crazy," Jane agreed. "So. I just found out I'm making this playlist for the benefit on Saturday?"

Nancy stopped stuffing envelopes. She looked surprised, and a bit horrified. "Caleb actually told you to do that?" she asked.

"Yeah. He did. He said *you* told him I have an 'encyclopedic knowledge of music.'"

Nancy's face fell. She motioned rapidly for Jane to go behind the cubicle walls, so they could speak more privately. Jane complied. Then she perched on the edge of Nancy's desk, and waited.

"So," Nancy said in a low voice. "Remember when we all went out for drinks last year? Around St. Patrick's Day? Just after you started working here?"

"Vaguely," Jane said.

"Well, we were in this bar, and you—well you were pretty drunk—but every song that came on, you yelled out what it was. You knew *every single* song. It was kind of amazing. But Caleb...."

Nancy looked around her cubicle as if Caleb might be hiding in it. Then she lowered her voice even more, so Jane had to lean forward to hear her.

"We had everything set for Saturday," Nancy said in an almost-whisper. "*Everything*. The music was planned. There was nothing left to do. And then this morning, Caleb gets this bug up his butt about having a playlist personally curated for the benefit. *This morning. Two days before.* He wanted me to hire someone to do it. Do you know how insane that is at this late date? There are so many other things I need to actually *do*. I told Caleb to have someone in the office do it. And he asked who. So I suggested you."

"Because I knew some songs at a bar when I was drunk that one time?" Jane guessed.

"I'm sorry Jane." Nancy looked chagrined. "I didn't think he'd actually ask you or anyone else to make a playlist. I figured he'd get distracted and forget the whole thing. Everything was already set," she repeated, looking a bit bewildered.

Jane sighed. It wasn't Nancy's fault. Being Caleb's assistant was a hard job. He was demanding and unpredictable. It was a bad combination.

She cracked a smile, to let Nancy know she wasn't angry with her. "I guess I know what I'll be doing Friday night."

"Holy fuck!" Jane yelled into her phone. "How am I going to pull together a four-hour playlist by Saturday?"

Felix meowed loudly through the other end of the phone.

"I'm sorry Felix," she apologized.

"Felix is fine," Bert assured her. "But he *is* worried about my lost hearing. Do you have to yell?"

Jane flopped on her bed next to her phone. "I'm sorry. I think I'm sick of this job. No. I'm not. But Caleb is warped."

"He does sound a bit eccentric," Bert admitted.

"Seriously warped," she insisted. "At least I'm going on vacation next week. Thank fuck." She began picking at the bedspread, then stopped. She would ruin it if she wasn't careful.

"There you go," Bert encouraged. "Keep your mind on your vacation. Happy thoughts. So anyway. You said you talked to him, again, right? Mr. Masterpiece? Before Caleb showed up and ruined your day?"

Yeah," Jane said, irritably. "Liam came over and talked to me, for like, two seconds. What about it?"

"Can I ask you a question?" he ventured. He sounded hesitant, which was unlike him.

"Sure," she said in a softer voice. "What's your question?"

"What does Liam Burns smell like, when he's up close like that?"

Jane sat up. "I'm hanging up the phone now."

"Jane," Bert sounded a bit petulant. "I'm serious."

"Oh, God, I don't know. Like a fucking pine tree. Like Eau-de-Man pine-tree cologne."

He sighed. "You'll pull off the playlist. You're the world class DJ no one's ever heard of."

"Gee, thanks."

"You know what I mean. You know tons of music and you're great at putting it all together. I still have that old mixed CD you made me."

"Do you really?"

"Absolutely," he said. "So—does he really smell like a pine tree?"

"Hanging up now." She pressed "end" on the call.

On Friday, the office closed early, at four o'clock. Just before closing, Sasha came up to Jane at the reception counter.

"What are you wearing Saturday?" Sasha asked without preamble.

"Clothes?"

"Don't be a smart ass."

"I don't know," Jane shrugged. "A dress, probably. That's what I always wear."

"So are you doing vintage cleavage, or vintage conservative?" Sasha probed.

"I haven't decided yet. Why, what are you wearing?"

"I don't know. I'm going crazy trying to figure it out. That's why I asked you what you're wearing."

Jane lowered her voice. "Is this about Liam?"

Sasha's face fell into a maudlin expression. "I've only had one conversation with him all week. Tomorrow's my last chance."

Jane cocked an amused eyebrow. "So make sure you talk to him tomorrow."

"Seriously Jane," Sasha groaned. "How are you not affected by him?"

"I don't know," she shrugged. "Not my type, I guess."

"What *is* your type?"

She forced a smile and said, "Good question."

4

"I can quit anytime," Jane reminded herself. "I can always get another crappy job."

She was stationed by the punchbowl at the far end of the buffet table. Someone she didn't recognize walked by. When she looked up, the person smirked and kept going. Jane dropped a sarcastic curtsy, then stirred the punch with the ladle.

When she'd arrived at the downtown luxury hotel where the benefit was being held, Caleb had pulled her aside. "People expect to see your face. Seeing you makes everyone feel at home. C'mon, Jane. Just hang out at the punchbowl for the first couple of hours. Then we'll make it self serve, and you can enjoy the party."

So this was her reward for delivering the '80s playlist to the benefit: exile at the punchbowl.

Enticing aromas from the silver serving dishes on the buffet table kept wafting in Jane's direction. She'd seen other people walk by with full plates, so she knew there was chicken Kyiv, nutted rice pilaf, and herbed mashed potatoes in the serving dishes. She was starving, but she couldn't eat yet, because she was stuck at her post.

Liam Burns, the guest of honor, arrived ten minutes before the benefit officially kicked off. From the moment he entered the room, event guests and Foundation employees mobbed him in the hesitant, understated way that was typical of people who worked for or were affiliated with the Foundation.

The event was a fashion free-for-all. Some of the men wore suits; some wore jeans and button down shirts. Many of the women were in party dresses, but others wore business casual outfits. A few were also wearing jeans. Jane had selected her own dress at the last minute: a forest green shift with a high scoop neck. No cleavage.

Caleb got behind a lectern on a small stage to introduce Liam Burns. Then, Liam proceeded to give a short speech filled with self-deprecation, wit, and solemn words of praise for the evening's cause, a benefit for local patients who suffered from Multiple Sclerosis. All the Foundation's benefits were tied to the Pacific Northwest in some way, and the region was notorious for having an unusually high number of MS cases.

Liam's speech was perfect, Jane knew, but again, he irritated her. It was his insufferable smoothness. She was certain he was masking a real human being beneath his veneer of studied calm. Why she wanted him to crack, she was not sure, but some part of her was hungry to see a less put together, less controlled Liam Burns.

When he ended his speech with a short anecdote about his friend who suffered from MS, Jane felt like an asshole for wanting him to crack. The cause clearly had real meaning for him. Even if his composure was artificial—as Jane suspected it was—he wasn't shallow.By the time everyone had eaten dinner, Jane had been on punchbowl duty for an hour and a half. Soon, she would be allowed to eat. If there was any food left by then. Her stomach rumbled.

Her '80s playlist was blaring in the background, but no one was dancing. Most of the employees and paying guests were standing around in groups with drinks, chatting. A few of them were seated at white-draped and candle-topped tables that had been placed around the edges of the room.

So far, Jane had served punch to only three people. Now, she looked down at the bowl. She didn't know who'd made the punch, but it was an unappetizing shade of red. There were small bits of ice still floating in it.

She watched Liam work the room. He moved from one social cluster to the next, engaging multiple people in conversation, doing more listening than talking. Occasionally, he would say something that made everyone around him laugh. He never stayed too long in one place. She wondered if he was having fun. If he wasn't, he was good at faking it.

Besides a grudging appreciation for his quirky physical magnetism, Jane remained unimpressed with Liam Burns. There was something too deliberate about him—the way he briefly put a hand on men's shoulders when speaking with them, or the way he stood at a measured distance from every woman he talked to. He seemed amused, as if he knew they were all secretly dying for him to invade their space.

Her stomach rumbled again, louder than it had before. Caleb, she decided, was an ass. She was considering feigning sickness when she saw Liam break from the group he'd been speaking with. He began walking in her direction. His gait was slow, and he gave off a dual vibe of wanting to seem invisible, but also of being aware that most people in the room were watching him.

Liam continued his lazy approach. His clothes fit the informal dress code: dark, well-tailored pants, and a light blue button down shirt, tucked in. He looked good with his shirt tucked in. His unruly dark hair had been tamed for the evening.

He was, without a doubt, on his way to the punchbowl. "Liam Burns drinks punch?" Jane muttered under her breath.

Then he was in front of her, wearing a half smile. "Do you always talk to yourself?" he asked.

"Only in public at social functions," she replied, promptly. She was gratified when the expression on his face did not change. Same half smile, no movement. A mask. It confirmed her assessment of him. He was careful and contrived.

Liam pointed to the punch. "Can I have a cup of—whatever that is?" The chunks of ice had almost melted, but the beverage was still blood-colored.

"You may." Jane picked up a cup and ladled punch into it.

When she handed it to him, their fingers touched. The moment of contact was fleeting, but she was sure he'd made it happen on purpose. She felt electric tingles run up her arm and spread across her chest. Yes. All right. He was magnetic, and attractive. But also slick, she reminded herself.

Liam thanked her for the punch as he took it from her, then, with the same half smile, said, "If I *may*, could I ask why you're hiding out here behind the punchbowl when everyone else…" he gestured to the rest of the room, where some of Jane's co-workers were starting to sneak looks over at the two of them, "…is over there?"

"I'm here to help," Jane explained. "I'm providing punch to the guests."

"No one is drinking punch," Liam pointed out.

"You are," she retorted.

"I haven't actually drunk any of this yet," he corrected. Then he grinned, and his whole face transformed. It wasn't one of his quick smiles; this one lasted. Warmth touched his eyes, and Jane felt her own face flush.

She gestured to his cup. "Maybe you should drink it then, since you came all the way over here to get it."

He took a sip of the punch, his eyes on hers. "That's not why I came over here," he said.

Inwardly, Jane rolled her eyes. Seduction-laced lines. Pointed looks. He could probably do it in his sleep.

"So, how's the punch?" she asked.

"Awful," he admitted, his eyes mirthful.

"Yeah, I figured."

"You should join the party," he told her, abruptly dropping his 'man-coming-on-to-a-woman' tone.

The shift in his demeanor was so quick, in fact, that Jane felt an almost physical jolt in her gut. She stared at him.

"You standing over here by yourself is bullshit." Liam lowered his voice. "Caleb is kind of an ass."

Jane grinned in spite of herself. "I was just thinking that."

Liam returned her grin. "So forget about Caleb and his punch. Come join the party."

A loud female voice interrupted them. "There you are!"

Sasha came over and stood by Liam. She'd decided on a royal blue wraparound dress that showed off her long legs and her cleavage.

She smiled and touched Liam's arm. "A few of us wanted to ask you a couple questions about your work with the Children's Theater Foundation? Would that be all right? I don't want to interrupt your conversation with Jane, of course."

She struggled to keep a straight face. Sasha was angling for more than interrupting a conversation. She'd been consumed with lust ever since Liam had arrived at the Foundation. Tonight, for Sasha, Jane was competition. In fact, tonight, for Sasha: everyone was competition.

Jane knelt and retrieved her purse and coat from underneath the banquet table, where she'd hidden them. When she straightened up, Sasha was still chatting to Liam.

"See you all later," Jane told them. "I'm heading out."

"Geez, Jane, what are you doing over here, anyway?" Sasha asked.

"It was Caleb's idea."

"Caleb is an ass," Sasha said, annoyed.

"So now we have consensus," Jane grinned, and saw Liam's lips quirk upwards. Then, his face resumed its usual mask.

"Don't you want to stick around, at least for awhile?" he said to Jane. "I insist you stay for dinner. You've earned it. I can vouch for the food. It's much better than the punch."

Jane hesitated. She looked across the room, to where a number of Foundation employees were observing the ménage à trois by the punchbowl—some surreptitiously, some with open curiosity.

And then, Caleb was there, busting up their threesome

with a burst of zealous energy. "Liam! I found you! So sorry we were cut off earlier..." Caleb began.

"Quite all right," Liam cut in, sounding more stereotypically British than he had for the entire week.

"Jane!" Caleb exclaimed, noting her coat and purse. "Are you leaving?"

"Yes." She gave Caleb a quick salute. "Punch duty completed. Punching out for vacation."

The CEO looked puzzled. "You're going on vacation? Why?"

Sasha cut in. "She's had it scheduled for months. People do go on vacation now and then."

Caleb sighed dramatically, then turned back to Liam. "As I was saying, I'm so sorry we were interrupted earlier, because I want to discuss future collaborations with you. Tonight has been such an incredible success."

Liam was polite. "Of course. Perhaps next week? We could set up a phone call?"

"Definitely," Caleb nodded vigorously. "We can hash out the details next week, but I would love to start brainstorming ideas tonight. I have three projects I think you would be perfect for. Maybe we could find a conference room?"

Liam smiled one of his most charming smiles. "Perhaps. What are your ideas?"

Caleb's eyes blazed bright blue. "Well, first of all, there's the matter of our Northwest salmon. Many are endangered species. They're essential for the livelihoods of commercial fishermen, and also for maintenance of the local food chain. Did you know the iconic Orca whale is almost completely dependent upon our salmon runs for its survival? Destroy the salmon, and there are no more whale-watching tours."

"That would be sad indeed," Liam agreed.

Jane stole a surreptitious glance at Sasha. But Sasha's eyes were glued on Liam. A tremulous smile appeared on her lips as she attempted to make eye contact with him from underneath her lashes.

"Well, it's been awesome catching up with you all," Jane broke in, "but think I'm going to grab a bite to eat, then head home." She smiled at everyone. "See you guys in two weeks."

Sasha's relief was palpable. "Have a wonderful vacation, Jane!"

"Yes. But make it a quick two weeks," Caleb added. To Liam, he said, "She's the most capable receptionist we've ever had."

"I don't doubt it." Liam turned to Jane. "You're really leaving?"

"Right after I hit the buffet, " she confirmed. "It was great meeting you."

Liam offered his hand, and Jane shook it, ignoring the half irritated, half bewildered expression in his eyes. Then she turned on her heel and walked toward the buffet, aware her hips were swinging more than usual. Liam might not be her type, but some primal part of her brain wanted him to see what she had to offer. And in the ass department, she had plenty. Definitely more than Sasha.

5

Liam had been right, the food did look better than the punch. Jane gathered a plate with chicken Kyiv, rice pilaf, a vegetable medley, and a couple mini-desserts from the dessert platter. She took her full plate in the direction of the white-draped round tables at the edge of the room.

Many of the tables, she observed with relief, were empty. After standing at the punchbowl for two hours, she didn't exactly feel like making small talk with her co-workers, or with strangers.

She settled at an empty table, taking off her coat and laying it over a chair. The tables were situated in relative darkness compared to the rest of the room, and each tabletop was set with a flameless candle inside a round, clear glass globe.

Now that she was finally seated, the room seemed more festive. Best of all, loosened up by alcohol, people were beginning to dance to her playlist. Nancy looked like she was having a particularly good time.

Jane watched her co-workers on the makeshift dance floor as they tried to figure out how to transition their moves from Taylor Dane's "Tell it to My Heart" to Poison's "Talk Dirty to Me." Then, without warning, Liam Burns slid into the empty chair next to her.

He pointed up toward the speakers in the ceiling. "This is your playlist?"

"Yup," Jane confirmed.

He gave her a quizzical look. "You've got a strange sense of humor, haven't you?"

She looked away from the dancers, who were doing their best to master the hair metal vibe. "What makes you say that?" she laughed.

"Your segues," he replied. "So many of them are...absurd."

She assumed a mock-serious tone. "We all do what we can for the world." She resumed eating. The music shifted again, from Poison to Squeeze.

"Absurd," Liam muttered under his breath, loud enough for Jane to hear. He raised one finger. "And you cheated. This song is from 1979."

Jane grinned, but remained silent. She wasn't going to acknowledge he was right. "What happened to Caleb and Sasha?"

"Caleb started lecturing about the harmful effects of dairy products. I'll confess I'm a bit fond of cheese, so I made an excuse and escaped." He gestured toward Jane's meal. "Aren't you drinking?"

Jane shook her head. "Never at work functions. That's how you end up sleeping with someone like Caleb."

Liam leaned toward her and lowered his voice. "You want to hear a secret? I'm hiding from Caleb. I'm more than happy to help with the cause, but if I have to listen to him lecture on the scourge of milk and cheese for even five more seconds, I'm going to shove him up a cow's ass."

Jane choked on her final bite of rice pilaf. Liam made a fist and pounded gently between her shoulder blades. She unceremoniously recovered the bite and swallowed.

"I'm sorry," he apologized. "That was my fault."

"It *was* your fault. Jokes about Caleb could literally kill me." She could still feel the imprint of Liam's hand on her back. She twisted her spine slightly to the right, then to the left, to try to shake off the lingering sensation, which, if she was honest, was not an unpleasant sensation at all.

"I hope you don't mind if I hang out here?" Liam asked. "I need to avoid Caleb and that nightmarish dairy-bashing scenario. I'm not kidding. I felt completely trapped. And, to be frank, a bit guilty about my cheese consumption."

"Don't worry," Jane patted his arm. "Caleb makes all of us feel that way sometimes." Then she pulled her hand back quickly, wondering what she was doing. Flirting? She didn't want to flirt with Liam Burns. It was on the tip of her tongue to tell him she was leaving, when he said:

"Could I ask what might sound like a rude question?"

She shrugged. "I guess? As long as I'm not obligated to answer." Without the receptionist's counter between them, she could sense a quiet intensity behind Liam's calm persona. She hadn't noticed that before. Suddenly, she had a hard time figuring out what to do with her hands. She reached instinctively for her purse, to get a cigarette. Then she remembered smoking was not allowed at the event.

Now Liam smiled. Crinkles formed around his dark eyes. "No obligation to answer my question whatsoever. So, are you ready?"

She tried to smile. "Hit me."

"Do you like your job?"

Jane stared at him, then admitted, "I don't know."

"I assume you went to university?"

"Sure. I graduated from college."

"To be the Foundation's eminently capable reception-ist?" he joked.

"No," she said, irritated. "To earn a white-collar paycheck. Why do you care if I like my job? Why do *you* act?"

"Because I love it," he answered. "And because it spares me having to hold a regular job."

"Well," Jane said. "That's great. I'm glad you love it and that you don't have to be, uh, regular?"

"Oh no. I am *all for* being regular. Fiber cereal every morning."

She laughed. She wanted to text Bert. *Mr. Masterpiece just made a joke about poo.*

But as her laughter died, she thought what she wanted most was to be in her car, on the way back home. Besides, Liam was probably just bored. He was likely needling her with questions just to avoid Caleb and pass the time. She stood up and forced a friendly smile. Then she retrieved her purse from the chair next to her, and set it on the table. "It's been good talking to you. But—I'm going now."

Liam's face fell. "I've pissed you off."

"No. I'm just tired. I was up late." She gestured to the speakers in the ceiling. "You know, making the playlist?"

He stood up, too. "I'll walk you to your car."

"You don't need to do that. I gave my key to the valet. I can wait in the lobby."

But Liam moved around her and took her coat from the chair where she'd left it. Then he held the coat open for her with a flourish. "So I'll walk you to the lobby."

Jane let him help her with the coat. The minute he was near, the heat from his body made her feel dizzy. He was businesslike and respectful as he helped her get the coat on, and he moved out of her personal space while she fastened the buttons. Still, the brief contact left her agitated.

For the past week, she'd assumed she was above the emotional and sexual freakout that had swept through the office because of Liam Burns. Emotionally, she still felt removed. But whenever he was near enough to touch her, he got to her. And, he could make her blush. Pretending she was immune to his physical magnetism was sort of the same thing as lying.

"Ready?" Liam asked.

She nabbed her purse and slung it over her shoulder. "Yep."

He extended his hand outward. "Lead the way."

Jane started through the room, trying to skirt the edges of it as she headed for the exit. She could feel Liam following her. Then, she heard him say "*shit*" under his breath. Suddenly, he came up behind her and put his arm around her shoulders. He turned her gently away from the exit. More tingles danced across her skin as he touched her.

"What are you doing?" she asked.

"I'm sorry," he said, quietly. "But please. Walk with me for a minute, will you?"

Mystified, Jane followed him back the way they'd come, around the edge of the room, past the white-draped tables. He'd let go of her, but she followed him anyway. It was curiosity, she told herself. What he was doing made no sense, so, she had to find out what he was up to. Right?

He led her to a back corner of the room, where there was a heavy metallic door with a small glass window on the top half of it. Liam opened the door, and gestured for Jane to follow him. Without thinking, she did. When the door slammed shut behind them, they were in a concrete-walled emergency stairway.

Liam slumped against the wall, then grinned triumphantly at Jane. "We lost him."

Her surprised laughter echoed in the stairwell. "Lost who?"

"Caleb. We were heading straight for him. There was no way we were getting out of that banquet room without another impassioned sermon about the evil practice of humans eating food intended for baby cows."

"Oh my GOD!" Jane laughed harder. "Are you actually that scared of Caleb? You could have told him you had to take a phone call or something." She went for the handle to open the door, but it wouldn't budge. Panicked, she turned to Liam. "We're locked in!"

6

Liam tapped his finger to his temple. "We're not locked in. We can exit at the lobby level. It's only ten floors down."

Jane cast a dubious glance at her shoes. Her heels weren't ridiculously high, but they were not the best shoes for traipsing down ten flights of stairs.

"I'll help you," Liam said, holding out his arm. "We can take it slow."

Why did that sound like an innuendo? Or was she reading too much into it? She looked up at him, and he gave her one of his quick smiles. She took a breath, then took his arm.

They started down the stairway. He matched her careful pace as they descended the stairs, side-by-side. His arm was warm, solid and strong. She had to admit, it was a relief to have his support.

"Are you all right?" he asked.

"Doing great!" she said, a bit too cheerfully. The stairway was narrow, and he was so close to her. With her hand on his arm, she could feel energy humming through him, and his subtle pine-scented cologne seemed to fill the stairwell. He did have an inviting vibe. If he'd been her type, she would have been swooning.

Suddenly, her heel caught on a stair and she stumbled. Liam steadied her.

"Thanks," she laughed. "Almost lost it, there. Maybe I should slide downstairs on my butt instead."

"I'm sorry." He sounded genuinely chastened. "This *is* a bit daft."

"Oh well, we're here now, right?" She'd lost count of how many flights they'd descended. There was a double flight of stairs between each floor, so in a way, they were actually hoofing it down twenty flights of stairs.

"You're taking it very well," he said.

"I don't have much choice at this point, do I?" she laughed. She stopped and called out, "HELLOOO!" Her voice echoed and bounced off the walls.

Liam chuckled. "What are you doing?"

"Just wanted to see how it would sound. I mean, since we're here."

"HELLOOOOOOOOOO!" he yelled, and his resonant voice reverberated through the stairwell.

"See, it's fun, right?"

"I've certainly had less fun," he agreed.

Just when Jane started to feel a burn in the muscles of her calves and thighs, they reached the end of the stairs. There was a big green "Exit" sign above the door. She sighed with relief as Liam went for the door and pushed on the handle. He wiggled it. Then wrenched it.

"What's going on?" she asked.

He looked sheepish. "Unfortunately, this door also appears to be locked."

She stared. "No. You've *got* to be kidding. You're kidding, right?" She went over to the door. "Let me try."

Liam stood aside as Jane attempted to open the door. But she could not make it budge. Through the small sliver of a window in the top of the door, she could see the hotel lobby. But only a glimpse of it.

"Shouldn't this open from the inside?" she demanded. "You said it would open from the inside!"

"Well. I assumed it would open from the inside. This is an emergency exit stairway. I don't know how anyone can exit in an emergency if the emergency exit door is locked."

"But it *is* locked," she pointed out.

"Obviously," Liam sounded irritated.

Jane gave him a baleful stare. "This was your idea." Before he could form a retort, she raised her fist and began pounding on the door repeatedly. "Hey! HEY! CAN ANYONE HEAR US? We're stuck in here! HEY! HELP! *HELP*!!!"

Liam took her elbow, gently. "Don't hurt yourself. There's got to be a better way."

Even in their predicament, his light touch on her elbow did things to her, inside. She had a strong urge to feel his hands on more of her. Not just on her elbow. To kill the urge, she went over to the concrete wall of the landing and leaned against it, then folded her arms across her chest.

"Someone's got to open the door eventually," Liam reasoned.

"Sure," Jane groaned. "Like, two months from now, when they have a fire drill."

"I am truly sorry," he apologized. "This wasn't the plan."

"What *was* your plan?" she asked.

Liam slid his hands in his pants pockets. He came over to her, and leaned against the metal railing, facing the locked door. "My plan was to walk you to the lobby, then out to your car."

"You know none of that was necessary, right?"

"I know," he smiled. "But that was the plan."

"I don't need anyone to walk me anywhere," she persisted. "I would have been perfectly safe."

He ducked his head. "Chivalry wasn't the reason I offered to walk you out."

She licked her lips, involuntarily. "So why did you? Offer, I mean?"

Liam looked directly at her, and their eyes locked. A crazy thought surfaced in her mind. What would it feel like if he kissed her?

Her lips parted as she returned Liam's gaze. Did people ever have sex in emergency stairwells? It had been awhile since she'd been with anyone. Too long. What was it people said about climbing mountains? That they did it just because they were there?

The exit door banged open, then, and a uniformed guard stood in the doorway. "How you folks doing?" he asked, amiably.

"Oh my God!" Jane exclaimed. "How did you know we were here! Did you hear us banging on the door?"

The guard, who looked barely older than a high school student, shrugged his shoulders. "Didn't hear a thing. But we saw you." He pointed above his head. Jane followed his finger, and spotted a tiny security camera mounted in a corner over the landing.

"Oh." She snuck a quick look at Liam. "Of course. We were on camera."

She felt silly about her sex-in-the-stairwell fantasy, then. If they'd actually done it, it would have been filmed. But of course, it never would have happened. She'd been reacting to Liam like a dopey fan, the same way everyone else at the Foundation had been doing all week. Apparently, she wasn't immune to his charm after all.

Liam spoke to the guard in a sharp tone. "It seems a bit odd that a door clearly marked with an exit sign should be locked. How can anyone leave the building in an actual emergency?"

Still amiable, the guard said, "The doors unlock when any sort of alarm goes off. It's automatic."

"Oh. I see." Liam was immediately contrite. "Of course."

They followed the security guard to the hotel lobby.

Liam shook the guard's hand. "Thank you very much. I'm sorry if we caused you any trouble. It was entirely my fault. I was trying to dodge a conversation."

The security guard grinned. "Happens more often than you think. You folks have a nice night." He ambled off.

Liam turned to Jane. "I apologize for putting you through all that."

She laughed, then shrugged. "I guess it turned out okay. Right?"

"Right." He grimaced. "I suppose I should go back upstairs."

"You *are* the guest of honor," she agreed.

Liam was decisive. "I'm walking you to your car. Then I'll go upstairs." "All right." She raised her eyes to his face. "I'll go to reception and tell them to bring the car around."

Once Jane had arranged for the return of her car, they both went outside to wait for it. It was cold, almost cold enough to snow, but not quite—typical for Seattle in January. It wasn't raining, but the air smelled wet. Jane's coat, a cream-colored three-quarter trench that looked perfect with her green dress, was not made for the weather.

She wrapped her arms around her body and tried not to shiver.

"You're cold," Liam observed. "Should we go back inside? We could wait there."

"It's okay. It'll be here any minute." She grinned. "When you do go back upstairs, what are the odds Caleb tries to guilt you into a late-night brainstorming session?"

"I'm not typically motivated by guilt," he said. "So that's not going to happen."

She looked up at him. "Good for you."

His eyes gleamed, but he said nothing.

Then, they were quiet. But Jane felt as if they were talking to each other anyway. Like something was happening between them beyond the verbal level. But it had to be in her head, right? She was tired, and stressed from being trapped in the stairwell. Which had, of course, been Liam's fault.

The sound of a car entering the driveway made them both turn. "That's me," she told him.

"Well," Liam said. "Maybe you thought this was unnecessary. But I'm glad I walked you to your car."

She smirked. "I do appreciate it."

He surprised her, then, by gently taking hold of her arm and brushing her cheek with a kiss. His dark stubble scratched against her skin.

"Good night," he said, pulling back from her. "Thanks for that insane playlist. It got me through several hours of well-intentioned silliness."

"You're welcome." Her voice had gone strange and soft. It was as if his chaste cheek-kiss had sucked the sarcasm right out of her.

"Ma'am?" The valet was standing at her elbow. "Are you ready to go?"

"Yes, thank you." She walked around to the driver's side of her car. Her legs were trembling slightly. Liam was still standing on the curb.

"Good luck with Caleb," she told him, over the top of the car.

"Thanks. Have a great vacation," Liam replied.

Suddenly, speaking seemed like too much effort, so she merely nodded at him, and got in the car. She positioned her purse on the passenger seat, then pulled on her seatbelt. When she glanced out the passenger side window, Liam was gone.

Maybe he wasn't so slick, after all. During dinner, he'd not only badgered her about her job choices, he'd also cheerfully alluded to constipation. It was quirky, and maybe even a little rude. Or gross. But Jane sort of liked it. And she'd seen his veneer crack, just a little. In the stairwell, when he'd realized the door to the lobby was truly locked and that they were trapped, his mask had slipped.

Once on the road, Jane lit a cigarette. As she drove, her brain vexed her with memories of Liam. His fingers brushing hers as he took the cup of punch from her. The warmth of his body next to her while he helped her descend ten flights of stairs. His stubble scratching against her cheek when he kissed it. Ridiculously, from that small amount of contact, she'd grown horny and restless.

"I need to get laid," she said aloud. "And I also need to stop talking to myself."

7

Four days into her vacation, Jane couldn't stop thinking about Liam. Even though he'd barely touched her, the annoying sexual desire he'd activated was not fading. She'd tried using a few sex toys to take the edge off, but just getting off was not enough. She wanted to have actual sex. Since it was unlikely she would ever see Liam again, he wouldn't be able to help her out.

So, Wednesday morning, she decided to take action. She sent a text to a friend in Seattle who was usually good for no strings attached sex.

Hey Mike. What's up? Haven't hung out in awhile.

Ten minutes later, she saw the message had been read. But Mike did not respond. While she was waiting, she threw herself into a frenzy cleaning the condo. "C'mon Mike," she muttered, as she scrubbed down a countertop. "I need you."

When she finally heard from Mike, it was three hours later.

I'm free tonight. Want to meet at The Mix?

The Mix was one of the few places in Seattle that Jane

truly liked. It had a small bar and restaurant with simple but great food. There was an adjacent room with a decent-sized dance floor, and the music was always eclectic. Jane sent a reply to Mike.

Sure. Meet you at eight?

That night, she showered and dressed, including a garter belt and stockings she knew Mike would like. The more eager she could make him to fuck her, the better.

She chose one of her most figure-flattering dresses, a cream-white fit and flare with small blue flowers. The skirt bloomed over her hips and fell loose, just above her knees. Unlike the dress she'd worn to the Foundation benefit, this one showed off her cleavage. But not too much. She could still dance without worrying about her boobs spilling out of the dress. Best of all, the dress had pockets.

When Jane arrived at The Mix, Mike was already seated at the bar. He stood up when he saw her, and smiled. He wore a small goatee, his homage to the long-gone days of the Seattle grunge rock scene.

"Janey," he held out his arms and gave her a hug, pressing his hands into her waist. He spoke in her ear. "You look amazing."

Jane felt her body respond, and, well, that's what she was here for. She sat on a stool to Mike's right. Behind the bar, bottles and glasses gleamed against dark wood cabinets.

All of the seats at the bar were full, but since it was Wednesday night, a few tables along the edge of the restaurant were empty. If it had been a Friday or Saturday, the whole place would have been packed.

"I've missed it here," Jane said. She caught the

bartender's eye and asked for a gin and tonic. While she waited for her drink, she and Mike launched in to their usual small talk ritual.

Mike would pay for their drinks. He always did. Jane would spring for breakfast in the morning, or, if she didn't want to stay the night at Mike's place, she'd leave him cash for breakfast on her way out. It was an ongoing joke between them that she was actually paying him for sex.

When the bartender put her drink in front of her, Mike held up his own glass. "It's good to see you. Cheers."

"Cheers," she smiled at Mike.

And then, beyond Mike's head, at a table in the center of the room, she thought she saw Liam Burns. She blinked, and the man who looked like Liam was still there. But it couldn't be him. The benefit was over, and Burns was a busy person with his own life. Besides, why would he be here, of all places, sitting by himself?

It had to be someone else, Jane decided. It was dark in the restaurant, and it was easy to be fooled. To think you'd spotted someone familiar. She looked away.

Mike was talking about his job, now. It was another part of their ritual. Mike would talk about his main job as an apartment manager (which he took seriously) and his second job as a part-time guitar teacher. Then he'd ask Jane about her job, and she'd make a joke without really telling him anything. Next, he'd ask if she wanted to dance. After they'd put in some time on the dance floor, they'd walk back to Mike's building and have sex.

"So, hey," he said, stopping mid-sentence. "Should we just—get the hell out of here?"

Jane blinked.

He leaned forward. "Seriously. You look so amazing. I can't wait to get you back home."

She smiled slow at him. "That's the plan, right?"

"Do you want another drink?" he asked.

"One more," she agreed. She stood up and put her hand on his arm. "I'll be right back."

Mike grinned. "I'll be right here." He signaled the bartender to order their second round of drinks.

On the way to the restrooms, Jane snuck a furtive glance over at the table where she'd seen Liam Burns' lookalike. But the table was empty. Maybe no one had been there at all. It was ridiculous that her brain was conjuring Liam Burns out of thin air, when she had Mike waiting for her—in the flesh—at the bar.

Once she was in the ladies' room, she walked up to the mirror above the sinks and stared at her reflection. She did look good. She'd put her hair up in a loose style that left a few flame-colored tendrils falling around her face. She was going to get laid. She wanted to. Her body needed sex. So why did she suddenly feel ambivalent about the evening? She considered telling Mike she was sick, and that she needed to go home.

There would never be anything serious between her and Mike. But she knew *him;* she trusted him on a basic level. After she'd had to take out the restraining order on Carl, feeling absolutely safe with her sex partners was imperative.

It had taken several months before she could acknowledge Carl was abusing her. She'd found a number of ways to rationalize his behavior. The first time, she'd told herself he had simply lost his temper. It would never happen again. The next time, she held on to the fact that he was never abusive during sex. It wasn't until he'd messed her up so bad she was ashamed to go to work that she'd admitted what was happening, and left him.

Sex with Mike was safe, and it was always good. Sex was the reason she'd come here. And she definitely wasn't sick. She left the mirror and banged inside one of the bathroom stalls.

As she made her way back to the bar, she couldn't help but glance over at the table where she'd thought she'd seen Liam Burns. A couple was sitting there now.

Jane slid onto her barstool.

"I was starting to worry you drowned in there," Mike teased. He was signing the receipt for their bar tab.

"No, I'm fine," she assured him.

He nudged her drink toward her. "Drink up."

She took a sip of the second gin and tonic as the bartender came over and accepted Mike's signed receipt.

"Hey," Mike said. "I've been thinking. Why don't we see each other more often, huh? I mean, we've been doing this for years. We're good together, don't you think?"

"Oh. Uh...." Jane felt a mild sense of alarm. Was Mike trying to say he wanted them to meet for sex more often? Or was he making a pitch for a more serious relationship?

"Don't you think we're good together, Janey?" Mike repeated. He slow-nudged her knee with his own under the bar.

"I always have a good time with you," she evaded. She took a sip of her drink, trying to figure out the best way to handle the situation. If Mike was going to get weird and possessive, maybe she *should* pretend to be sick.

"I think we're good together." Mike's tone was emphatic, more emotional than his usual "chilled-out-guy" routine. Jane began to wonder if he'd tucked in an extra shot while she'd been in the ladies' room.

"Listen," she put her hand on his arm. "Maybe we should..."

"JANE!" boomed out a loud voice.

They both swiveled on their barstools to see who it was. Jane had to blink several times before she was certain: it *was* Liam Burns. He'd done something with his unruly dark hair, had slicked it down, so that he looked a bit nerdish.

He planted himself in front of them. "Hello *Jane.*" Liam's eyes gleamed with mischievous intent. Then he extended his hand to Mike, and said, "I'm *John Burns*, Jane's boss."

"I'm Mike."

Liam shook Mike's hand vigorously.

Jane stared at Liam. What was he doing? Inserting himself into the situation, obviously, but why? Why was he pretending to be her boss, introducing himself as "John Burns?" And why had he dropped his British accent? He sounded like any run-of-the-mill speaker of non-accented American English. Whatever he was up to, his ability to shift accents was impressive.

"So," Liam-pretending-to-be-John said, "you kids having a good night out on the town?"

Since the evening had been heading in a weird direction anyway, Jane decided to play along. "Yes," she said, "we're having a great time. It's good to see you, but why are *you* still in town *Mr. Burns*? I thought you were traveling to LA for meetings this week."

Liam-as-John's face went blank for a split second, then he beamed at her. "It's a good thing you're on vacation, Jane. You've been working too hard. I'm not traveling to LA until *next* week."

"Oh," she demurred, "Guess I read the schedule wrong."

"So, uh, John," Mike said, with pained politeness. "Do you want to join us for a drink?"

"Oh, no, no," Liam-as-John protested, "I don't want to intrude. Though, since you're here, I did want to ask you,

Jane, when you get back to the office, will you be able to help out with the salmon benefit?"

She widened her eyes in surprise. "Are we still doing the salmon benefit? I was certain we nixed it *weeks* ago."

Liam's eyes burned with an emotion she could not place. Jane wanted to laugh out loud, but she kept her hilarity suppressed. Next to her, Mike shifted uncomfortably on his barstool.

"You really do need your vacation time," Liam-as-John said. "It was the *halibut* benefit we decided to cut. Remember?"

"Oh right." She touched her hand to her head. "I forgot. Screw halibut. Save the salmon. Well, *of course*. I want to help in any way I can. What exactly needs to be done?"

There, she thought. Let's see if he can pull this out of his ass.

"Well," Liam said, launching into a perfect imitation of Caleb, "we're going to need to reach out to partner organizations, such as The Center for Whale Research, since the future of our salmon is so inextricably bound up with the plight of our Orca whales. We want to get as many relevant organizations involved as possible, though, of course, as always, we have a limited budget."

Jane nodded gravely. "Of course."

Liam-as-John beamed. "Reaching out to Orca-focused organizations would be something of an extra project, but I think you'd do well with it, Jane. It would be a fantastic chance for you to develop your networking and fundraising skills."

Mike started to fidget and jiggle his leg under the counter. He looked around the bar, then back to Jane, then to Liam.

"Count me in for the salmon," Jane said. Then she laughed. "When I'm back from vacation, of course."

"Fantastic. I think you'll enjoy the challenge." Liam turned to Mike. "Did you know our northwest salmon and our Orca whales are edging toward extinction?"

"I think I'd heard something like that, yeah," Mike said, stroking his goatee. "On NPR or something?" He tapped Jane on the shoulder. "Can I talk to you outside for a minute?"

Jane glanced quickly at Liam, then back to Mike. "Sure."

She slid off the barstool, and Mike stood up with her. Liam claimed Jane's empty seat.

"I'll keep your places for you," Liam-as-John said, helpfully.

"Thanks man." Mike put his hand at Jane's back, guiding her to the door.

She wanted to look back to see if Liam was watching them, but she squashed down her curiosity and let Mike lead her out the door to the street.

8

Outside, Jane folded her arms over her chest. She tucked her hands below her armpits to keep them warm.

"Where's your coat?" Mike asked.

"I checked it when I got here."

"Want to go back and get it?"

"No. What's up?"

Mike looked toward the door of the club then back at Jane. "What's up with that *dude*?" he asked. "What's his deal?"

"You mean, uh, John Burns?" Jane stammered. "He's just excited about Orcas. And salmon."

"Do you really work with that goofball?" Mike groaned.

Technically, Jane thought, she did. Or she had, since Liam had been working with the staff at the Foundation last week. Technically, one could say they worked together.

"Yeah, I do," she said. "Why do you ask?"

Mike made an almost comical grimace. "He seems kind of weird, that's all."

"Most of the people who work at the Foundation are weird," Jane defended. That, she told herself, was also true.

Mike gave her a sad look. "Did I kill the mood?"

"What do you mean?" But she knew what he meant. He'd broken their code. Their arrangement had always been based on friendship and casual hookups. He'd hinted that he wanted more, and in an instant, it had changed everything between them.

"Yeah," Mike answered his own question. "I killed the mood."

"Kinda," Jane admitted. She shivered and wrapped her arms more tightly around her body.

Mike sighed and stroked his goatee. "What are you going to do? You gonna go back in and talk to your boss?"

"Maybe," she said. "Just for a few minutes. There's this, um, promotion coming up at work? Can't hurt to schmooze a little bit." How could it be so easy to lie, she wondered, and why, exactly, was she lying?

Mike held his arms open for a hug, and Jane stepped into them. He held on to her longer than a friendly hug would last, and when she started to pull away, he said near her ear, "I'm sorry, Janey. Forget what I said. We can keep it casual. You sure you won't change your mind?"

She shook her head against his chest and looked up at him. "You know what? My stomach is bugging me. I'd be crappy company. No pun intended. I'm just going to go kiss up to the boss and go home."

Mike let her go. "Yeah," he frowned. "I fucked up."

"We'll hook up some other time," she told him. But she was not sure she meant it.

"Bye Janey." Mike turned around and started walking in the direction of his building. She watched him for a few moments, even though she was freezing cold. Mike was a good guy. She felt bad about lying to him.

Mostly, though, she was relieved.

She turned around and went back inside. A deep twinge of excitement ran through her when she saw Liam still sitting at the bar. The stool to his left, the one Mike had been using, was empty. Jane slid in beside him.

"Hey, *John Burns*," she said. "How's it going?"

"Why'd you keep trying to fuck me up?" Liam asked. His British accent had returned.

"I don't know," she retorted. "Why the fuck did you even do that?"

He looked at her with a huge grin, and she found herself returning it. She felt like they were co-conspirators in some undefinable scheme. She liked the feeling.

"Where's your friend? Mike, was it?" Liam asked.

"He went home," Jane said.

"Was he pissed?"

"Maybe a little. But he figured he killed the mood because of something dumb he said."

Liam gave her a direct look. "So I *did* interrupt your date."

"It wasn't exactly a date," she corrected, then wondered why she was being honest with him.

He raised an eyebrow. "So what exactly was it?"

"That's none of your business."

The expression in his eyes told her he knew all about her arrangement, without her having to say another word. He smiled then, a kind smile.

"Mike and I have this thing..." she started.

"We all have needs," Liam said, stopping her from saying more, but leaving her feeling completely understood.

They sat together, not talking, but aware of each other. Of the rise and fall of breath, the movements of hands. Her hands, as she retrieved her drink from in front of Liam, then scooted it within her reach. His, as he drummed his fingers once on the countertop, then tented his hands in a "V" shape in front of him.

Liam broke their silence. "You know, one thing I've noticed about this place. You can hear other people speak, even though there's music playing. It doesn't drown out conversation."

"That's one thing I've always loved about it," Jane agreed.

She took another sip of her drink, and stole glances at her new drinking companion. Liam was wearing dark slacks and a button down pale yellow shirt. His hair had begun to curl into its typical unruly shape. Jane figured he must have wet it down in order to assume the role of John Burns, her slightly nerdy boss.

"Do you ever get recognized?" Jane asked, keeping her voice low. "When you go out like this?"

"Sometimes." Liam shot her one of his quick grins. Then a laugh bubbled out of him. "I'm really not that famous. Plus I've always been good at hiding in plain sight." He gestured quickly to his clothes. "Dressing like an uptight office worker helps. It's not what people expect."

"But it must happen sometimes," Jane pressed.

"Sure. It happens more in LA. Or when I'm in the UK. But the work I do tends to have niche audiences. Unless I run into those exact people, I'm just another bloke at the bar. So," he said, dropping to a stage whisper, "you don't have to lower your voice when you talk about my job."

Jane made a face at him. "I was just curious."

"No, please. Ask me anything you like."

"Okay," she ventured. "You figured out why I'm here. Why are *you* here? Why are you still in Seattle?"

He held up a finger. "One question at a time."

"Why are you still in Seattle?" she repeated.

"I had some time between projects. I've never spent much time here, and I wanted to check it out."

"What do you think?" Jane asked.

"The city's surrounded by an incredible amount of natural beauty," Liam said. "I was not prepared for the visual feast. The first day the sun came out it was absolutely gorgeous."

"I hate it here," Jane blurted. "Sorry," she amended. "I try to save that kind of bitching for people who know me better."

"Lived here all your life?" Liam guessed.

"Basically."

"Familiarity breeds contempt. As they say." Liam signaled the bartender. "I'm going to get a drink. Do you want one?"

She shook her head. "Still working on this one."

"Scotch and soda," Liam told the bartender. Then he turned his dark eyes on Jane. "Do you want to know the answer to your other question?"

"Why you're here? At this specific bar? Sure," she shrugged. "Tell me why you're here."

"I met Sasha for dinner."

Jane let out a quick snort of laughter. "Of course."

He made quotation marks with his hands. "Informal business meeting."

"Business?" she scoffed. "You know Sasha works in human resources, right? What'd she do, sign you up for our retirement plan?"

Liam chuckled. "She framed it as a discussion about the

potential benefits of joining the Foundation as a part-time permanent employee."

Jane raised her eyebrows. "Right. Like that makes sense." She glanced around the restaurant. "So where's Sasha now? Is she on the dance floor?"

"No," Liam shook his head. "She left. Just before you got here. I think I might have made her angry."

"Were you rude to her?"

The bartender set Liam's drink down in front of him. He said 'thanks,' and took a sip. "Sasha is a lovely person. But the trouble is, she somewhat reminds me of my ex-wife. Honestly, it's a bit painful to be around her."

Jane felt a need to defend her co-worker. "Sasha's her own person. I doubt she's anything like your ex-wife. But you can't help how you feel, I guess."

"No," Liam said, smiling at her with a strange expression. "I've found it's very difficult to change what one feels."

He held her eyes with his, and Jane felt her pulse quicken. It was physical attraction, of course. But she was feeling something else, a sensation just behind her heart that was unsettling.

In one quick motion, she downed the rest of her drink. "I'm going to hit the dance floor before I get out of here. Want to join me?"

This time, Liam's smile was rueful. "Is it all right if I dance like a middle-aged person?"

Jane smirked. "That's another thing I love about this place. It doesn't matter how you dance." She asked the bartender for two glasses of water, which he provided in pint glasses. "Drink up," she told Liam, picking up her glass. "It gets hot in there."

When Jane had finished her water, she stood up and

thumped the empty pint glass on the bar. "Ready?" she asked.

Liam held up a finger while he downed the rest of his water, then set his pint glass on the bar next to Jane's. "Ready."

9

Jane and Liam walked away from the bar to the narrow doorway that separated the restaurant from the dance space. Inside the doorway, to the left, a guy stood behind a beat-up podium. Jane pulled a mildly rumpled ten dollar bill out of the pocket of her dress, and handed it to the podium guy.

"For both of us," she said, indicating Liam.

They stepped inside, and suddenly the music, which had been faint at the bar, was overwhelming.

Jane began to move to the song that was playing, an old dance classic from the 90s. Liam performed the quickest up and down take of her body she had ever seen anyone do. Then he began to move with her. They circled around and near each other like shy kids at a school dance, making minimal eye contact. Checking each other out with surreptitious glances.

They'd started dancing at the edge of the room, but as the song came to an end, they were deep in the crowd of gyrating bodies. A new track began playing, a more recent one, and a cry of pleasure went up from the crowd. Jane started moving to the new song. Liam, however, stood with his hands at his sides, looking a bit forlorn.

"What's the matter!" she yelled, laughing.

"Where's the beat in this song?" he yelled back.

Just then the beat appeared in the form of handclaps, and Jane, along with almost everyone else in the room, raised her hands above her head and began to clap with the beat. Liam stayed where he was.

Laughing harder, Jane began moving backwards, further into the crowd, still clapping. A girl got in her face, and they yelled the song's lyrics at each other.

By the time the song burned out its long intro and took off, she had lost Liam in the crowd. *Good.* Colored lights spun over the dancers, and she threw her body in among them, into a zone where she was nothing but movement and color.

And then he was there. Liam. Dancing with her. Throwing himself into it with as much fervor as she was. He stopped and did a quick pirouette, then spread his hands wide with a quizzical expression. She laughed and motioned for him to keep going. He danced with her until the bridge of the song.

The bridge also lost the beat, but it was Jane's favorite part, when she could keep the beat with her body. Liam stopped dancing again. But once the beat kicked in, he moved in close and put his hand on her waist.

It felt like being stung, him touching her like that. Her skin was hypersensitive and flushed, and her heart ached the same way it had earlier, at the bar. The sensation was mixed with an explosion of sexual need, so strong it made her tremble.

They swayed together, his hand on her waist, her hands on his shoulders. Then they would fall away from each other. Then another slow collision, then another, over and over, until he reached out and gripped her forearms gently to pull her whole body close to him.

Now he would feel her shaking, she thought. She looked up, and his eyes were dark and intense. The music was still pulsing and thumping, but they were no longer dancing. He let go of her arms and slid his own around her. She dropped her head to his chest, and rested against him. They stayed that way until the song ended, then he said, near her ear, "Do you want to get out of here?"

She nodded. He put his hand between her shoulder blades to lead her out of the mass of moving bodies on the dance floor. After settling the tab and retrieving their coats, they stepped out into the cold night air. Jane stopped and pressed her hands to her cheeks. They felt hot.

Liam stopped, too, and looked down at her. "You all right?" he asked.

"I'm fine." She smiled up at him, and was surprised to see a shadow of uncertainty cross his face. But it could also have been the shadow of a passing car.

Liam looked down the street, then back at her. "Where do you want to go?" he asked.

"Do you mind if we walk a little?"

"No. Not at all. Lead the way."

They began walking down the street, past the doorways of other bars and restaurants that lined the block.

"You're pretty good on the dance floor," Liam remarked.

Jane laughed. "You think so?"

"Definitely. And that wasn't even '80s music."

"I don't normally listen to the music they play in that club," she explained. "But it's different when you're danc-ing. Especially at The Mix. The whole place has such a great vibe."

"Yeah I picked that up." Liam stopped on the sidewalk, causing Jane to stop, too.

"Look," he said. "I'll walk with you all night if you want. Or we can go have a late dinner, if you want that. But did I misread you back there? Did we connect, or did I imagine that?"

Jane grinned. "*Connect*? You mean, did we agree to have sex tonight?"

A group of people were coming toward them, talking and laughing. Jane and Liam moved to the far edge of the sidewalk so the group could pass. When they were gone, Liam turned so that he was facing Jane.

"Yes," he said, with a smile that was half confident, but also half hesitant. "Sex was what I meant by 'connect.'"

Jane moved toward him, stood on tiptoe, and kissed his cheek, the way he'd kissed hers the night of the Foundation benefit. "Yes," she said. "We connected."

"Good," he let out a breath, as if he'd been holding it in. "So—what next? My hotel's nearby. Do you want dinner? A five mile hike? Right to the hotel? What do you want?"

Jane began walking again. After a moment, Liam fell in step with her.

"I don't want to go to your hotel." She hoped he would not ask her why. She didn't want to explain her need for comfortable territory in order to have sex. A relative stranger's hotel room was not comfortable for her. Since leaving Carl, she'd devised new rules for relating to men. Sometimes, they were difficult to explain.

"All right," Liam said. "Where do you want to go?"

"I have two ideas. We could pick another hotel. I'll help pay for it," she said, hastily.

"Well if you want your own hotel, you can pay for the whole damn thing," he retorted.

When she looked up at him, he was smiling, and she was relieved. He seemed to be taking her needs in stride. So far.

"I'm kidding," he assured her. "All right. Another hotel, or—what's your second idea?"

"Or we could go back to my place."

"Another hotel? Or back to your place?" he repeated. "Those are the choices?"

"Right. Oh, and about my place, I don't have security cameras, in case, if you were worried I would..."

"...capitalize on my massive fame for your own selfish gain?" he finished, with a hint of self-mockery.

"Right," she said.

He frowned. "You're not a serial killer?"

"That's always a useless question, but no," she laughed.

"Good enough for me. Let's go to your place."

"Okay. So the problem with that is I maybe shouldn't drive my car for at least an hour."

"I'll drive," he said. "I barely touched the drink I ordered, and the other I had with Sasha was ages ago. We had a full meal."

"Fine. My car's back that way." Jane turned on her heel to retrace her steps.

Liam came up behind her, draped his arm around her shoulders, and gave her a squeeze. "So where is your car, and how far away do you live?"

"About forty minutes."

"We have to walk for forty minutes to get to your car?" he exclaimed, horrified. He stepped away from her and onto the curb, yelling "Taxi!"

"Nobody takes taxis," she laughed, pulling him back from the curb. "Anyway my *place* is forty minutes away. My *car* is parked across from The Mix."

"Well then, let's run."

He grabbed her hand and bolted down the sidewalk. She laughed and tried to keep up. Liam led her between the cars parked on the curb alongside The Mix. Together they watched for traffic, then ran across the street, laughing. She took him to her car, pulled the keys out of her purse, and hit the electronic lock. Then she tossed him the keys, which he fumbled, then caught.

"Don't wreck it," she said, and walked around the passenger side to get in.

10

Jane got in the passenger side of her car, and looked over at Liam. He was adjusting the driver's seat for his legs.

"You'll have to tell me where we're going." He checked the mirrors and stuck the key in the ignition.

"I'm just north of Seattle," Jane informed him.

Liam was sarcastic. "Well give me a compass then, and I'll cut a path due north through the city."

She laughed, while he looked over his shoulder and began maneuvering the car out of its parking spot. His wit was a bit acidic. But she liked that.

Liam drove her uncle's car well. He was also good at following her driving directions. When she gave him an instruction, he understood it, and executed it.

They fell into a rhythm, with her telling him where to go, his quiet agreement, then performance of what she told him to do. The sound of his voice coupled with his skillful handling of the car began to send tremors through her thighs.

"We stay on this road for awhile," she said. "About five miles. Then there's an exit to the town where I live."

"So I can just drive for a bit, then?" Liam asked.

"Just drive," she agreed.

"I like your car," he announced. "It's more powerful than it looks."

"It was my uncle's. He left it to me."

Liam shifted gears, and the car purred forward. Jane studied his profile. His jaw was already sprouting dark stubble. The harsh lights along the side of the highway flashed over the planes of his face as they sped down the road.

She liked being the passenger while Liam was driving. She hadn't had the urge for even one cigarette. Which was, frankly, amazing.

After they exited the highway, they took the long road down to the small waterfront town where Jane lived. She guided Liam through the streets to her garage, which was off an alley and detached from her condo building. She opened the garage door with the opener in her purse.

Liam parked the car. Instead of immediately getting out, he sat still. The safety lights in the backseat went out, making a faint whirring noise, and they sat in almost total darkness.

Jane began unfastening her seatbelt. Liam reached over, cupped her chin in his hand, and turned her head toward him. "You can back out if you want," he said.

"Well, gee thanks. So can you." When he didn't respond, she asked, "Do *you* want to back out?"

"No." He dropped his hand. "Definitely not. Can I kiss you? Before we go inside?"

"It's kind of uncomfortable in here. But sure?"

He undid his own seatbelt, then turned back to her, and

pushed a few tendrils of her hair away from her face. In the dark, even with the garage door open, she could barely see him.

"Are you going to kiss me, or what?" To her surprise, her voice shook.

Wouldn't it be funny, she thought, *if he's a terrible kisser. After all that, the bar, the walk, the drive up here. Then: the worst kiss ever!*

She laughed aloud at the thought. That was when he went in for the kill. His lips covered hers, and he kissed them softly a couple times. Then, he braced his hand behind her head and pressed his mouth against hers with a little more force. She heard her own sharp intake of breath, and a sweet rush of sensation flooded through her body as he teased her mouth open with the tip of his tongue. Each time his tongue touched hers, she felt a stab of pleasure inside. Her breathing grew heavier, and she shifted in her seat to get closer to him. Then, abruptly, Liam pulled back.

"So?" he asked. "Are you in, or are you out?"

"I'm in. I've been in the whole time. You're a freaking sadist."

"No, not a sadist. Just a tease."

"Get out of my car," Jane ordered. She stepped out of the vehicle.

"Whatever you say." He got out, too.

Once they were both outside the garage, he handed her back the car keys. "I guess I'm following you."

Outside, it was quiet. Her heels and his dress shoes clicked on the pavement as she led him around to the front of the building. While Jane unlocked the door, he pressed his hand against the small of her back.

They went up the stairs, and Jane could feel her heart pounding. It sounded loud in her ears. As she opened the door to her condo unit, Liam slid his arm around her waist and pressed his lips to the top of her head.

They burst inside together. Jane's thighs trembled with arousal, but her stomach lurched. It had been years since she'd slept with anyone she didn't know as a friend or acquaintance.

She shut the door, dis-entangled herself from Liam, and shrugged off her coat. Then she went to the coat closet and slid the coat on a hanger. She reached out her hand.

"Want me to hang up yours?"

He smirked, then removed his dark overcoat and handed it over. Jane found a place for it in the closet and shut the door. She moved past Liam to the kitchen.

"Do you want anything?" she asked. "A drink? A soda? A sandwich?" She stood poised with her hand on the refriger-ator door.

Liam entered the kitchen, and put his hand over hers, prying it away from the door handle. Then, with his eyes on her face, he backed her against the nearest kitchen counter.

"Can I tell you something?" he asked. His legs were pressed against hers, flooding her body with warmth and electricity. She was having trouble breathing properly.

"Sure?" she managed.

"I was hoping this would happen since the day you brought me coffee at the Foundation."

She rolled her eyes. "You don't have to say stuff like that. I told you. I'm in."

"Well, fuck you," he said, in a soft voice. "It's true."

Her own voice was suddenly hoarse. "Good for you. Way to be honest."

He reached for her waist again, to pull her closer to him, and kissed her. First her mouth, then along her jawline, then down the side of her neck. She sighed with relief, and pleasure.

Liam reached down and lifted the hem of her skirt, tracing his fingertips over her legs as he moved the skirt up past her hips. He laughed when he discovered she was wearing a garter belt with stockings and no underwear.

"I know you put this on for someone else and I don't even fucking care," he said.

With a sudden movement, he plunged two fingers deep inside her. She was wet, and her breathing grew ragged. He sighed, and leaned his head against hers.

"Just fuck me," she breathed.

He began moving his fingers inside her, and she moaned, clamping her internal muscles around him.

"I'm going to fuck *with* you a little first," he said. "I hope you don't mind."

"Like you care. Oh, God." He rolled his thumb over her clit, moving in circles, sending deep, sweet sensations all through her body. Then he thrust his fingers inside her again.

"Please just fuck me," she begged.

"Show me where your bedroom is," he said in her ear.

"We can fuck here."

"No, show me," he insisted. "I want you there."

"Okay. Let go of me."

Liam slid his fingers out of her and she shuddered. His face was a mix of smug satisfaction and something that looked like tenderness.

"C'mon," she said. She pushed past him and into the hall. Then, stopping, she reached back, pulled the zipper on her dress, and stepped out of it. She left it on the floor and continued down the hallway, to her bedroom. Liam followed her.

Once they were in her room, he pushed her back on the bed, gently, and stretched his body over hers. He began covering her with sweet kisses, like he was trying to convince her to have sex, something he didn't need to do. It was somehow too emotional. She didn't want this much sweetness. Sweetness was dangerous. She wanted to get off.

"What are you doing?" she whispered.

Instead of answering, he kissed between her breasts, then unhooked the clasp at the front of her bra and pushed the cups away from her body. He took one of her nipples in his mouth, and sucked. His tongue stroked its sensitive tip, and she arched her back as he moved to her other breast, giving it the same attention. Her nipples grew tight and hard, and she bucked against him.

"How are you feeling?" he asked.

"You're driving me nuts," she said irritably.

"Good," he smiled. He reached down and unhooked first one, then the next of her thigh-high stockings from her garter belt, tracing his fingers between her thighs and pushing them apart. She thought he would fuck her, then, but instead he dropped to the floor, and rolled one of her stockings down and off her leg, tracing his fingers over her calf.

She writhed, impatient, on the bed. He was going too slow, making her feel things she didn't want to feel. Delaying her gratification, when gratification had been her entire aim for the evening.

After Liam removed her second stocking, he put his hands on her knees, stretching her legs further apart. Then he pushed his head between her legs. The straps of her garter were in his way. He flicked them aside and touched his tongue to her clit. The teasing strokes of his tongue felt good, but he didn't know her body or exactly how to please her. She didn't want to take the time to educate him; she wanted him to hurry up and fuck her.

Liam started laughing between her legs. Feeling his hilarity infect her, Jane laughed, too, and said, "What is it?"

He pulled his head up. "I know when my tongue isn't wanted."

"Your dick is though," she said.

"You've said it enough. I should have it by now: just fuck you." Suddenly, he stood up, gripped her waist, and flipped her over on her stomach. She yelped in surprise then giggled. He unfastened the hooks on her garter, pulling it off and exposing her ass, which made her feel vulnerable. She turned back over, slowly, and stared up at him. He stared back.

"So, are you going to fuck me *now*?" she asked.

His eyes changed. The only light in the room was coming from the kitchen down the hall, so she was not sure, but she thought he looked sad. It was confusing. How could he be sad, when he was on the verge of getting some?

Liam unbuttoned his shirt and shrugged it off his shoulders. Then he began unfastening his pants. Jane's thighs shook in anticipation. She watched him remove a condom from his discarded pants pocket, open it, and put it on. Then he pressed the length of his body against hers and buried his face in her neck, kissing under her ear until she arched against him.

"You don't have to be tough," he said, so soft she almost wasn't sure she heard him say it. "I don't need that from you. But I'll give you what you want."

He slid his hands down her back, and grasped her hips. Then he thrust into her.

That was it.

It was what she'd been craving: the sensation of being filled, steady strokes, his hot skin on hers. She wrapped her legs around him and dug her fingers into his ass. She whispered in his ear. "Can you go faster?"

For a moment, he stopped moving, and she wondered if he was sad again, or maybe angry. But then he kissed her mouth and said, "Alright," in the same calm tone he'd used for following her driving directions.

He began moving faster, pounding her hard, making it feel more like punishment than making love. It was exactly what she wanted. She cried out with each thrust, and to her delight, it excited him more and he fucked her even harder.

Her orgasm ripped through her body in harsh waves. He came a few seconds later, and pressed his lips to the side of her neck. "Do you want me to go?"

"What?" she said, surprised.

He pulled out of her, then rolled onto his back. "That was fantastic. But somehow, I feel like a human dildo."

Her voice raised. "Because I wanted it? Are you some kind of weirdo who thinks women shouldn't like it?"

"No!" he said, vehemently, then, more calmly, "No. But that's not what I mean. Do you—do you know what I mean?"

After several moments she admitted, "Getting laid was my mission tonight. You took Mike's place. But you knew that, right?"

"I gathered," he said. "It's great you like sex. Believe me, I'm not complaining. But maybe you're done with me now?"

"No," she turned her head toward him. "I mean if you *want* to leave, leave, but you can stay. If you want to."

He raised himself up on an elbow and looked down at

her. Then he smoothed her hair back from her face. "Then I'll stay."

She scrambled underneath the covers. "Get in so you don't get cold."

With a sudden burst of energy, he joined her, and wrapped her body in a giant bear hug. Then, with no warning, he let her go, and rolled on his side.

"What was that?" she laughed.

From over his shoulder, he replied, "You needed to be fucked and I needed that, so consider us even. Good night."

"Good night," she said, softly.

11

Jane slept soundly and woke at six. Liam was on his side, snoring lightly. It was strange seeing a man in her own bed.

Since breaking up with Carl, she'd kept men out of her personal space. If she trusted someone enough for sex, she would go to his place. For most of the last nine years, with a couple exceptions, that person had been Mike. If not Mike, it had always been someone she already knew. She didn't date strangers. She didn't like to date at all. But she did like sex.

When Jane realized Liam wouldn't wake up any time soon, she shuffled out of bed and snagged her blue bathrobe from a hook on the back of the bathroom door. Then she slid her feet into slippers and took another peek at Liam. She wondered if he was feigning sleep, hoping she'd make him breakfast. If so, he'd be disappointed. She wasn't much of a cook.

In the kitchen, she made coffee with fresh beans. She ground extra, in case Liam wanted some. After that, she'd have to figure out how to send him on his way. Then again, maybe he'd want to leave as much as she wanted her space back.

While the coffee was brewing, she opened the blinds. The windows in the living room overlooked the Olympic Mountains and Puget Sound. She was fortunate, she knew, that her uncle had left her this place. She would never have been able to afford it on her own.

Of course, she would have traded back the condo and the car, just to have Uncle Chuck alive again. Sometimes she felt guilty having both possessions. She'd told Bert about the guilt, once, and he'd pointed out that everyone dies eventually. He'd helped her to think of the car and condo as tangible reminders of how much her uncle had cared about her.

Jane heard the coffee maker sputter to a finish in the kitchen, and went to pour herself a cup. As she stood in front of the machine, taking her first sip, Liam emerged from the bedroom. He was wearing his clothes from the night before.

"Heading out?" she asked.

He continued his approach, then stopped at the edge of the kitchen. "Getting rid of me?" he countered.

She waved her hand in the direction of the coffee pot. "Do you want coffee? I don't have breakfast food, so there's no breakfast. But there is coffee."

"Sure," he smiled. "I'll take a cup of coffee."

Jane got another mug out of the cupboard, filled it, and handed it to him. "I don't have anything for it."

"I don't take anything in it." Liam took a sip. "It's very good."

"I buy good coffee beans."

"It's the beans, is it?"

She half grinned. "It's at least ninety percent the beans."

Liam gestured with his coffee mug. "You're not drinking yours."

Jane raised her own mug to her lips and took a large gulp. She and Liam locked eyes. He stepped further into the kitchen, and set his mug down on the counter. Then, he pried Jane's from her hands and set it on the counter, too.

"Hey," she protested weakly. "I was going to drink that."

He hooked one finger in each of the belt loops of her robe, pulled her forward, and kissed her.

Her body responded so fast it was a shock. Just moments earlier, she'd been wondering how to get Liam to leave. Now all she wanted to do was drag him back down the hall to her bedroom.

So she did.

"You're addictive," Liam said. "I don't want to move." He was absently stroking one of her nipples. Jane felt it stiffen under his fingers as they lay side-by-side on her bed.

She said nothing. She wasn't used to feeling this connected to someone after sex. It made her uncomfortable. The sense of connection was probably an illusion, though. She had nothing in common with Liam. They were from two completely different worlds.

"You must have somewhere you need to be, right?" she guessed.

Liam turned over on his stomach. "Not immediately. I've got an audition in LA in a little over a week. It's for an American TV series filming in Vancouver. My original plan was to hang around Seattle until then."

"An audition?" She turned on her side so she could look at him. "That sounds—exciting." And there it was. An audition. He definitely did not inhabit the same world she did. Even though he tried to play it down, he was a famous actor. That was just a fact.

He made a dismissive noise. "It's routine for me. I was already rehearsing for the role in Seattle. At the hotel."

"It sounds important, though. I don't want to keep you from that."

He grinned. "Right. Actually, I forgot, I also have a number of phone calls to make. I really should wash my hair. Plus I have a manicure and a pedicure on the schedule for this afternoon, so I can't possibly stay here in bed with you for one more minute."

Jane found herself grinning back at him. "You have a mani-pedi appointment? Today?"

"Of course. Perfectly groomed cuticles have always been the secret to my low-key success."

"Are you serious?" she laughed. "I can't tell if you're being serious."

He smiled into her eyes. "Not serious. I'll get out of your hair soon, I promise. But I would like to see you again. If that's all right."

His words were a jolt to her gut, because she hadn't been expecting them. "Sure," she faltered. "We should, umm, exchange numbers."

"It's a plan." He gathered her in his arms, making her feel liquid. She laughed as he poked tickling fingers into her sides.

"Would it be all right if I used your shower?" he asked, releasing her.

"Go ahead. There's a linen closet in the bathroom with fresh towels. Help yourself."

He gave her a quick kiss. "Thank you. Don't get up. Stay in bed and relax. It's your vacation."

He heaved himself out of bed and disappeared inside the bathroom. A few moments later, Jane heard the sound of the shower turning on, then Liam humming something tuneless as he stepped under the spray.

She stared at the ceiling, trying to decide how she felt. There was something so cheerful about the sound of a man taking a shower in her bathroom. It was even a little bit exciting. But there was a thread of terror weaving through her excitement. No one had been this much in her space for years. After so much time, it was unfamiliar territory.

Before Liam left, he and Jane exchanged phone numbers. He promised to call her within the next couple days.

After he was gone, she took her own shower, then dressed in old jeans and a fisherman's sweater. She'd been planning to spend the afternoon watching dumb TV shows, but she was too restless to sit still. She wanted a cigarette. Then she decided to call Bert, instead.

But when Bert picked up, he was busy. "Can you give me a half hour? I'm on the line with a client."

"Okay," she sighed.

"Half hour," he promised. "Then I want to hear all about whatever the hell is going on with you. Because it sounds like something's going on. Am I right?"

"Kinda," Jane admitted.

"Half hour," Bert repeated, then hung up.

Jane was still restless, so she put on her coat, jammed a knit hat on her head, and walked down to the ferry dock on the waterfront. When she reached the train tracks that ran alongside the water, she looked both ways for a train. There was supposed to be a warning blast before a train showed up, but she always looked for trains, anyway.

Once she'd crossed the tracks, she turned right, taking a paved path alongside a small beach that stretched to the south of the ferry dock. The dock was empty, and the creosote covered pilings looked lonely, waiting for one of the big green and white state-run ferries to return. There wasn't much wind today, and no rain. It was the perfect day for a walk at the waterfront, even though it was very cold.

When Jane had traveled the full stretch of the asphalt walkway along the beach, her phone rang. She pulled it out of her coat pocket.

"So," Bert said. "Lay it on me. What's going on?"

"Can you hear me?" she asked. "I'm outside."

"I can hear you fine," Bert assured her. "Stop stalling. What's up with you?"

"Um. So, I kind of slept with somebody last night."

"No!" he exclaimed. "Are you telling me you actually followed my advice and went out in the big, wide world to search for the real relationship you deserve?"

"Chill out," Jane huffed. "It was just one night. I'm not getting married, or anything."

"But *something* is going on. I can hear it in your voice."

"Shut up, Bert," she said, automatically.

"So who's the guy?" he sounded curious. "Anyone I know?"

"Kinda." Jane's voice was faint. She stopped walking and looked out across the water. A ferry was now cruising toward the dock. There were seagulls flying with it. She'd read somewhere, once, that seabirds could travel more easily in a large boat's wake.

Bert groaned. "Please tell me it's not your weird-ass

boss. Or that guy you meet for sex? You don't want to turn either of those guys into a 'thing,' trust me."

"No," she said. "It's not my boss. And it's not Mike. And I don't even know if this is a 'thing.'"

"Who else do I know?" Bert mused. "I mean, most of our mutual friends in Seattle are gay, so I think I'm out of guesses."

"It's Mr. Masterpiece," Jane said.

"Mr. Who?" he asked.

"Mr. Masterpiece," she repeated. "The guy is Mr. Masterpiece."

Bert went quiet. "You're lying," he said, finally.

"Actually I kind of wish I were." She shivered and realized she was much warmer when she was walking. She began to head for the railroad tracks.

"Okay. Let's say for a minute that you're not lying. How the hell did Mr. Masterpiece happen?"

"I met him while we were working on the benefit," Jane replied. "I told you that."

"You also told me you thought he was sort of annoying," he reminded her.

"I did think that. And then last night I went to meet Mike at a bar, and Liam was there. I ended up having sex with Liam instead of Mike. No big deal."

Bert started laughing. "I hope you know how insane that sounds. Guess how many people I know who've had sex with Liam Burns? That number would be zero. Until a minute ago."

"It's not a big deal," Jane insisted. "I met a guy at a bar. Liam Burns just happened to be the guy."

"So. You had sex with Liam Burns, and it's no big deal. End of story?"

"I don't know." Her voice crumpled. "He wants to see me again. He's said he's going to call in a couple of days."

"That's—fucking fantastic!" Bert exclaimed.

"What if he ghosts me?" she fretted. "That would just —suck."

"Oh Janey," his voice softened. "You like him."

"How could I like him?" she demanded, exasperated. "We spent one night together. I don't know him well enough to like him."

"It's not a logical thing," Bert explained. "You just like the people you like."

"I can't believe I'm waiting for a damn phone call." She hit a button affixed to a light pole, triggering the signal to cross the street. "I can't remember the last time I was waiting for someone's stupid phone call."

"If he doesn't call you, then call me. I'll tell you what an asshole he is."

"No, you won't," she contradicted. "You love him. *And* you think he's hot."

"I've been pretty jealous that you got to meet him," Bert admitted. "Look. I know it sucks to wait, but he's either going to come through, or he's going to bail. If he bails you're better off knowing what he's like now, right?"

"What if he comes through, but bails later, and it sucks then?" Jane asked.

"Then," Bert said, "sounds like maybe you need to decide if *you* want to bail."

12

After she and Bert hung up, Jane returned home and made a cup of chamomile tea to get warm and calm down. But when she finished the tea, she still wasn't calm. So she fired up one of her '80s playlists and started dancing around the living room. She hoped losing herself in music and movement would take her mind off waiting for Liam to call. She hated waiting for phone calls. She was shaking her ass to "Never Say Never" by Romeo Void when her phone rang.

When she looked at the phone, she saw an unfamiliar number light up the screen. It was a call from Houston, Texas. Her heart stopped. Last she'd heard, Carl was living in Texas. She let the phone keep ringing.

The call went to voicemail. Jane stared hard at her phone. She hoped whoever had called wouldn't leave a message. But to her dismay, a minute later, a notification popped up on the screen, telling her she had one new voicemail.

With trembling hands, she went to check the message from the Texas number. It was long, almost two minutes.

She hit "play," and recognized Carl's voice immediately. But he sounded different. He was speaking much more slowly than she remembered.

"Hi Jane," his voice crackled through the phone. "Long time no talk. Listen, uh, I don't want to freak you out. I'm still in Texas, just so you know. I'd rather do this face to face, but I know you don't want to see me, so. So I'm calling you. I'm glad you didn't change your number. "I just wanted to tell you I know I hurt you. When I hit you—I was wrong—I was wrong and I'm sorry. I'm really sorry. You don't have to respond, or answer, or anything, if you don't want. But I uh—wanted to tell you I know it was wrong. I'm trying—I'm trying to take responsibility for my life. And uh, if you ever do want to talk to me, if there's anything I can do to make it up to you, you can call me. You know, anytime. But I uh, I understand if you don't want to talk to me. So, yeah, that's it. Take care of yourself, Jane."

There was a beep, and the message ended.

A deep, confusing torrent of emotions welled up inside her. He hadn't threatened her, so she was partially relieved. She knew him well, or she had, once, and she wanted to believe it when he said he was trying to take responsibility for his life. Some part of her still wanted the best for him. But in addition to the relief and charitable feelings, she was also livid.

How dare he insert himself back in her life, even with a voicemail? The restraining order had expired long ago. She supposed it was possible he was trying to do the right thing. But had he even considered how it would make her feel to hear his voice? How many bad memories and feelings it would dredge up?

Jane had a knee jerk urge to call Bert again, but she didn't want to talk to him until she'd had more time to process Carl's voicemail. Instead, she went for a drive, blasting her car stereo as loud as she could stand it.

She drove to a beach north of town, and parked where she could look out over the water. Then she smoked one cigarette, but stopped after that. The emotions she was feeling were beyond cigarettes. She needed—something else.

What would it take to be a different person? To be the kind of person who wouldn't get thrown off course by a voicemail from an abusive ex? She also knew she should cut herself some slack. It was normal that Carl's voicemail would fuck her up. But still, she wanted to be free of the effect he had on her. Of the effect he was having right now. Of feeling like she needed to run to Bert, so he could save her.

For nine years, Bert hadn't just been her best friend, he'd also been her hero. And he hadn't only helped her pick up the pieces after Carl, he'd defended her from Carl.

At the beginning of their friendship, Bert had come over to her new apartment to hang out. The apartment had been cramped and was always dingy, no matter how much Jane cleaned it. But it had been the best she could find after fleeing from the place she'd shared with Carl.

That night, however, Bert had lit up her small, depressing space with his personality and wit. They had just finished a meal that he'd cooked for her, and she was marveling at his culinary talent, when Carl showed up at Jane's door.

He'd been drunk, and had pounded on the door so hard it shook the walls. Seeing how scared Jane was, Bert had told her to stay put, then answered the door himself. He'd asked Carl, politely, to leave. Carl had told Bert to go fuck himself. Bert had asked Carl to leave again, this time not so politely. Then, Carl had tried to push into Jane's apartment.

Next, Bert had dragged her ex in to the hall and landed several strategic punches that rendered Carl temporarily harmless. Bert's threat to do it again, plus the restraining order, had finally kept Carl away from Jane. A few months later, he'd moved out of state. By then, she had already abandoned her depressing apartment and moved in with Bert.

She stifled a sudden sob: she still needed her hero. Grabbing her phone, she dialed her best friend's number.

When he picked up, he teased her. "Geez, Jane, twice in one day? I'm going to have to start charging you by the hour."

"I'm sorry, but I really need to talk to you."

"I was kidding. Bad joke. You can call me anytime, you know that. What's going on?"

She gazed out at the bright, sparkling surface of the water. In the wintertime sun, it looked inviting. But she knew it was deathly cold.

"I need to talk to you about Carl."

For the next couple of days, Jane inhabited a strange, limbo-like space. The laid-back staycation she'd planned, with overindulgence in sleeping, bad TV, and takeout was no longer what she wanted. Carl's call had shoved the past into her present, disrupting her life with tumultuous emotions she'd thought she'd left behind a long time ago. But apparently, she hadn't. She'd only buried them.

Bert had been adamant: she didn't need to call Carl back unless she wanted to. Her first priority was to take care of herself, and, if Carl kept calling her, she could look into getting another restraining order. Bert had assured her there were circumstances in which you could get a restraining order against someone in another state, and promised he would help her again if she needed him. She was grateful. But he couldn't make her feel calm again. One unwanted voicemail had her questioning everything.

Adding to her confusion, by Saturday morning, she still hadn't heard from Liam. Jane suspected that, as she'd feared, he was ghosting her. But maybe that was for the best. She didn't truly know him or anything about him. Maybe, she should simply think of her encounter with Liam as a good story—one she could tell when she was old and grey—and move on.

But then, Saturday afternoon, he called.

"Hello Jane, it's Liam. Liam Burns?"

"It's good to hear from you," she said, a bit stiffly.

His tone was apologetic. "I'm sorry it took me awhile to call you. Some unexpected things came up. Is now an all right time?"

"Yeah, now's fine," she said. She meandered down the hall to her bedroom, where she sat cross legged on the bed.

"I wanted to tell you," Liam said, "I had a great time with you the other night."

"I had a good time too," Jane told him.

"You did? Good. Good, I'm glad to hear it."

Was he nervous? Maybe she was imagining it, but she thought she could hear a hint of nervousness in his voice. "So, are you getting ready for your audition?" she asked.

"Yes. I am. About that. Before the audition, I was wondering, if it wouldn't be too forward, I mean, if you think you might enjoy it—I was thinking we should go somewhere? Spend some time together. How does that—I mean, does that interest you?"

He *was* nervous, she could hear it in his voice. It was kind of adorable. For the first time in two days, she started to feel a little bit good.

"You're still on vacation, aren't you?" Liam pressed.

"For this weekend and all of next week," she confirmed.

"Maybe you have plans already. I shouldn't presume."

"I planned to take a staycation," she informed him. "I really wanted some time to myself."

"Ah. So I did presume."

She started to say that if she went away with him, it could only be for a couple days. She needed her time alone. But then she wondered why. What was she going to do alone? Freak out about Carl for another full week, without even her job to distract her? Maybe a trip with Liam was just what she needed to take her mind off Carl's re-intrusion into her life.

Jane began picking at the bedspread, then immediately stopped herself. "Where would we go?"

"I was thinking somewhere warm. Or maybe there's someplace you have in mind? It's up to you. My treat."

"That's a pretty big treat," she objected.

His tone became playful, and she could imagine him grinning on the other end of the call. "Well, you did pay my cover charge at The Mix. Then, I drove your car. That's your gas money. Plus you put me up for a night *and* made me coffee in the morning. I think I owe you."

Jane laughed. "There is this place I like that's relatively near here. I guess it's kind of—rustic? But it's close enough to drive." She didn't like the idea of Liam paying for plane tickets, a hotel, and who knows what else. It was too much; the kind of thing that introduced feelings of obligation. She didn't want that.

"So how rustic is this place?" he asked. "You don't mean camping, do you? I'm not much of a camper, I'm afraid."

Jane stretched her free arm above her head. "It's not camping," she assured him. "They have cabins you can rent. It's on the coast. Winter's not the busy season, so there might still be cabins available. I mean, it rains a lot."

Liam laughed. "Sounds absolutely gloomy. So you're in?"

"I'll see if I can get us booked," she said.

"Just give me the information and I'll book it. My treat, remember?"

"All right," she relented. "But we're taking my car."

13

The next morning, they went to the coast. Liam had insisted on driving. Jane wasn't sure if he truly loved driving her car, or if he just didn't trust her behind the wheel. Either way, she was unbothered. If she drove, she'd want to smoke. She wasn't sure how Liam would react if she smoked in front of him. Besides, she was quitting. In theory.

Liam had given her a long kiss when he showed up at her apartment. Then, he'd helped her load her car with food she'd purchased the night before, for their stay at the cabin. But so far, since they'd been on the road, he'd been quiet. Jane figured he wasn't a morning person.

It was, she thought, truly odd she was taking a trip with Liam Burns (of all people) to one of her favorite childhood haunts. When he'd said she could pick their destination, she'd instinctively chosen a place where, as a kid, she'd been able to be herself. In a way, she felt she was using Liam, or at least the trip itself, for her own reasons.

"You know," he glanced over at her, then put his eyes

back on the road. "Don't take this the wrong way, but you're a nice person to be around when no one's talking."

Jane laughed. "Is there a right way to take that?"

He sounded contrite. "What I mean is, it's easy to be around you without saying anything. It's a bit rare."

"I'll try to remember to be sensitive to your word aversion."

He chuckled. "I'll be able to talk once we're settled. I'm just not big on talking while I'm driving."

It wasn't until they were traveling through National Forest land, which was the last stretch of the drive, that Liam's tongue loosened up.

"It's a bit spooky through here," he remarked, as they passed through a particularly dense stand of tall evergreen trees. Even though it was the middle of the day, the trees blocked most of the light. All of the tree trunks were covered with deep green moss. Lighter green lichens hung like cobwebs from the trees' feathery branches.

"Yeah, lots of rainforests," Jane agreed. "It is kind of spooky. Full of life, though."

"I wouldn't have imagined this. It's a real presence, isn't it?"

"Definitely." She looked over at him, and watched his eyes travel from the trees back to the road. He seemed enveloped in a sense of awe. She turned back to her window, smiling. It made her feel good that he seemed to sense the beckoning magic of one of her favorite places.

"Are we getting close?" Liam asked.

"Pretty close. When we break out of the trees you'll start to see the ocean." To demonstrate what this would be like, Jane raised her arms to the sky and made an angel choir noise.

"It's that good?" he asked.

"*I* think so."

"Well, if you think so, then I suppose I shouldn't argue —oh God—is this it?"

They came around a curve, and the dense trees receded to the left. To the right stretched open fields of wild grass. The clouds, which had followed them all morning, split apart, and winter sun burst through the openings. The escaped rays danced over the grass, and the blades undulated in the ocean breeze. Further in the distance was a churning slate blue line: the Pacific.

"Beautiful," Liam said.

Jane raised her hands and made the angel choir noise again.

"All right," he agreed. "It's that good."

After they checked in at the lodge, they got back in the car and drove the short distance to their cabin, which sat on top of a bluff, just above the beach. They parked next to the cabin and unloaded the car.

"It's not fancy," Jane warned, as they went inside. "But we're right on the water."

Liam went straight to the breakfast nook, which was set against a large picture window that looked out over the ocean. He peered outside. "I see the Pacific all the time in LA. But this feels different."

"It's more lonely here," she agreed. "And more eerie. I'm going to put the food away. Do you want a beer?"

"Sure." He slid on to one of the benches at the breakfast nook. "Aren't you going to join me?"

"After I put everything away." She knelt by the mini cooler, retrieved a beer, and took it to him.

"Thanks." Liam gave her an amused smile. "You don't have to play housewife."

"I'll be right back."

There was a slight hiss as he opened his beer bottle. Jane began unloading the contents of the mini cooler into the half-sized refrigerator.

The kitchen was pre-stocked with plates, mugs, glasses, silverware, and cookware. She found a large mixing bowl, and arranged the fruit she'd brought inside it. Then she nabbed the other chilled beer. Taking the bottle in one hand, and the bowl of fruit in the other, she joined Liam at the breakfast nook, then set the fruit on the table. She opened her beer bottle and clinked it against his. "Cheers."

"Cheers," he repeated, softly.

The ocean below them was a constant roaring drone. Jane felt tension ebbing from her limbs as she listened. Whether the weekend with Liam turned out well or not, it would be worthwhile, just to be near the ocean. She was feeling the pull of it deep in her gut, and she wanted to go outside, to explore and see if this place was how she remembered it. Or to see if it had changed.

"I'm so glad we came here," she said.

"So am I."

Then she warned, "There's not much to do."

"So what do you typically do when you're here?" he asked, taking a sip from his beer bottle.

"Walk on the beach. Eat. Read. Make a fire and stare into it." She laughed. "Then stare at the ocean. Listen to it roar. Hours of excitement."

Liam stood up, came over to her, and held out his hands. She looked up at him. He took one of her hands and tugged, and she let him pull her to her feet.

He smiled. "I'm just glad to be here. Thanks for agreeing

to disappear with me for awhile." He brushed his finger over her cheek. Then he kissed her, a slow, sweet kiss that sent pleasant shivers through her body.

There was an invitation in his kiss, and she wanted to accept. But she was torn. The pull of the place and her desire to explore was just as strong.

"Do you want to go out with me and look around?" she ventured.

"I was actually wondering if you wanted to take a look at the bedroom."

She grinned up at him, and he chuckled.

"You *really* want to go outside, don't you?"

"I haven't been here in years," she apologized. "I'm dying to see what it's like."

"I could do with a rest," he confessed. "If I'm honest, driving here wore me out."

"It's a long drive," she agreed, quickly.

"Why don't you go look around, and I'll grab a quick nap," he suggested. "We can have a good dinner at the lodge later. I take it that's the only place around here to get a meal?"

"Unless you do your own cooking."

"I can cook," he told her. "At least a halfway decent omelette." He was still holding on to her hand.

"Go sleep," she told him. "I won't be long. I just need to scratch my curiosity itch."

He dropped another quick kiss on her mouth, squeezed her hand, then let it go. As he started for the cabin's bedroom, he said, "Don't let me sleep through dinner."

After Liam had disappeared into the bedroom, Jane found the thermostat and turned up the heat. Then she put on her navy blue rain parka and went out.

She started along the trail that wound along the top of

the bluff, noting the strange-shaped evergreen trees that clung to its edge. Their branches grew mostly in one direction, because they faced the constant wind blowing in from the ocean. She decided against going down to the water. Although she would have loved being on the beach with a few other solitary souls, it seemed deserted today. She was not sure she wanted that much solitude.

After her long hike along the bluff, she walked back toward the highway and was pleased to find that a small gas station and mini grocery store was still there, and still in business, just as she remembered it. On a whim, she picked up a dozen eggs, a brick of cheddar cheese, and a ripe tomato. She left the store carrying a small paper grocery sack.

The wind howled past her ears on the way back to the cabin, and the ocean was a quieter rumble in the distance. The air tasted and smelled like salt water and woodsmoke. She inhaled the fragrant air, and felt a deep sense of relaxation come over her. Being here made her feel reconnected to a part of herself she had almost forgotten. It felt good. Suddenly, she was excited to get back to Liam, and began walking quickly toward the cabin.

Inside, it was still. She peeked in the bedroom, and saw that Liam was still asleep. Staying quiet, she put the eggs, tomato, and cheese away in the kitchen.

She took a shower, staying under the hot spray until she felt like a lump of warm jelly. Then she dried her hair, wrapped herself in a big white towel, and pushed quietly into the bedroom, where Liam appeared to still be sleeping.

Jane knelt by her suitcase and pulled out fresh clothes. She laid them on the bed, then sat on the edge and dropped the towel so she could get dressed.

"You look so lovely from this angle," Liam said.

She grinned. "So you *are* awake."

"It was the hairdryer. That high pitched whining sound —impossible to sleep through."

She heard him shift his position on the bed, then felt his warm hand on her shoulder. He pushed her hair aside and pressed his lips to her neck. Jane felt a sweet, urgent ache between her legs.

"I'm sorry I woke you up," she said, without turning around.

"I'm rested." He drew a torturously slow line down the middle of her back with his finger, and she shivered.

"You're a sadist."

"You like fucking more than you like playing," he retorted.

She turned around and looked at him. "Isn't fucking the point?"

"Of course," he smiled. "I admire your ability to get to the point. But playing can be fun."

"You're naked," she observed.

"It got warm in here while you were out."

"Maybe I turned the heat up too high." She shuddered as he began to trace his finger back up her spine, from base to top. Then he tilted her head toward him and kissed her.

"Can we play later and get to the point now?" she asked.

"All right." Moving with lightning quickness, he took her by the shoulders and lowered her to the bed. Then he moved over her, nudging her legs apart with his knee.

She looked up at him, half surprised, half amused.

"So did you mean right now?" he asked. "Or a little bit later from now?"

"I'm ready now." Jane felt her cheeks flush. She'd

always been able to get aroused quickly, but Liam seemed to have the ability to send her body into overdrive.

He put on a condom, then pushed inside her, with a quick, rude movement. Her body rose to meet him as she clenched her muscles around his dick. After a few slow strokes, he fucked her fast and hard. She clung to him as she began to cry out, reveling in the almost savage rhythm of their bodies. He came first, and she shattered around him a few moments later. He rolled to the side and cradled her against him. They were both breathing hard.

"Was that too rough?" he asked.

"No," she said.

"It seemed like what you wanted."

"It was."

"Can we try it my way at least once before we leave here?"

"The sadistic way?" she scoffed.

"The playful way," he corrected.

"Sure," she said. "We can try it."

But she felt insecure. Liam seemed to want more from her than she was used to giving. She wasn't afraid he would hurt her, or force her to do anything she didn't want to do, but she was afraid she might disappoint him. She was used to having sex on her own terms. Then Liam tightened his arms around her, and she tried to relax.

14

At the lodge restaurant, Jane and Liam sipped on glasses of wine while they waited for their dinner to arrive. They talked about the few things they had in common: the recently concluded benefit at the Foundation, the weirdness of Caleb's obsessive personality, and the drive from Seattle out to the coast.

When the wait-staff brought their meals, she said, "We're stuck with the food for a few days. Hope you like it."

"I'm sure it will be delicious." Liam sat back in his chair and smiled at her. "So. Tell me something. About you."

She stopped with her fork poised above the seared salmon on her plate. "Could you make that question a little more specific?"

"We've essentially just met," he apologized. "I'm not sure what specifically to ask."

"Well, that's unfortunate." She took a bite of salmon. "Oh my God. This is so good." She wrinkled her nose. "How's the lamb?"

"Very good."

Jane shuddered. "How can you even eat a lamb?"

"How can you eat salmon?" he countered. "Aren't you depriving the local Orca population of one of its main sources of food?"

"I *work* at the Foundation. It's my job, not my religion," she retorted. "Besides, there's a delicate balance between ecosystem conservation and the maintenance of the local fishing industry."

"Tell yourself whatever you need to, salmon thief," he shot back. "Whatever helps you sleep at night."

She grinned, and took another bite.

"All right," he relented. "You want me to ask a specific question?"

She nodded. "It would help."

"How about your parents? What are they like?"

"Both gone," she said. "They passed before my uncle did. Quite a few years before."

That was not quite true. Jane's father had taken off when she was nine years old. It was possible he was still alive out there, somewhere. But Jane had not heard from him since. After her father's departure, her mother had gone through a succession of boyfriends. It was her mother who had eventually died. But the real story was too complex to explain over dinner.

"I'm sorry," Liam said. "See. This is why it's difficult to ask specific questions. You never know when you're going to wade into a minefield."

"No." Jane waved her fork. "No minefield. It's okay. It was a long time ago. I was closer to my uncle, anyway."

"What was he like?" Liam asked. "If you want to talk about him, that is."

"Yeah, I like to talk about Chuck," she assured him. "I don't know. I used to hang out at his place—my place now —and we'd have these long rambling conversations.

Usually about whatever was on his mind, not mine, but he was always thinking about interesting stuff, so—that was okay."

"What did he do? I mean, what was his profession?"

"He was a Boeing engineer," Jane said. "He got a sweet retirement package. After he retired, he spent most of his time reading. He loved literature, and history. Science. He just loved to learn, and he loved talking about everything he was learning." She laughed. "Once he got going it was hard to make him stop."

"So, did you live with him?" Liam asked. "Your uncle?"

"No, not really. I was already living away from home by the time my mom died. Uncle Chuck's place became home base for me, but I didn't actually live there. I just visited. He didn't have anyone else, I mean, not family, anyway. He never got married. He was my mom's brother, but they didn't get along."

Jane felt weird, then, like she'd said too much. But Liam's face was lined with sympathy.

"You must miss him a lot."

"Well, of course." Jane took a sip of her wine. "I miss him all the time."

Liam smiled so the skin around his eyes crinkled. "That wasn't so bad, was it?"

"What?" she asked.

"Answering a few personal questions?"

She narrowed her eyes and gave him a guarded smile.

"Well, now it's your turn," he told her. "You can grill me."

"I don't want to grill you." She dug her fork into her herbed mashed potatoes. "I want to finish my food."

"Really?" He looked more amused than offended. "You don't want to know anything at all?"

She looked up at him, a bit embarrassed. "I wouldn't know what to ask. I mean, everyone at the Foundation was like, your biggest fan ever, but umm, I've never even seen anything you've done."

His face broke into a broad grin. "Really? Absolutely nothing?"

"PBS and BBC dramas aren't really my thing. I like TV that's a lot less, uh, cerebral?"

Liam snorted with laughter. "It's not cerebral. It's just another brand of entertainment. It's entertainment for people who *think* of themselves as cerebral."

Jane smirked. "Like the people who work at the Foundation, you mean?"

His eyes danced with merriment. "I said no such thing." He took a sip of wine, then put down his glass. "You don't have to ask me anything about my job. Just ask me something general. Or personal. Whatever you want."

"All right," Jane gave in. "Actually, there is something I want to know about your job."

Liam motioned for her to go on.

"You know how Caleb is kind of annoying?" she said. "I mean, how he gets on everyone's nerves?"

"I still remember what it was like to work with Caleb, yes. I seem to also remember getting us both stuck in a stairwell in an attempt to avoid speaking to him."

She grinned. "So, when you're on a film set, is there an equivalent to someone like Caleb? You know, that person who makes everybody roll their eyes, or go out of their way to avoid them?"

"Yes," Liam said, without hesitation. "Method actors."

"Method actors?"

He nodded. "The most annoying people on the planet. Worse than Caleb. Exponentially worse."

"What's a method actor?" Jane asked. "Wait, are they the people who try to like, live the role?"

"They try to become the character, wallow in the character's emotions, live the character's reality on and off the set. It's extremely tiresome. Method actors give the most annoying interviews. 'I just felt I became one with my character, there's a part of my soul that will *always* belong to King Lear.'" Liam rolled his eyes. "It's complete rubbish. And it tends to excuse those who use it from acquiring solid technique, which I find inexcusably sloppy."

Now it was Jane's turn to grin broadly. "Why don't you tell me how you really feel?"

He flashed a rueful grin back at her. "You managed to hit a sore spot. I'm not one hundred percent against method acting, it's got a respectable history rooted in theater. It's a useful tool to have in one's repertoire. But actors who turn it into a gimmick?" Liam made a face. "It's a definite pet peeve."

"Are you thinking of anyone specific?" she asked.

He leaned forward. "I won't name names. But there was a—colleague, I'll call him—who was an overenthusiastic member of the cult of method acting. On the page, his character was supposed to be repellent to all others. So this colleague consumed raw garlic before showing up on set each morning. He was literally repellent, to all of us, to the crew, to anyone who crossed his path. It was horrific."

"That's just rude," she objected.

"Exactly. It had nothing to do with acting, and everything to do with being a massive cunt."

She gave a surprised laugh.

"I shouldn't use that word, I'm sorry," Liam apologized.

"That particular word doesn't bother me," she reassured him.

He reached out and took her hand. "I'm glad. Because it's one of my favorites."

Jane grinned at him. She was having a good time, she realized. Liam wasn't just attractive, he was fun to be with. Somehow, she hadn't expected that.

"Speaking of annoying people," she said, "Caleb seems convinced you're going to come back to the Foundation for another benefit. Are you really going to do that?"

Liam arched an eyebrow. "I'll likely do one more. I have a feeling Caleb wants to make me an honorary employee, but that's not feasible."

"It's good of you to even consider it."

He beamed one of his quick smiles at her in response. Then he moved his fingers gently over hers, a light touch that she nevertheless felt all through her body.

"Should we get dessert?" he asked.

She was decisive. "No. I brought chocolate. Let's go back."

In the cabin, they sat at the breakfast nook, nibbling on the chocolate bar, again falling into comfortable silence. The ocean was a rhythmic drone in the background, rushing in to shore, then pulling back.

"This place is wonderful," Liam said. "Peaceful. Thank you for sharing it with me."

"I brought you a coat to wear," she told him. "For the beach? Your overcoat isn't really the right thing, it won't cut the wind. It's my uncle's old parka. Hope that doesn't weird you out. It might be a bit big, but I think…"

He reached across the table and took both her hands firmly in his own. "I don't have a parka with me. Thanks for bringing one. I'll wear it."

She was silenced by the feel of his warm hands closing around hers. Any touch from him made her ready for sex. Such an intense attraction could not last forever. But she doubted it would wear off soon. For sure not during the weekend.

"So," Liam said slowly. "Fancy a quick fuck?"

"Yeah." She stood up, and started for the bedroom.

He was learning her body. He knew what she wanted and was giving it to her. Hard. Fast.

And then he said her name.

"Jane."

She opened her eyes and looked at him. He twined his fingers in her hair, pulling gently on it, covering her mouth with his. Then he slowed his thrusts and changed his rhythm. She moaned into his mouth.

"Do you like that?" he asked.

Her body responded, surprising her with its hunger for the slower pace. When she came, it was in shuddering, deep waves, leaving her clinging to Liam afterwards.

She felt good, but vulnerable. He was stirring up a cauldron of dormant emotion, and she wasn't sure how long she'd be able to handle it.

15

In the morning, Liam found the eggs in the refrigerator, and cooked an omelette. As it turned out, he hadn't made empty boasts about his cooking skills. He made a mean omelette.

After breakfast, they left for the beach. They took the wide, wood-lined steps from the bluff down to the ocean. A massive wall of weatherbeaten and surf-tumbled logs, higher than their heads, was jumbled and pressed up against the bottom of the bluff. This portion of the beach was on National Park land, so park employees had chain-saw-cut a path several yards wide through the logs to make the beach accessible.

Liam thumped his hand on the cut edge of one of the logs as they walked past. "How do these get here?"

"They wash up on the beach during storms," Jane explained. "Mostly during the winter."

"Must be dangerous."

"You wouldn't want to be on the beach during a storm," she agreed. "Well, unless you're the kind of person who likes Russian Roulette. Then you might."

"Not anymore," Liam said, under his breath.

Jane looked over at him. "You actually used to do that? Play Russian Roulette?"

"Not literally," he said. "But my personal life definitely used to resemble a deadly game of chance." He gave a tight, quick smile. "Those days are over now."

Jane wasn't sure if she should ask more questions, so she left it alone. She was a private person herself, and she understood if Liam preferred not to be interrogated about his personal life.

Once they had passed through the logs, they turned to the left and started walking down the beach. The mist was heavier near the water, and it was difficult to see more than a few yards in front of them.

"Now this *is* eerie," Liam remarked, as they plowed through the soft, dry sand above the tide line.

"Let's get closer to the water," she urged. "At the edge, where the sand is wet? It's easier to walk down there."

They traveled a few yards down toward the water, and began ambling along the packed wet sand.

"The tide's going out," she observed. "I should have checked the tide tables before we left."

"Thanks for the parka," Liam told her. "It was good of you to bring it. You're right, my coat would be useless in this weather."

"It's windy right?" Jane grinned and spun around in a circle, then stopped.

"Hey," he said, smiling at her.

Suddenly the sight of him in her uncle's parka hit her in a strange way. He looked nothing like Uncle Chuck, and the parka was too large for him. Chuck had had a pot belly. He'd also been a few inches taller than Liam. But seeing a living person—seeing *Liam* wear Chuck's clothes—gave her an odd sensation. For the first time, it hit her in a concrete, visceral way: her uncle was gone. He was never coming back. Jane began walking faster down the beach.

Liam called out after her.

She turned around, and saw him trailing behind. "I need to run for awhile!" she yelled. "I'll catch you on the way back!"

"Be careful!"

"I will!" She kept going, then turned back around. "Don't let me get lost!"

She took off.

It felt good to run on the hard sand, with the thrum of the surf in her ears. But nothing was as loud as the wind rushing past her. It was constant but not too strong, providing just enough resistance as she ran.

She ran until the howling wind and crashing surf blended into one sound. Her chest began to hurt and she stopped, taking in large gulps of air. She wasn't a regular runner, and she was out of breath.

Jane turned and looked back up at the bluff, which was barely visible through the wispy mist. At the top of the bluff, here and there, the dark green shapes of the weather-beaten evergreen trees poked through the grayness. She looked back to where she'd left Liam and saw nothing but mist.

Slowly, she turned toward the ocean, and watched the water roll forward, then draw back, away from the shore. The tide was still going out. Tiny seabirds skittered across the sand, looking for food. She hoped they were finding it.

An uneasy sensation stole over her. She felt as if the sand under her feet might give way. The actual dangers on the beach, she knew, were getting stuck in a riptide while swimming, or getting hit by a log when a strong wave washed it up on the sand. She was in no immediate danger. But the sense that the sand was precarious under her feet remained. Worse, she felt paralyzed, as if the tide would claim her, once it made its slow turnaround and came rushing back up across the beach.

Being here was bringing up feelings that were too dark for a romantic getaway with Liam. She wanted to snap out of it. But the overwhelming sense of uncertainty would not leave her alone.

"Jane," said a soft voice.

It was Liam. He encircled her in his arms, and wiped tears away from her cheeks with his fingers. She hadn't known she was crying.

She looked up at him. "I love it here. I love this place. Why do I feel like this?"

"I don't know the answer to that. But how about we get you back inside where it's warm? We can have some of that generic tea I spied in the kitchen."

She nodded, and he nudged her back in the direction of the beach stairway. Then he took her hand in his.

"I'm sorry," she apologized. "I'm not much fun right now."

In answer, he simply squeezed her hand as they continued to walk.

"This beach almost feels haunted," Liam said, presently. "It's gorgeous, but it's got a weird intensity to it."

Jane swung their clasped hands forward. "It's more cheery in the summer. Especially if the weather's nice. Then it's perfect. Never too hot. Never too many people. And kids fly kites."

"Did you fly a kite here as a kid?" Liam asked.

"Yeah."

"I can picture that. Your red hair. Chubby cheeks. Staring up at the sky. Snot running down your nose."

She nudged him, hard. "Hey!"

"Real kids make snot," he said solemnly.

"That's probably how it was," she conceded.

They continued the rest of the way down the beach in silence. When they entered the path carved out between the logs, the sound of the ocean was temporarily muffled. They started up the wood-lined stairs, Liam still holding on to her hand.

Back at the cabin, Jane put on a pot of water to boil for tea while Liam thumbed through the assortment of complimentary tea bags.

When their tea was poured, they settled at the breakfast nook with their mugs.

"I'm truly sorry," she started again, but he shushed her.

"Sometimes people experience strong emotions for unpredictable reasons. It's nothing to be ashamed of."

"I know. But you wanted to have fun and get away, and right now I'm not any fun."

He frowned. "That's not true. I told you I wanted to spend time with you and that's what we're doing."

"Are you for real?" she laughed, incredulous.

He seemed puzzled. "For real?"

"You aren't—you don't—I didn't expect..." She gave up. "Never mind."

"Why don't you get some sleep?" he suggested.

"Won't you be bored?"

"I'll join you."

She sighed. "Does this mean we're old?"

"Well," he smiled. "I'm old. You're distraught."

"This is really so pathetic," she protested. But she allowed him to steer her in the direction of the bedroom.

"Not really," he said. "I've been on a crazy schedule for weeks without proper sleep. I need to catch up. And: you're distraught."

She kicked off her jeans. "Why do you keep saying that?"

"Just a hunch." He had not yet removed any of his clothes.

She peeled off her sweater, then crawled in bed wearing only her long sleeved tee-shirt and underwear. "Do you want to elaborate on your hunch?" she asked. "Because it sounds like something men say to women to keep them in their place. 'Sit this one out, honey, you're too *distraught*.'"

He sat at the edge of the bed, on what was becoming 'his' side. "I don't want to butt into your life."

"What's your hunch?" she pressed. "I want to know. I'll tell you if I think it's bullshit."

Liam reached over and pushed a lock of her hair away from her face. "Do you promise to tell me if you think it's bullshit?"

"Are you being sarcastic right now?" she asked.

He laughed. "A little."

"So what is it?" She curled her body in a tighter ball under the covers. "What's your hunch?"

"I'm guessing what you feel might have to do with your uncle," he said. "That you handled everything after he passed, then you got on with life and assumed you were doing well. Which I'm sure you were. I'm sure you have been—except for, maybe, the grieving part?"

When she didn't answer right away, Liam touched her shoulder. "Jane?"

"I heard you," she said, in a quiet voice.

"So," he asked. "Am I close?"

"It's not bullshit," she admitted. "But I don't want to

talk about it right now." Other than Bert, she hadn't spoken to anyone about her uncle's death. Even though Liam was offering a sympathetic ear, she didn't know how to begin talking about Chuck's passing. It was easier to say nothing.

"All right. We don't have to talk about it. But let me know if you change your mind." Liam stretched out alongside her, without getting under the covers, and put an arm around her.

"What are you doing?" she asked. "Why aren't you getting in bed?"

"I want to let you sleep. If I get in bed with you I won't leave you alone."

"Fucking and sleeping go together pretty well." She turned her head and grinned at him. "We could do both."

"Fine," he agreed. "I'll give it five minutes. If you're not asleep in five minutes I'll fuck your brains out. Deal?"

"Deal." She yawned. "You'll have to make good on that. Set your watch."

He moved his arm off her, and she heard a series of beeps. Then he put his arm back around her again. "Done."

She never heard the alarm go off.

16

Jane opened her eyes. Liam was no longer curled around her, but stretched out on his back, asleep and breathing quietly. For awhile, she watched him sleep.

He was turning out to be more than she'd expected. She'd agreed to go away with him for the sex, and, to have a distraction from Carl. But Liam wasn't just a distraction. He was funny, and also kind. She knew if she were a normal person, she'd be feeling all gooey and stupid about him. But instead, his kindness filled her with uneasiness. She had an uncontrollable urge to call Bert, so he could help her sort through her thoughts and emotions.

Jane got up and knelt by her bag, where she'd left her phone, and checked the time. It was already four in the afternoon. She pulled on her jeans and sweater, then took her phone and left the bedroom.

Through the cabin's windows she saw daylight was beginning to wane outside. She grabbed her parka from the hook by the door and went out. She headed to the side of the cabin that faced toward the lodge, so she'd be out of the wind.

It was often difficult to get cell reception at the coast, but she decided to call Bert, anyway. If she could reach him, it was meant to be. The phone rang several times, and just when she thought it would go to voicemail, Bert answered.

"What's going on?" he asked, worried. "Are you okay? Carl didn't call you again, did he?"

"No," Jane said. "He hasn't called again. Not so far. Anyway, that's not why I'm calling you."

"Where are you? Are you home? Are you sure you're okay?"

"I'm fine." She looked out toward the ocean, where the waves were crashing on the beach in the fading light. "I'm uh, actually out at the coast. With Liam Burns."

"You're at the coast with Liam Burns?" Bert exclaimed. "That's great! I mean, is it great? You're with Liam Burns, but you're calling me. Is there a problem?"

"No," she reassured him. "It's going really well."

Bert sighed, sounding relieved. Then, abruptly, he became irritated. "So why *are* you calling me, then?"

Jane raised her eyebrows high. "Because I wanted to talk to you. What's the problem? We talk all the time."

"Yeah, but you're with *Mr. Masterpiece*. You just told me you're having a good time. Aren't you being kind of rude to him?"

"No." She started to get angry. "Why can't I talk to you while I'm here?"

"How would you feel if Liam was on the phone while you're with him? Wouldn't you think that was rude?"

"I'm not being rude." Jane raised her voice. "He's asleep right now. How is that rude?"

"Look," Bert sighed. "Is something wrong? Because I don't know why you'd call me in the middle of a fling with fucking Liam Burns—unless something's wrong."

Jane opened her mouth to tell him what she was feeling. How she'd started crying on the beach. How Liam's kindness made her uncomfortable, and how messed up that was. But then she heard another male voice through the phone. Someone else was with Bert.

"Yeah, just a second," Bert said, his voice muffled. "I have to finish this phone call. I'll be right there."

"You have company," she sighed. "That's why you don't want to talk to me."

He lowered his voice. "Don't be like that. Yes, I have company, and yes, I'd like to enjoy my company. But I'm always here for you if you need to talk. You know that."

"Just forget it," she said. "Forget I called. Go have fun."

"Jane." There was frustration in Bert's voice. "You're being an ass-pain. Stop being an ass-pain."

"Have fun," she repeated. "I'm hanging up now."

"Well likewise. Go enjoy your super-great fling with Liam Burns."

"Goodbye." She hung up.

Jane stared at the phone for a second, feeling lonely. She'd wanted Bert to help her make sense of her tangled feelings, and instead, talking to him had made her feel worse. She slipped her phone in her pocket. When she turned to go back inside, she saw Liam. He was leaning against the wall of the cabin.

"Hey," she said, walking up to him. "You're awake."

"Is everything all right?" he asked. "That didn't sound like the happiest conversation."

"It's no big deal," she assured him. "It was just my friend Bert. We have—spats—sometimes."

Liam looked like he was about to say something, then stopped himself. "It's a bit chilly out here," he said. "Do you want to go inside?"

"Sure." She started for the door of the cabin and Liam followed. She could feel subtle tension emanating from him.

Once they were inside, she retreated to the couch. The couch, as well as several chairs, were arranged around a small coffee table, near the cabin's wood-burning stove.

Jane gestured to it. "We haven't even made a fire yet. We should do that." She looked over at Liam, who was still standing near the cabin door. "Are you going to sit down?" she asked.

He seemed agitated. "Can we talk?"

"Okay," she agreed, warily. "But could you maybe sit down, first?"

Liam came over, but instead of joining Jane on the couch, he sat in one of the chairs opposite her, then leaned forward. He started to speak, then stopped. Flashed a smile that was more like a grimace. Finally, he spoke.

"Look, I know I'm just a guy who showed up in your life a couple weeks ago. I have no right to pry into your business. But, you were upset earlier today, and just now, you sounded upset on the phone. Is anything—bothering you?"

"What do you mean?" Jane let her eyes wander to the wood stove. Without a fire going, it looked as if it would be cold to the touch. There was a small rack of fire utensils next to it, with a shovel for ash, a pair of fire tongs, and a small broom. When she moved her gaze back to Liam, she saw a concerned look in his eyes.

"I'm just wondering—I don't want to overstep—but I get this feeling there's something going on with you. Something troubling you, or maybe scaring you?"

She held his eyes this time, but kept her face carefully blank. "Thanks for asking," she said, politely. "But no. There's nothing going on."

She wasn't being truthful, of course. Under the surface, things *were* going on. She had a new, acute awareness of losing Uncle Chuck. In addition, Carl's voicemail was still on her phone. For some reason, she hadn't deleted it. She could tell Liam knew she wasn't being honest, and that he was bothered by her lack of candor. But she didn't want to talk to Liam about her problems, and especially not about Carl. Liam was supposed to help her *stop* thinking about Carl, if only for a few days.

"Are you sure?" he pressed.

Her voice went cold. "Yes, I'm sure. Nothing's going on. I meant it when I said it the first time."

An uncomfortable silence filled the room. Liam looked away from her, then back, and smiled, a bit sadly. "Are you hungry?" he asked. "Do you want to go have dinner?"

"I am hungry," she said, "but I don't know if I'm in the mood for the lodge."

"What else are we going to eat?" he asked, laughing. "Fruit and hardboiled eggs?"

Jane sighed and stood up. "Fine. Let's go." She went to retrieve her coat, but Liam stopped her with a light hand on her arm.

"You know what," he said. "I spotted fish and chips on the menu last night. I'll get the restaurant staff to pack it for us." He got up from his chair. "We can eat here. I'll go now."

"Okay." She felt awkward, and wondered if he felt it, too. "Guess I'll try building a fire."

He raised his eyebrows. "You know how to do that?"

"I'm pretty good at it, actually," she snapped. Then she wished her tone had sounded less harsh.

"I trust you." He kissed the top of her head, then went to the door and took Uncle Chuck's parka off one of the pegs. "I shouldn't be too long," Liam promised. "I'll text you if it takes more than half an hour."

The door banged lightly when he left. She watched through the windows as he walked in the direction of the lodge. When she lost sight of him, she wandered over to the wood stove. Maybe she didn't know how to open up to Liam, but she definitely knew how to build a fire.

Jane opened the stove's glass paneled doors, and made sure the flue was open, too. Beside the stove were two small bundles of wood, and a basket filled with old newspapers and a few matchbooks. That would do it.

She set about arranging newspaper, kindling, and fire-wood inside the stove. Then she struck a match, and put it to the newspaper in several places. She sat back on her heels and watched as the paper blazed and caught the kindling on fire. Once everything was burning well, she shut the stove's doors, satisfied. It was a small thing, but building a successful fire made her feel good.

Then, she moved to a chair by the fire to relax. But she couldn't, she was too restless. So she got up and retrieved her phone from the pocket of her parka, to see if Liam had sent a text. But there was no cell service now. So even if he'd tried to text, he wouldn't have been able to reach her. She wasn't sure what time he'd left, and wondered how long he'd been gone.

Unsettled, she returned to her chair. As she stared at the blazing fire, she wondered if Liam truly wanted her to confide in him. Would he actually want to hear her talk, in depth, about how she missed Uncle Chuck? Would he even want to know about Carl's voicemail and how much it had messed her up? And if she shared these things with him, could she trust him?

Behind the glass-plated doors of the wood stove, the

fire crackled merrily. She decided to open one of the bottles of wine she'd brought. If Liam took too long getting back, she'd have a glass without him.

She went in the kitchen and set one of the wine bottles on the counter, then started hunting through the kitchen utensils for a corkscrew. But she couldn't find one. Feeling a bit frantic, she opened every drawer and every cupboard, hoping a corkscrew would appear. But she came up empty. She could buy one at the little grocery store, but it would be closed now.

"This sucks," she said, aloud. She suddenly wished she was back in her apartment, alone, watching bad television and eating microwave popcorn. She knew it was strange to feel that way. Any number of her co-workers would have given anything to be in her place. Sasha, especially. But Jane still felt a yearning to be alone. Alone was lonely, maybe, but it was always easier.

17

She lifted the bottle of wine off the kitchen counter, and studied it, wondering if she could use one of her keys to get the cork out. Was that desperate?

The cabin door opened. Jane turned around, still holding the bottle, and saw Liam in the doorway. He was carrying a large paper bag, and he held it aloft.

"Success!"

She faced him, gripping the wine bottle with a pained expression on her face.

"Are you all right?" he asked.

"We don't have a corkscrew," she mourned.

"Oh." His face relaxed. "Well, that's easily fixed."

He set the paper bag down at the breakfast nook, and pulled a small ring of keys from his pants pocket. Then he held out his hand. "Give me the bottle."

"That's what I was thinking," she laughed, nervously. "I was going to use my house key."

"No, not a key, a corkscrew." He showed her a silver-colored cylinder attached to his key ring, and popped the cylinder off to reveal a small but adequate corkscrew. Then he went to work on the wine bottle. It took a bit of wrestling, but he got the cork out. "There," he said, handing the uncorked bottle back to Jane.

She laughed. "Thank you. I can't decide if it's nerdy or sleazy that you have something like that on your key ring."

"Well in this case it's providential, isn't it?" he said. "Let's eat before the chips get cold."

"I built a fire. We could, umm, watch it burn?"

"Sounds good," he agreed.

There was still tension between them. She hated it.

"If you get the food," she told him, "I'll bring everything else."

They perched on the edge of the couch with plates of deep fried cod, chips, and glasses of wine. The silence between them remained uneasy. For awhile there was just the sound of their utensils clinking against their plates, and the fire crackling.

"I didn't mean to make you uncomfortable earlier," Liam ventured. "With my questions? I was just concerned."

"I know. I'm not very good at talking about stuff that's bothering me." She threw him an apologetic smile. "I guess I need to get better at that."

"You shouldn't tell me anything," he contradicted. "Not if you're not comfortable confiding in me."

Jane placed her almost empty plate on the coffee table, and looked at him. "You were right, when you said I didn't grieve after Chuck died? I didn't. There wasn't ever time. Or I felt like there wasn't. But when I saw you wearing his parka today, something just clicked."

Liam frowned. "I was wondering about that."

"It's not your fault," she assured him. "It's not like I thought you were him, or anything." She gave a self-conscious laugh. "I don't know how to talk about this. About death? I don't know what else to say."

"I think it's common not to know how to talk about it," Liam observed. "Death makes people uncomfortable." He laughed then, and raised his eyebrows high. "Can't imagine why."

She laughed with him. It felt good, like the awkwardness between them was starting to melt away.

"Do you think that's why you were crying on the beach this morning?" he asked. "Your uncle?"

"Mostly."

"So there was something else?"

She looked at him. Could she tell him about Carl? Should she? She was afraid of being judged. And, on a deeper level, she also feared Liam could be just like Carl. He certainly didn't seem that way. So far. But Carl hadn't seemed abusive at first, either. There had been warning signs, but she'd been blind to them. What if she was experiencing the same kind of blindness now?

"I'm pushing you again," Liam said. "You don't have to tell me what it is."

She drew in a long, quiet breath. Then she took the plunge. "It's all right. Someone I used to know left me this voicemail. An old boyfriend. When I was with him, it was a —bad time."

"A bad time?" he repeated.

Jane forced the words out. "He was violent. To me. I had to get a restraining order."

"And the same ex-boyfriend is contacting you now?"

She nodded.

"Do you feel safe?" Liam asked.

"I think so. His message wasn't threatening. He told me he's still living miles away. And he said he understands if I don't want to get in touch with him. That's what he said, anyway."

"Why did he bother you at all?" Liam was speaking calmly, but there was an angry, dangerous edge to his voice.

Jane knew instinctively that the anger was not directed at her. It was for Carl. She laughed without humor. "He sounds like he wants to make amends. His own version of it, anyway."

"You don't owe him amends," Liam said, tersely.

"I know that," she agreed. "I'll get another restraining order if I have to. But it just, you know. It really shook me up when I heard his voice."

"Of course it did. I'm sorry, Jane. That must have been —it must be—incredibly difficult for you."

She shrugged. "I got through it." Then she tried to laugh. "Bet you didn't know you were on vacation with Ms. Baggage."

He took her hand. "Everyone has baggage."

The sensation of their clasped hands was enormous. It was more than a physical thing, though it was that, too. Her whole body was alive with the unfamiliar feeling. She was afraid if she moved, her awareness of it would go away.

Liam squeezed her hand, gently. "Is there anything personal you want to ask me?"

"Like what?"

"Anything. You haven't asked me one personal question. Not since I ran into you at The Mix. Not even *at* The Mix."

"That's not true," she protested. "I asked you why you were still in town."

"But that's not personal."

"Umm. Okay. Do you have—kids?"

"Yes. One. I have a nine-year-old daughter with my ex-wife. In fact, I was just talking to my daughter, while I was at the lodge. It's easier to get a signal there."

His *daughter*. His *ex-wife*. How did they fit into his life? Was he good friends with his ex? Or were they sworn enemies? Did his kid live with him? Were those even appropriate questions to ask?

She decided on a neutral question. "What's your daughter's name?"

"Ingrid."

"That's a nice name," Jane faltered.

Liam studied her for a few moments, and she began to feel uncomfortable.

"What?" she asked.

"This is difficult for you, isn't it?"

She slumped against the couch. "I haven't been doing tons of actual dating," she confessed. "I think I've forgotten how to do the get-to-know-you small talk thing."

He touched her knee. "It's all right." But he looked a bit sad and lonely.

Jane tried again. "Does your daughter live with you?"

He smiled at her. "Part of the time. Her mother has the more stationary life, so Ingrid's with her more than she's with me. But she comes for long visits. Sometimes she flies out to see me where I'm working, if we can manage it."

"I don't know anything about kids," Jane admitted.

"You haven't got any?"

"No. And I don't want any, either." She peeked at him to see if he was horrified, but he merely looked thoughtful.

"It's not for everyone," he allowed. "Actually, I'm not sure it's for me. But it happened, and now I can't imagine my life without my daughter."

"That's honest," Jane said.

Liam leaned forward and put his empty wine glass on

the coffee table. He gave her a quick smile. "I try to be. Enough people find it charming that it works for me. Until it doesn't."

"It's still better to be honest."

His eyes crinkled. "I'll keep that in mind."

Jane got up and took their plates. When she came back from the kitchen, she knelt by the wood stove and peered inside it. The fire was beginning to die down, and she glanced over at Liam. "Do you want to hang out here by the fire for awhile? If I put another log on, it'll burn for a few more hours."

"Sure," he said. "Let's stay here. We can finish the wine."

Jane opened the stove's doors and a blaze of heat rushed out at her. She used the fireplace tongs to maneuver two medium sized pieces of wood onto the fire. When she was done, she shut the doors and dusted her hands on her jeans.

Liam beckoned her over, and she sat near him, just close enough for their legs to touch.

"You're a very conscientious person," he chuckled.

"Um, thanks? More wine?" she asked.

"I'll get it." He leaned forward and poured wine into each of their glasses.

They fell into silence, an easy one this time. Jane watched the fire and sipped her wine. She moved into a sort of trance as she felt the slow warm buzz of the alcohol steal over her. Soon, she was under a spell of complete contentment.

When Liam pried the glass from her fingers, it shook her out of her reverie. "It's empty, luv," he said, returning her glass to the table. His glass, also empty, was already there.

She let her head fall on his shoulder. The wine made it easy.

"That's it," he coaxed. "Just sit with me."

The crackling of the fire, the fainter roaring of the ocean, and the feeling of her head resting against Liam's warm shoulder blended in to one sensation. She was so relaxed she could have fallen asleep, but she also felt alive, and wide awake.

"Jane."

She loved the way he said her name. He could turn her on just by saying a few words. "I'm here," she said.

Liam put his hand against her cheek. "Are you sleepy?"

She met his eyes. "Not really."

"Neither am I." He cupped his hand behind her head, and pulled her closer. Then kissed her. It felt different. Maybe it was the wine. Maybe it was because she'd told him about Carl. But it was different.

He deepened the kiss, and she slipped her arms around him. When he began kissing her neck, she arched her back and sighed. He pulled her closer. Her heart was beating fast, but he was restrained, teasing her with slow kisses, on her mouth, her neck, just beneath her ear.

She grew impatient, and pushed away from him. Keeping her eyes on his, she pulled her shirt over her head.

"In a hurry?" he laughed.

"Is that okay?"

He took her shoulders. "*You're* okay."

"Okay," she said, softly. Then she stood up. Slowly, she began to remove the rest of her clothes. While Liam watched, she stepped out of her jeans, and kicked them to the side. Then she reached back and unfastened her bra, and let it drop to the floor. She slid her underwear down her legs then stepped out of them, and she was naked in front of Liam in the flickering firelight.

"You're truly lovely," he breathed, then motioned for her to come near him again.

She took a few steps forward. He reached out and grasped her hips, and looked up at her with lust, tenderness, and a hint of humor. "So you probably want me to 'just fuck you,' yeah?"

A slow smile curled across her lips. "Yeah. That would be ideal."

Liam tugged her closer. Then he flicked his tongue over her clit, tasting her. She closed her eyes and let him tease her. Tried to let him take his time. Her legs began to tremble.

He raised his head and looked up at her. "Are you doing all right?"

"Yeah." But she was dying to have him inside her.

He tugged on her hand, and lowered her to the couch. Then he pushed her gently on her back and began removing his clothes. Her legs continued to shake as she waited for him. When he finally entered her, she cried out with relief and satisfaction. She curled her legs around him as he thrust slow and hard inside her, and a rush of unfamiliar emotions surged through her limbs. More emotion. Being here with Liam had switched on an emotional spigot. She didn't know how to shut it off.

He seemed to sense the shift in her, and stroked his hand across her face.

"Are you all right?"

"Fine," she gasped. "Don't stop."

He sped up his pace, the way she liked it. The orgasm that finally seized her had a note of sweetness she had not ever felt before. Or at least, she hadn't felt it in a very long time.

They curled up together on the couch under a blanket, and watched the fire go down. Once it was out, Jane followed Liam back to their bedroom, where the surf lulled her to sleep.

18

Jane and Liam passed the rest of their time together like a couple who had settled in to a comfortable routine. During their last dinner at the lodge, they lingered over dessert and coffee.

"So if I ask you a question I've asked before," Liam said, "will you get mad?"

"I don't know," Jane grinned. "Did I get mad the last time you asked?"

"Annoyed, I think. But I was hoping I could give it another go?"

She took a sip of coffee. "Okay. Shoot."

"I'll try to phrase it differently this time," he said. "So here goes: Are you happy in your job?"

"Oh, right!" Jane burst out laughing. "You want to know if I'm living my best life."

"Sure," he smiled. "Or just if you're happy."

"I actually thought about this," she admitted. "And okay, no, being a receptionist at the Hope Project Foundation isn't my passion. Umm, this will sound bad, but I don't have some big dream I'm afraid to pursue. I know everybody's supposed to have one. But I don't."

"You don't?" he asked.

"Not really. I love my home. Thanks to Uncle Chuck there's no mortgage, but there are condo dues and taxes. Utilities. Car maintenance. Groceries. I need a job. My uncle always believed there was dignity in work, you know, all work and any work? That probably makes him sound like a simpleton."

"No, he sounds like a solid person," Liam said. "Good work ethic, all that. Sounds like my father. I didn't appreciate him much when I was younger, but as I get older, I do."

"I'm a lot like my uncle, I think," she said. "I don't need my job to fulfill me emotionally, you know? I just need the paycheck and the health insurance."

"So what does fulfill you?" Liam asked.

The question caught her off guard, and she turned her head toward the window. They both fell silent. She looked out in the darkness, in the direction of the water. Even unseen, the ocean's presence was palpable.

"I'm sorry," Liam said, low. "You don't have to answer that."

Jane turned away from the window. "I'll tell you what fulfills me. It's survival. That's it. And anyone who doesn't like it can fuck off." She rolled her eyes, then, mocking herself. "That sounds so melodramatic."

Liam reached across the table and took her hand. "It's not melodramatic. But it does sound a bit bitchy." He smiled to soften his words.

She smiled back at him gratefully. "I'm fine with being bitchy."

He squeezed her hand, and let it go.

"What fulfills *you*?" she asked.

He held up his hand, then counted off on his fingers. "My work. My kid. Beyond that, I suppose, those rare and good friendships that sometimes come along—the ones that surprise you."

"Those are all good things," Jane agreed. "I'm a fan of rare and good friendships."

Their waitress, who had been making the rounds in the room, stopped at their table. "Do you folks need anything else? More coffee?"

Liam smiled up at her with understated charm. "I might take a bit more. That is, if we're not monopolizing the table?"

"Oh, absolutely not," the waitress assured him. "The dinner rush is over. Take all the time you need."

"Thank you," he said, as the waitress filled his cup with more coffee.

"Can I ask you another personal question?" Jane said to Liam.

"Of course. What do you want to know?"

"The other day, on the beach, you said something about how your life used to resemble a 'deadly game of chance?' Or I thought I heard you say that."

"I did say that," he agreed. "Or rather, I said my *personal* life used to resemble a deadly game of chance."

"What did that mean?" she pressed. "Unless you don't want to talk about it."

"No, I can talk about it. It's just the usual cliched rubbish. I had a difficult time handling my first taste of fame." Liam cracked a sardonic smile. "You know the story. Fast living, too many women, trying to fill the vast emptiness inside." Now he rolled his eyes.

"What changed?" Then she laughed. "Or, maybe it didn't change?"

He looked rueful. "I was hoping marriage would change the way I felt about myself. It didn't. But having Ingrid helped. And I eventually came to a place where I realized I'm lucky to do the work I do, even if I haven't ascended to the level of fame I once thought I deserved. I got my priorities straight, that's all. That's what really changed things."

Jane's smile echoed his ruefulness. "That sounds so —mature."

He gave a quick grin. "Well, now, I have a question for you that won't sound mature at all. About this Bert character. Is he an old boyfriend of yours? I'm trying to figure out who my competition is."

Jane laughed. "No. Bert's my best friend. But he was never my boyfriend. He's gay."

"Well," Liam smiled, and picked up his coffee cup. His eyes sparkled over the rim. "That's lovely."

The morning they left the coast, they packed the car early. Liam drove from the cabin to the main parking lot in front of the lodge. While they were checking out in the gift shop, Jane examined a rack of souvenir keychains displayed at the front counter. All the keychains were attached to a small rubber toy, and all the toys were different marine creatures: seagulls, octopi, salmon, and Orca whales.

"Look," Jane said, pointing at the keychains. "Do you think I should get one for Caleb or would that...."

The young woman behind the counter cut across Jane's words. "I'm sorry if I'm being rude," the girl said, as she handed a credit card receipt to Liam for signature. "But are you Liam Burns?"

"Well, yes." He smiled at the girl. "I am. I see you read the receipt."

Suddenly, Jane was fighting hard to keep from engaging in more eye-rolling.

"I don't want to take up your time," the cashier apologized. "But I just have to tell you, that one movie, *Slim Chance?* It's like, my spirit movie. I love it so much." She giggled then, self-conscious.

"That's an old film." Liam was amazed. "Can it even be found anywhere?"

The girl nodded. "I tracked down the DVD. I had to order it from the UK."

"Well, thank you for your patronage and your kind words," Liam said gravely, signing the receipt and handing it back to her.

"Would you mind if—could you give me an autograph?" she pleaded. "I know it's a lot to ask, but it would be *so* amazing. I'm sorry."

"No need to be sorry," Liam told her. He slipped an arm around Jane's waist and gave her a reassuring squeeze. "Give me something to sign, and I'll sign it."

The girl provided Liam with a piece of paper. He signed it, and she thanked him profusely. Then he and Jane went out to the car.

He stopped her on the sidewalk. "Was that weird?"

Jane shrugged. "Everyone at the Foundation acted the same way. I mean, it's normal. It's part of your job, right?"

"But it made you feel weird," he said.

It seemed petty to admit that it had. So instead of admitting it, she changed the subject. "When's your audition, again?"

"Friday."

"So when are you flying back to LA? Or is it Vancouver?"

"It's LA. The show films in Vancouver, but the audition is in LA. I'm flying out tomorrow morning."

Jane put out her hand. "Give me the keys. I'm driving us back to Seattle."

"I'm well-rested," Liam protested. "I can drive."

"But you won't be rested once we get back. And then you have to get on a plane. That's a bad idea. Keys please."

He gave in and handed them over.

As she was pulling on her seatbelt, Liam said, "Thank you for a lovely time, Jane Daniel."

"Thank you too, Liam Burns," she returned.

"We should do it again sometime."

Did he mean that? Or was he being polite? "Sure." She kept her tone light. "Next time you're at the Foundation for a benefit, and I go on vacation, and we run into each other at a bar, let's do it."

"It's a date." He settled in to the passenger seat, adjusting it for his height.

Jane started the car. She wanted to believe this was the beginning of something between her and Liam, because, for the first time in years, she felt ready to try. However, the exchange between Liam and his fan in the gift shop had reminded her how different his life was from her own. The idea of continuing any sort of relationship with him seemed absurd. Surely, he would prefer to go out with women in his business. Women who would understand him. Women who, if they weren't out and out celebrities, still had much more glamour than Jane.

The fantasy was over. It was time to drive back to reality.

19

Liam remained quiet as they traveled back through the dense forest. He kept his eyes on the window, peering through the lichen-covered trees. His silence gave Jane a chance to adjust to the fact that, after today, she probably wouldn't see him again—unless he returned to help the Foundation with another benefit.

Presently, however, the silence in the car became too intense for her. Unlike Liam, she did enjoy talking when she was behind the wheel. Especially on a long drive.

"Can I ask you something?"

He turned away from the window. "Sure. Of course."

"How do you prepare for an audition so close to when it actually happens? You only have one day left, right?"

"It's plenty of time. I don't like freaking out right before I audition. And I've done most of the prep already. Research. Going over the script. Working out the physicality. I did most of that while I was in Seattle, when I had free time at the hotel. I'll review my notes. But the character's already in me."

"Do you want the role?" she asked. "I mean, is it a good one?"

"Yes," he nodded. "It's a good one. I want it very much."

"Can you talk about the, um, the character? Or what the TV show's about?"

"I'd rather not." He sounded apologetic. "It's a bit like sharing your plans for the future before you take any concrete steps to make them happen. Jinxes it."

"Totally understand," Jane assured him. "Forget I asked."

"What I *can* say," he offered, "is that the project has the potential to be something I'm proud of. That's always the ideal. I've had to take a few mediocre parts to stay employed. But for the most part, I've been fortunate." He laughed. "There are worse things in life than being a D-List celebrity, I suppose."

"You're not a D-List celebrity," she scoffed.

"Not yet," he laughed.

They stopped at a fast food restaurant for breakfast sandwiches and coffee. At first, Jane headed for the drive-through, but Liam said he preferred to go inside, to stretch their legs.

While they were ordering food, the girl at the cash register recognized Liam from the PBS *King Lear* presentation. They chatted about it while she rang up their order.

"D-list celebrity," Jane teased, as they sat down at a table with their trays.

"She said she had to watch it for a class in school!" he exclaimed.

"But she *recognized* you," Jane pointed out. "She even called you 'King Lear.'"

"Exactly! She said, 'Oh my GAWD. It's *King Lear*.' Poor girl was still suffering from the experience. As far as she's concerned, I *am* King Lear. I ruined weeks of her life. She'll never forgive me."

Between their breakfast stop and getting back on Interstate 5, Liam fell asleep. By now, Jane was certain she was mere hours away from never seeing him again. They'd had a good time together, but he was obviously out of her league. He'd already been recognized twice that morning. Maybe she should think of their trip to the coast as a test run? She'd "put herself out there." She'd taken a risk. That was worth something, right?

But if she was honest, it was no longer enough. She liked him. A lot. He made her feel emotions she hadn't experienced in years. Why did the person who finally made her feel this way have to be someone like Liam Burns? Why couldn't it be somebody who wasn't famous?

When they were close to the airport, Jane called his name several times to wake him up.

He straightened in his seat. "I'm sorry. I didn't mean to fall asleep."

"It's all right," she said. "Listen, we're not far from the airport. Did you want to check into a hotel there? Or do you want to go back to Seattle?"

"I need to speak with you," he said, abruptly. "Can you have a semi-serious conversation while you're driving?"

"Yes?" She was puzzled. "I mean, I can't look at you, I have to look at the road, but...."

He broke in. "I suppose this is a bit sudden, but we need to have this conversation now, before we possibly part ways."

"Okay," she said, keeping her eyes on the road. "So, what do you want to talk about?"

"I enjoyed our time together, and I want to see you

again," Liam said. "As soon and as much as possible. But do you—is that something you also want?"

She was instantly awash in sensations of disbelief, happiness, and...was that hope? Was she actually hoping this thing with Liam could—just maybe—be worth pursuing?"Before you answer," he continued, quickly, "I should tell you, I can't say for sure when I'll be back. It depends how the audition goes, and if there are callbacks. I can't make a definite plan. But I will be back, likely within the month. I want to spend time with you, if you want that, too."

Jane gripped the steering wheel tightly and stared straight ahead. "Yeah," she said. "I want that."

"Really?" Liam sounded relieved.

He was relieved *she* wanted to spend more time with *him*? A broad grin spread across her face. "Yeah. Really."

"Well. Fantastic."

Jane glanced over at him, quickly, and saw his grin was as big as her own. Then she put her eyes back on the road.

"About tonight," Liam went on, "I could take a hotel room at the airport if you prefer. But I'd be just as happy to spend tonight with you."

Another small thrill went through her. "You could stay with me. If that's truly what you want?"

"It is. Question for you. Would it be all right if I took a shower at your place?"

"Of course."

"We should both take one."

Jane smirked. "What do you have in mind?"

"Just good hygiene. And maybe a little delayed gratification."

"Delayed gratification?" she repeated. "Can you elaborate?"

He chuckled. "Just shut up and drive. I'll elaborate later."

Jane's hand opened and closed against the wall of the shower. Liam stood behind her, with his body pressed against her back. His left hand held her steady, and his right hand was massaging the tip of her clit. Every few seconds he slipped a teasing finger or two inside her, and she tightened her muscles around him. She was breathing hard as the water ran over their bodies, and she could feel his erection pressing against her.

"Let's fuck here," she said, breathless.

"Not yet."

"Okay, but can't we....oh, God," she moaned, as he began sliding his finger rhythmically in and out of her cunt. She bucked her ass and her hips backwards against his legs.

"You really want to come, don't you?" he laughed.

"Duh, you fucking sadist," she panted.

He stopped, pushed his finger against her clit, and held it there. "I'm not a sadist."

"So what are you then?"

Liam began swirling his finger over her in a slow, circular motion, building up the tension. "I'm just playing. I'm showing you what I like."

He began to move his finger over her clit more quickly, driving her to the edge again. Then he pulled his hand away. She gasped. Tremors ran down her legs, and she whimpered as the sensations of an almost-but-not-quite orgasm tormented her.

"Please," she begged. "Please just make me come."

He pushed one finger inside her again, then two, then finger-fucked her, slow, as the water continued to pour over them. When she finally came, she felt it over every inch of her skin. Like her whole body was having an orgasm.

Liam held her against him while she rode it out, like he wanted to feel what she was feeling. When her breathing became somewhat normal, he reached around her and turned off the water. Then, he got out of the shower, and extended his hand to help her out. Her legs were still shaky. She raised her eyes to meet his as she stepped out of the shower stall.

Her nipples tightened as his eyes roamed over her body. She examined him, too, realizing she hadn't actually *looked* at him before. From his round, muscular shoulders, to the dark hair springing from his chest and trailing down his stomach, to his erect dick, framed by wide-set hips that tapered to strong legs. She dragged her eyes back up to his face.

Then she pushed past him, grabbing his hand and tugging on it as she aimed for the bathroom door. With her free hand, she opened the door and took a few steps toward the bed.From behind, Liam slapped her on the ass.

The slap revived all her arousal from the shower and then some. She turned around and trained her eyes on his erection. "Don't you need to do something about that?"

He wrestled her to the bed, and began kissing her, deep heavy kisses that left her breathless again. Then he pulled back, and looked down at her.

"Thanks for letting me play." His eyes were dark and full of emotion. She felt connected to him, and the feeling was strange, but welcome.

"There's a condom in the nightstand," she managed.

He straddled her, and reached over to the nightstand drawer. Then he kept his eyes on her while he rolled the condom on, and she watched while he focused on her face.

When he penetrated her, she closed her eyes in triumph. Maybe she was up for this, after all.

Jane woke to Liam brushing her hair from her forehead. He'd already dressed and was wearing his overcoat.

"What time is it?" she asked, then yawned. She put her fist to her mouth to stifle it.

"It's seven," he said. "I didn't want to wake you. I've got a car coming in a few minutes."

"Do you need coffee?"

"I'm fine. I'll text you when I know more about my return trip to Seattle."

"Ok." She pushed herself to a sitting position in the bed, shivered, and drew the blankets around her shoulders.

"Don't be upset if you don't hear from me right away," he cautioned. "You can text me if you want to. I just won't be too available until after the audition."

"I won't bug you." She yawned again. "Good—I mean break a leg."

"Saved it just in time." He bent down and kissed her. "I'll be in touch. I promise."

He left the room. She heard him open the door to her apartment, the sound of him hefting his bag on his shoulder, and then his footsteps on the stairs. Outside, a car was idling. Her bedroom windows faced the street, and she could hear Liam talking to the driver. Car doors opened, then shut, and finally there was the sound of the car driving away.

"He'll be back," she said aloud. And the amazing thing was, she actually *wanted* to believe it.

20

J ust before noon, Jane rolled out of bed and shuffled to the kitchen. As she waited for her coffee to finish brewing, she realized she wished Liam was there. She missed him.

"Dammit." She poured herself a cup of coffee, muttering "dammit" repeatedly under her breath. She was already starting to wonder if he would truly get back in touch, or if he'd fed her a line. One good thing about fuck buddies was that you never had to wonder where you stood with them.

When she opened the shades to survey the view, the day was grey and overcast, and the mountains were buried behind dreary clouds. She sipped her coffee, hating the empty feeling in the condo.

She had an urge to call Bert, but stopped herself. She hadn't spoken to him since their sort-of-fight on the phone. She knew they'd make up eventually, but for the first time ever, she allowed herself to consider that Bert might not always be a phone call away.

He would never disappear from her life completely, and

she knew she could always count on him in a pinch. But what if Bert got married? What if he and his husband adopted a child? Or what if he landed a job in another country, which was something he sometimes talked about doing? If any of those things happened, she might not be able to pick up the phone and reach him any time.

Gulls flew against the grey sky, barely visible except for the bits of white on them. She wondered how Uncle Chuck had lived alone here for so many years. But her uncle had always seemed content with his life. Jane was no longer certain whether she was content with hers.

From the bedroom, an unfamiliar noise startled her. It sounded like a request for a video call. "Oh crap," she said. "I left my phone in there." Who was it, she wondered. Liam?

But when she got to the phone, she saw it was Bert. That was odd. He didn't like video calls.

She accepted the call and her friend's face appeared on the screen. Fifteen years ago, Bert had been in the Navy. He was a veteran of the war in Afghanistan. He didn't talk about his experience overseas much, but he still wore his hair in a close-cropped military style.

"So are you alive?" Bert asked.

"Yes," Jane said. "Obviously."

"Can we talk?"

"Umm. Sure. I need to get my coffee though. I'll be right back." She went to the kitchen to retrieve her coffee mug, and took it to the bedroom. Then she settled on the bed, cross-legged, and picked up the phone. "Okay. I'm back."

"Where's Mr. Masterpiece?" Bert asked.

"He flew out to an audition this morning."

"Oh," he laughed. "Of course he did." A loud meow sounded in the background. Bert switched to the voice he used to speak to his cat. "Do you want to say hello to Jane? Do you? Come look in the phone. Come here, come look in the phone, sweetie, there you go."

His face went off camera, and a large fluffy-white cat appeared in his place. Felix meowed several times, loudly. Then he began alternating purrs with piercing meows. Jane started laughing. Felix was so ridiculous. And adorable.

Bert appeared back on screen. "It's good to see your face," he said.

"Yeah?" she asked, wary.

"Listen. About the last time we talked: I'm sorry. You were right. I didn't want to be interrupted. But I shouldn't have made you feel weird for calling me."

She began picking at her bedspread. "It's okay. Everything worked out."

"I'm glad, but I'm apologizing here. Could you let me know if you're feeling that?" he asked.

She grinned. "It's okay, Bert. I know you need to get laid, too."

"Amen to that," he said, brightening. Then his expression shifted to concern. "You say everything worked out. What does that mean? Where are things with you and Mr. Masterpiece?"

"He said he wants to see me again, and I don't believe him," she blurted.

"Sweetie," Bert soothed. "Why would he say that if he didn't mean it?"

"I don't know, to be polite? British people are usually polite, right? Maybe it's a matter of form. You know, just something they say after lots of fucking?"

"Hmm. Did he toss it off on the way out the door? How'd he say it?"

Jane told Bert about the conversation she'd had with

Liam on the way back from the coast. How they'd talked about seeing each other again. "So?" she asked, when she'd finished.

"I think," Bert said slowly, "that unless he's a sociopath and he's messing with your head—which I doubt—I think he really wants to see you again."

"I'm waiting for a text," Jane groaned. "I'm waiting for a damn text." Her voice shook a little. "I don't know if I can do this."

"Are you sure this is about Liam? Or is there something else going on with you?"

"Maybe," she admitted. "I kind of lost it while we were on the beach. Liam was wearing Uncle Chuck's parka and it just hit me—I mean—Chuck was kind of my stability, right? And, you know. He's gone now. My stability is gone."

Bert's face looked troubled. "Hey," he said. "I've been thinking. We haven't seen each other in awhile. I should come out there and visit."

She smiled into the phone. "That would be great. And fun. When were you thinking of coming out here? What works with your client schedule?" Then she added, "And your personal life?"

"Well," he said, "my personal life will just have to understand I need to go see my friend Jane. But my client schedule—February would work. March is even better. Less busy."

"Why don't you come out in March?" she suggested.

"All right," he agreed. "I'll plan a trip for March."

"Felix looks healthy," Jane observed. In the background, Felix let out a loud "meow," as if he were agreeing with her.

"Listen," Bert said. "Just wait for that text, okay? Unless he hasn't been good to you, in which case I'll have to go find him and hurt him."

"He was," Jane assured him. "Good to me, I mean. It was, you know. A really good time."

"Good. Then wait. Go running. Get a dog. Watch a horror movie. Do whatever you need to, but don't write him off. Give him a chance to send that text. I could be wrong, but I don't think he's going to string you along."

"Ok," Jane sighed.

"Are we okay?" Bert pointed from himself, into the phone, then back to himself.

"Yeah," she cracked a smile. "We're okay."

"Well given that everything is so super ok, I need to get back to work. Ok?"

"Fuck off," she grinned.

"That sounds like the Janey I know. Call me anytime."

"You too."

She felt relieved. It was always better when she and Bert were in sync. His visit in March would be something to look forward to. And, she knew, he was right about Liam. His request to see her again was more than mere politeness. She needed to give him a chance to contact her.

Everything was good. So why did she feel like shit?

That afternoon, Jane partially followed one of Bert's suggestions. Instead of going for a run, she went for a long walk through the neighborhood above the waterfront. Then she wound her way back down, crossed the train tracks, and ambled along the beach for awhile.

There was a group of people getting ready to go diving at the beach's scuba park. They were talking excitedly amongst themselves. Looking at the divers standing around in their wetsuits in the cold winter air made Jane shiver.

When she returned to the condo she was restless. She

tried to relax and watch a movie, but she kept refreshing her phone, looking for a text from Liam. Finally she gave up on the movie and fixed a frozen meal.

After dinner, she treated herself to a long bath, and when she got out, she spent time carefully working moisturizer in to every inch of her skin. Then she put on a pair of clean pajamas and crawled in bed. Bliss. She was tired, full, and clean. Self-care for the win.

She checked her phone on the nightstand, the way she always did before she went to sleep. It was early, only eight p.m. Suddenly her heart was racing.

Liam's audition was tomorrow. Should she text him? Wish him well? Or should she leave him alone? She knew if Liam were anyone else, she would text him without thinking about it. But what if he didn't respond? She'd feel terrible if he didn't.

She pulled up a text window and held her finger over it for a few seconds. Then she began typing.

I already said this, but break a leg tomorrow.

She hovered over the "send" button. Took in a deep breath. Let it out slowly. "Fuck it," she said, and hit "send" on the text.

It made a noise as it went, then showed as "delivered." She reached over to turn off the sound on her phone, then stopped. If she left the sound on, she might hear Liam's response before she went to sleep; or, it would wake her up; or, she would see it in the morning. Or, of course, there would be nothing.

She carefully put the phone face down on the nightstand, stretched her arms behind her head, and prepared to wait for a reply. But after several seconds of staring at the ceiling, she groaned. "This is nuts."

She picked up a book. It was one she'd been reading off

and on for awhile, an absorbing story about espionage during World War II. It helped divert her attention. It was not putting her to sleep, however.

Swoop.

It was the sound of a return text message. She threw the book down on the bed and flipped the phone over. There was a message from Liam.

Thanks. x. How are you?

She typed, slowly, to avoid mistakes.

I'm good. Going to bed early.

After another minute or so, Liam sent back a response.

Same here. Sleep well. I'll let you know how it goes. We'll talk soon.

Jane turned off the sound on the phone and lay back down, feeling relieved and happy. Sleep came easily after that.

21

Liam phoned Jane from his place in LA on Saturday evening to tell her he'd been called back for a second audition the next week—and, that his daughter was staying with him, unexpectedly, for the weekend.

"It's good you're hanging out with Ingrid." She tucked her feet under her on the couch, to get more comfortable.

"Yes. It is. But I also wanted to remind you I'll be in touch, as soon as I can, about coming to Seattle to see you." His tone was apologetic and a bit tense. "I wanted it to be sooner."

"It's all right," she assured him. She wondered how she could sound so nonchalant, when only a couple days ago, she'd been climbing the walls waiting to hear from him.

"How are you, are you all right?" he asked.

"I'm thriving," she joked.

"*Are* you all right?" he pressed.

"I'm fine. It'll be good to see you. Whenever it works out for you to be here."

"I'm hoping it will be very soon. I'm definitely looking forward to seeing you."

Something about the way he said "seeing you" implied more than seeing, and even though she was alone in the room, she blushed.

"This can't be a long phone call," Liam went on. "Ingrid's mother is dropping her off any minute. But I'll call you after the next audition. Text if you need something."

"Break all your legs," she replied, for something to say. Then she felt stupid. Like a teenager who'd said the wrong thing to a crush.

But Liam replied, "I'll do my best."

Jane was relieved to get back to work on Monday, if only to have a distraction from her Liam-generated emotions. She hadn't heard from him again over the weekend. Since she wasn't sure exactly when his callback was, she hadn't sent him a text to wish him well. He'd said to "text if she needed something" but what, she wondered, would be a real need, rather than just needy?

"I really fucking hate this," she said aloud, as she sat in traffic Monday morning. "I fucking hate this so much." Then she heard Bert's voice in her head, the voice of reason, reminding her this was standard when you started dating somebody new. It would take awhile for she and Liam to find a comfortable communication rhythm. They were still feeling each other out.

"This is good," she told herself, trying to see the best in the situation. "I'm giving him space, he's giving me space. We're getting to know each other. This is healthy. Right?"

Back at the Foundation, there was a pile of clerical work waiting for her at the reception desk. Apparently, none of the office assistants who'd been filling in for her had kept up with it. Her email in-box was overflowing. She was going through her email when Sasha approached her desk.

"How was your vacation?" Sasha's hair was pulled back in a dramatic style that seemed to emphasize the elegance of her long limbs.

"Pretty...boring," Jane said. "Just the way I wanted it."

Sasha studied Jane with a shrewd and appraising eye. "You look great. Rested."

"That's how I feel. Hey, I like your hair that way."

"Thanks." Sasha leaned forward and said in a low voice, "I went on a date with Liam Burns."

"Oh?" Jane shifted uncomfortably. "Really?"

"Yeah. He stayed in town for awhile after the benefit. We had dinner."

"So," Jane asked. "How was it?"

Sasha rolled her eyes. "He was an ass. Completely self-absorbed. He didn't come off that way during the benefit, right? But I guess once he was done playing his part, his true self emerged."

"That sucks. I'm sorry he was such a —disappointment."

Sasha waved a hand, as if she were brushing Liam Burns off a shelf. "Whatever, it's fine. Now I know. It'll be awkward if he comes back and works on the salmon benefit, though."

Jane's voice was faint. "That probably would be super awkward."

"Well, anyway," Sasha grinned, "I'm glad you're back. I didn't have anyone to be bitchy with while you were gone."

"I find that hard to believe," Jane smirked.

"See?" Sasha pointed at her. "That is what I missed."

The main doors burst open and Caleb entered the office, carrying his stainless steel travel mug.

"Jane!" he lit up upon seeing her. He pounded on the reception counter several times as he passed. "Jane's back!" he yelled as he went down the hall to his office. "Jane is back!"

Sasha glanced sideways at her. "You probably didn't miss that."

She shook her head. "I even missed that. It's good to be back." Then she gave a crooked grin. "But maybe ask me again in two weeks."

She didn't hear from Liam until Wednesday. It was evening when her phone lit up with his number. She headed for the bedroom and sat down on the bed. "What's up?"

"I'll just get straight to it," Liam said. "I have good news. I got the part."

"Oh, that's great!" she cried out. She was more excited for him than she'd expected to be. "When did you find out?"

"This morning," he said. "Which brings me to my next piece of good news. Or, hopefully it's good."

"What is it?"

"I'm flying out to Seattle in the morning, and I'm staying through the weekend. Would you like to get dinner while I'm in town? Before you answer, there's another part to it."

"Another part?" she asked, confused.

"Yes. Ingrid's coming with me. I've got a new flat in Seattle, and I want her to see it. I'm putting her on a plane back to her mother on Saturday, but I was thinking the three of us could get dinner Friday night? Then you and I could spend Saturday evening and Sunday together."

"You have an apartment in Seattle?" Jane exclaimed.

"It's only been for the last couple of weeks," he explained. "I haven't even spent a night there, yet. So what do you think about dinner with Ingrid and me? On Friday?"

"Where's your new apartment?" she asked, ignoring his question about dinner. "It's not downtown, is it? You wouldn't think so, but that's kind of a terrible place to live. Well, in my opinion, anyway."

"No, it's not downtown. It's a bit north, near one of the marinas."

"Do you know which one? There are like, a zillion marinas north of downtown."

"Not off the top of my head." He let out an impatient chuckle. "Did you hear my question about dinner? You, me, and Ingrid? Friday night?"

Her heart pounded uncomfortably, and she forced out her next words. "Sure, I'd love to have dinner with you and your daughter. It sounds—great."

"Jane," his voice softened. "She's a kid. She'll love you."

"I would like to meet her," she said. "But I'm not a 'great with kids' kind of person."

"That's why I think she'll love you. Can you recommend anywhere for dinner?"

"Somewhere in Ballard," she said, immediately. "If your new place is north of downtown, and near a marina, that might be the neighborhood you're talking about, anyway. There's a ton of funky small restaurants that come and go. I could make a reservation if you want."

"Text me a list of three choices," he said, "and give me a general idea of what they are. I just want your local expertise. I'll have my assistant take care of the rest."

"Oooh, fancy, an *assistant*," she said, before she could stop herself.

"Just a virtual assistant," he corrected. "But I suppose it is a bit fancy."

"No, it's good," Jane laughed. "Now that I know you pay people to make your restaurant reservations, I'll never offer to book anything on your behalf without asking you for compensation, first."

"You really are a massive smart-ass," he said.

"Guilty," she admitted.

Liam lowered his voice. "Once we're alone, I really can't wait to fuck you senseless."

"*Oh.*" She felt her knees go weak even though she was sitting down. "Yay for fucking."

"Text me that list." His voice was crisp and amused. "I'll see you Friday night."

"See you then."

He hung up, and she stared at the phone, feeling horny and terrified. She hadn't anticipated meeting his kid. At least, not this soon. She hoped she wouldn't fuck it up. *Mess it up*, she admonished herself. *You're going to meet someone's kid. Better get "fuck" out of your vocabulary for a few days.*

When she checked in with Bert, she didn't tell him everything. She told him only that Liam would be in Seattle for the weekend, and that she was going to see him. She left out the part about meeting his daughter. She wasn't sure why.

"Well that all sounds good!" Bert enthused, when she finished telling him about her weekend plans.

When she didn't answer, he pressed: "Isn't it?"

"You know, we hardly ever talk about you," Jane mused.

"We only talk about me. Me and my job. Me and the things that annoy me. Me and my fuck buddies. Me and this—thing—with Liam. We don't talk about the people you're dating. We don't talk about your life at all."

This time, Bert was subdued.

"Bert?" Jane said. "Are you still there?"

"Yeah," he sighed. "I heard you. I know. You're right. That's one of the things I want to talk to you about when I see you."

"There's not something wrong, is there?"

"No, I'm fine," he reassured her. "Don't worry. We just need to catch up on a few things, and I want to do it in person."

"Okay," she said. "I'm still a little worried."

"Well stop. Go have a great weekend with Mr. Masterpiece, then talk to me after you're all stupid from fucking him for forty-eight hours."

She opened her mouth to tell him it would not be forty-eight hours, because she'd be having dinner with Liam and his daughter Friday night. Then she stopped. "Okay," she agreed. "I'll call you."

22

Jane drove to Ballard, one of Seattle's many neighborhoods, on Friday night. Earlier, Liam had sent a text, saying Ingrid had picked one of the restaurants from Jane's list. She'd chosen a pizza place.

It started to rain while Jane was searching for a parking space. She'd promised to meet Liam and Ingrid at six, but she'd left work late, and it was already ten minutes past the hour.

After circling the pizza restaurant for fifteen minutes, she spied someone coming out of a parking spot on the street. She stopped and put her flashers on to wait for it. The person in the car behind her started honking.

"Go around asshole," she said through gritted teeth.

But the person kept honking. She rolled down her window and made a sweeping gesture with her arm, indicating they should drive around her car. But the driver kept blaring their horn at her. Realizing her efforts were pointless, she pulled her arm back inside and rolled up the window.

The car Jane was waiting on finally left, driving away

with a glow of taillights. She pulled forward to parallel park. "Don't take my spot. Don't you dare."

The car behind her seemed poised to do just that, following close on her bumper. But then, at the last minute, it drove around and passed her with an angry rush of movement.

"Idiot," she muttered.

Fortunately, she was good at parallel parking, so she managed to maneuver into the spot. Then she looked at her phone. There was another text from Liam, sent a half hour ago.

We're here early. Take your time.

"Shit," she groaned. She sent a text back.

Trouble parking. Just got a spot. On my way.

The rain picked up as she walked the three blocks to the pizza place, and she hadn't brought an umbrella. She was going to get soaked. By the time she arrived at the restaurant, her coat was dripping wet.

Jane walked in the door and immediately inhaled the aroma of fresh baked pizza. To her right, a gas fire glowed in a mammoth fireplace. Wood tables stretched down the length of the restaurant all the way to the back of the room. To her left, there were pizza slices for sale under hot lights. Behind that was the kitchen.

She went up to the cashier. "Has Liam Burns, a party of two or maybe three checked in?"

"Yes!" said the woman behind the cash register. "We put them all the way in the back."

Jane thanked her, then made her way to the back of the long room, where she saw Liam sitting at a table with a little girl who looked seven years old, instead of nine. The girl had light brown hair that fell down her back. *So that must be Ingrid*, Jane thought. Heart pounding, she approached the table.

"You made it!" Liam smiled and stood up to greet her, then embraced her with one arm, not seeming to mind that she was drenched. He kissed her cheek.

"You're dripping water on the floor," Ingrid observed.

"I know," Jane said, making a face. "It started raining after I parked my car."

She unbuttoned her parka. Liam helped her out of it, and hung it on the back of an empty chair.

"There doesn't seem to be anywhere else to put one's coat," he explained.

"That's all right. I'm so sorry I'm late. The traffic was terrible."

He shushed her. "We could see that on our way here. But we walked, so we didn't have to deal with parking. Ingrid. This is my friend Jane. Jane, this is my daughter."

Ingrid put out a small hand and Jane took it.

"Nice to meet you," said the girl. Her speaking voice was a strange combination of a British and American accent. Her delicate features and light coloring were probably from her mother. But her eyes were hazel green, and shaped exactly like Liam's. It was a striking contrast with the rest of her face.

"Nice to meet you too," Jane replied.

Liam held out a chair at the side of the table for her. "Have a seat."

Liam and Ingrid were already working on salads. "We were pretty hungry," he apologized, as he saw Jane take note of their food.

"I'm so sorry I'm late..." she began again.

He stopped her with a warm smile. "Hush. Do you want one too?"

She shook her head. "I don't want to hold you up any longer. Just order dinner."

"Should we decide on a pizza?" Liam suggested.

"No meat!" Ingrid cried out.

"Ingrid just became a vegetarian," Liam explained.

"Well, that's a good way to be," Jane said. "It's kinder to animals."

"Dad thinks it's rubbish. But he's from a different generation, so he doesn't see things the same way I see them."

Jane glanced over at Liam. "Well yeah. I guess that would be true?"

Liam smirked. "My daughter is a great help in reminding me of the generational divide."

"Dad likes to tease me," Ingrid added. "But he's not serious."

Before Jane could decide whether to respond to Liam, or, to his verbally precocious nine-year-old, he pulled his phone out of his pocket.

"I'm sorry," he said. "I have to take this. It's about the job. I'll be right back. Order the pizza without me if the server comes by." To Ingrid, Liam said, "Be good while I'm gone."

"All right, Dad," she sighed.

He started for the door of the restaurant, holding his phone in his hand.

Jane turned, and spotted the pizza menu sitting off to the side of Ingrid's salad plate. "Do you know what kind of pizza you want?"

"I think the one with the peppers and onions," Ingrid said. "They fill you up, and I love peppers and onions."

"Well great, let's order that." Jane was relieved the kid at least knew what she wanted.

Ingrid picked up a glass with soda in it. Ice clinked as she raised it to her lips, took a sip, then set it back down. "How do you know my Dad?" she asked.

Uh oh. Here we go. "We worked together," Jane said. "But not for very long. He came and helped us at the company where I work."

"Do you like him?"

Jane paused, not sure how to answer. She noted that Ingrid had quick-changing facial expressions, just like her father. One minute she looked forlorn, the next mischievous, the next, a bit frightened.

"You know," Jane said, on impulse. "You don't have to like *me*."

That got Ingrid's attention. She looked up, confused, as if she didn't know whether she should declare that she did not, in fact, like Jane at all, or if she should stay neutral. She began to play with her salad, pushing croutons around the plate with her fork. She maneuvered each crouton through a small lake of bleu cheese dressing, and lined them up next to each other in a neat, dressing-covered row. "I don't know you," Ingrid said, finally. "So I don't know if I like you or not."

"That's a very honest answer," Jane replied. "Honesty is a good thing."

The server arrived then, interrupting them. "Are you ready to order now, or do you need more time?"

Jane looked up and smiled at him. "No, we're ready. We'll get the largest pizza you have, the one with onions and peppers?"

"They're jalapeño peppers," the server warned. "We go light on them, but they're very hot."

"I like spicy food," Ingrid declared. "But," she looked at

Jane, "if you don't like spicy food, maybe we should get something else?"

"I like spicy food too," Jane assured her. "Let's go for it."

As the server left with their order, Liam returned to the table.

"I'm sorry," he said, sliding back in his seat. "I needed to pick up that particular call, but I'm turning off the phone, now, so we can enjoy our dinner. Did you get a pizza?"

"Yes, the spicy pizza," Ingrid piped up. "Jane likes spicy food, too, so you're just going to have to manage."

Jane looked sideways at Liam. "You don't like spicy food?"

"Not really, no," he grinned.

"Good to know."

"I'll make do," he assured her. "It's just pizza."

The rest of the evening remained awkward, but less so. Ingrid let go of her reserve and shared that she was entering a short story contest at her school. She was nervous, she admitted, but also excited. Jane asked her how she liked her dad's new apartment.

Ingrid wrinkled her nose. "It's all right. He needs more furniture. But it's got a pretty view of the city and lots of boats. Dad," she said, "can we get dessert? I'm leaving tomorrow. Shouldn't we make the most of our time?"

"Of course sweetheart. What would you like?"

When they'd finished dessert, the three of them walked outside together. It was dark, and small rivers of water were running down the gutters. The air smelled fresh, and Jane took in a deep breath.

Liam looked up at the sky and held out his hand. "The rain's stopped. We'll walk you to your car."

He walked between Jane and Ingrid, keeping hold of his daughter's hand. Jane was glad he didn't take her hand, too. It would have felt like pretending the three of them were a family, and they weren't.

"Well, this is me," she said, when they got to her car. "Thank you for dinner. And nice meeting you, Ingrid."

"You too," Ingrid replied. She furrowed her brow, then added, "Thanks for the honest talk. I liked it a lot."

Jane was startled, but then she grinned. "You're welcome. So did I."

Liam looked from Jane to Ingrid. "I'm glad the two of you had a chance to get to know each other a little."

As Jane searched for her keys, Liam leaned in to her, and put his arm around her waist. Then he kissed her on the cheek, and whispered in her ear, "I want you to tell me all about this 'honest talk.'" He stepped away, saying, "I'll call you tomorrow afternoon, around three?"

"Sounds good," she said. "Talk to you tomorrow."

As she pulled away from the curb, Jane waved at Liam and Ingrid. Then she drove home in silence, feeling strange. She didn't bother to listen to one of her mix cds, or even turn on the radio.

After showering and changing into pajamas and her robe, she was still wide awake. She couldn't stop thinking about Liam eating pizza with his daughter like any normal dad. The image was completely incongruous with the excitement he'd generated at the Foundation, or the reactions of his niche fans when he ran across them in public. Jane thought it was weird that she still had never seen any of his films or TV shows.

She logged on to her computer and looked up the catalog of Liam's work in film and television, then started searching where she could stream his stuff online. She chose the most recent PBS production of *King Lear*, and one BBC TV movie. She meant to watch only *King Lear* that night, and possibly the movie the next morning. But she stayed up until three am to watch them both.

Liam had been made to look much older to play the role of King Lear. Hearing him speaking Shakespearean English made her laugh at first, but then she got lost in his performance. By the time Lear was carrying Cordelia's lifeless body into the frame, Jane was wiping at her eyes.

"I'm such an idiot," she sniffled, as the play ended. Then, after a second of hesitation, she started the BBC movie.

In the film, Liam had a prominent, though not starring, role. The character he played was younger, animated and energetic. At the beginning of the story, he seemed to be a heroic type, but by the end he was the villain.

What amazed Jane, however, was how he could put a "bad guy" across in a way that was so human, and so sympathetic, she almost wanted to root for him. As the movie credits began to roll, she stared at the screen, impressed, fascinated, and freaked out. She wondered what she was getting herself into.

Liam liked to downplay his fame, and it was true that he wasn't insanely famous, like George Clooney, or Danny Glover. But he was definitely famous, with a capital 'F.' And he was *good*. She'd always assumed he was a talented actor. But after actually watching him work she knew he was exceptionally good. Better than most.

What if it was only a matter of time before he hit his stride and his fame ballooned, transitioning him overnight into someone who *was* on the same level as Danny Glover or George Clooney? Would she still fit into his life if that happened? And even if she did, even if he still wanted her, would she be able to handle it?

She liked to think she could handle it, but if she was

brutally honest with herself, she wasn't sure she could. She wanted to feel safe in a relationship. So far, the situation with Liam had been promising. He'd made her feel safe. But if he were to become astronomically famous, would she continue to feel that way? Even if Liam didn't change one bit with massive fame, his life would change, and so would hers. Hounding by the press. More visibility than she was used to. More than she wanted.

She knew it was ridiculous to worry about these things. They were still getting to know each other, and there was no reason to assume they'd even be together if and when he became more famous. She was projecting trouble into the future, which was pointless.

Still, her thoughts continued to plague her. Because of the fallout from her relationship with Carl, she'd spent the last nine years effectively living in the shadows. It was hard enough to leave the shadows behind and try to start living a normal life again. The potential threat of also living in the limelight—even reflected limelight—felt like more than she wanted to take on.

23

Jane was eager to see Liam on Saturday—but she was also dreading it. She felt a creeping emotional numbness, as if the events of the past several weeks had happened to someone else. And if they hadn't happened to her, then none of them mattered much.

In a mild daze, she went through the motions of starting her day. She no longer worried Liam wouldn't call; she knew that he would. Nevertheless, anxiety gnawed at her.

He called while she was cleaning up the kitchen. The sound of the phone made her jump.

"I was thinking," Liam said, without preamble, "would you be interested in coming to stay at the flat?"

Jane leaned against the kitchen counter. "So why'd you get an apartment in Seattle, anyway?"

"The job," he said, quickly. "Seattle's much closer to Vancouver than LA."

Her mind was swirling with questions. Why had he really moved to Seattle? He'd said it was the job, but since he'd found an apartment so quickly, maybe he'd decided to move to Seattle *before* he was certain about the job. Besides, if the move was about the job, why hadn't he simply moved to Vancouver? She wondered if he was hiding anything from her, and if that thing would be any of her business.

"Did Ingrid fly home by herself?" she asked.

"Yeah. It's not a perfect arrangement, but she's used to it. The airline provides a chaperone. We book her on nonstop flights, then keep tabs on her until she's safely at her destination. Her mother collected her just under two hours ago."

"I guess it will make her independent," Jane mused. "Flying by herself, I mean."

"Jane," Liam said. "You changed the subject. Do you not want to see the flat? I can come up there to see you if you prefer."

"I thought you didn't have any furniture?"

He laughed. "I have what I need. Ingrid just wants that complete look. I'll fill it up eventually."

She made up her mind. "I'll come to your place. What's the address?"

As she drove to Seattle, her nervous feelings got worse, and her thoughts were a confused jumble. After making a study of Liam's acting the previous night, she felt newly insecure and out of her league. And yet, strangely, she also had a growing sense that Liam was truly into her. She wasn't sure which scared her more: her own insecurity, or her gut feeling that Liam was serious about her.

"I make no sense," she said aloud. "I make no sense at all."

As she'd expected, Liam's building in Ballard was one of the newer ones that had gone up in the last several years. She remembered having admired it previously while driving by. Unlike some new buildings in the city that had a cheap, impermanent appearance, this one looked solid, with attractive brickwork adorning the facade.

He'd given her a code to park in the garage. At the garage door, she reached through her open car window and punched the code on the keypad, then parked on the second level, which Liam had said was for guests. Then she took the elevator from the garage to the building lobby.

From the lobby, she rode the main elevator to the fifth floor. She was warm, so she unbuttoned her trench coat, the same one she'd worn to the Foundation benefit. The hallways were carpeted in an understated navy and gold pattern. Jane wandered down the hall until she found Liam's apartment, rang the bell, and waited.

She could hear nothing inside. Just as she was beginning to worry that maybe she'd misunderstood something —either about Liam's apartment number, or the time he'd wanted her to come over—he opened the door. He was wearing a button down shirt over jeans.

"Jane," he said, with one of his full smiles. He held the door open and stood to the side. "Come in, please."

Her heels clicked on the wood floor as she entered. Liam closed the door behind her, then put his hand on her arm, stood back, and took her in. She'd worn a navy blue dress that showed off her figure, but had a conservative neckline. It wasn't a dress she wore to work. She liked it too much to make it a part of her work wardrobe.

"What?" she asked.

"You look lovely," he said. "That's all."

She met his eyes. "Thanks." Then she peered past him, trying to see the rest of the apartment. At the end of the hall, there was a large open room with picture windows, but all she could see was the hint of the room. She couldn't determine its shape.

He smiled. "It's just a flat."

"Right," she said. "Just a place to live."

"Let me get your coat. I'll hang it up for you."

She shrugged off the coat, and Liam came up behind her and took it.

"I have a couple things to tell you," he said, as he secured her coat in the hall closet, and closed the door. "And I want to show you the flat. But right now, I just want to take you to bed."

Jane grinned. "That works for me." Despite her earlier apprehension, now that she was physically close to Liam, it was easy to feel good. Because he was hot, sure. But also because she just liked him.

He took her hand. "C'mon."

In his bedroom, there was a bed, and a nightstand with a lamp, but nothing else.

Jane sank down on the bed, which was covered with a simple neutral toned comforter. That was a relief. Hyper masculine or kinky bedding would have triggered her funny bone and weakened the sexual thrall she felt around Liam. Then again, that might also have been a relief.

"Where do you keep your clothes?" she asked, looking up at him.

"Suitcase, for now," he said. "And the wardrobe."

He held out his hands. She took them, and let him pull her back up on her feet. They stood close together, eye to eye.

"You seem, I don't know, I can't quite describe it." He smiled, but he looked puzzled. "Almost shy."

She knew what was happening. She was going numb. Somewhere inside, her emotions were starting to shut down. With her fuck buddies, it'd been easy. There had never been a need for intense emotion. But Liam made her acutely aware of her emotions, and it was starting to feel like too much, too soon. Still, no matter what was going on with her emotionally, as long as she felt safe, sex was always easy for her. It was the one way she knew she could connect. So she put her arms around Liam and kissed him.

He crushed his mouth over hers in response, and she felt life flow back in to her limbs. She pressed closer to him and he moved his hands to the zipper of her dress. He pulled it down, past the slight catch at the waist, then the rest of the way. She worked her way out of the dress while he watched her. Then she let it fall to the floor.

"You and your garters," he laughed.

"I like how they feel."

"I'm not complaining. I like how they look on you. But I also like them off."

"So take them off," she told him.

She was wearing a simple garter, two straps in front, two straps in back. He knelt down and slid his hands up her calves, over her stockings, then onto the bare skin of her thighs. His fingers felt hot on her skin. He unhooked one strap, then the next, then grasped her hips and coaxed her to turn around. Next, he unfastened each of the back straps, then slid one stocking down her leg. He tapped his finger against the side of her foot.

"Lift, please."

She lifted her foot so he could remove the stocking.

After he'd taken off the second stocking, he stood and

unfastened the hook and eye closure at the back of her garter belt. He pushed the belt off her body and let it drop to the floor. Then he leveled a slap on her bare ass. He pulled her back against him, and asked, "Do you like that?"

"Yeah," she laughed, a little embarrassed.

"Thought so. How come?"

"It makes things more intense," she said. The slap echoed through all the nerves in her lower body. But it was more than that. It was the exercise of a certain kind of authority. It was something she did not want in her daily life. But during sex, it made her feel wanton and crazy to be fucked.

He slapped her ass again, on the other side, so both her buttocks felt warm and slightly stung.

"I'm not into that dungeon crap though," she said. "I mean, if you are, I'm not judging. But I'm..."

"Just shut up and let me make you feel good." He slid his hands over the cheeks of her ass. "Do you want more?"

"Yes. Please," she managed.

He walked her to the bed, then maneuvered her onto it, facedown, so her ass was over the bed's edge, exposed. She turned her head to the side, so she could breathe. Liam sat down next to her, and pressed one hand firmly but gently against her back. Then, with his free hand, he leveled several more rhythmic slaps on her bare ass.

Her breathing grew ragged as the slaps continued, stinging, then hurting, each one turning her on more than the last. Then he stopped and slid his finger inside her.

"You're so wet," he breathed, sounding satisfied. He began moving his finger in and out of her cunt. She clenched her internal muscles around his finger and bucked her ass against his hand. Just when she was about to come, he grasped her hips and flipped her over. Then he pulled her to a sitting position and stood in front of her.

With her ass planted on the bed, she felt the soreness from the spanking. She had a hunch she'd feel it even more later. "Why'd you stop?" she asked, looking up at him.

"Touch yourself," he told her. "The way you do when you're alone."

When she hesitated, he added, "I want to watch you."

Slowly, Jane spread her legs open at the edge of the bed, and reached her hand down to her clit. Keeping her eyes locked with Liam's, she began massaging the sensitive tip with her fingers, in slow circles. She started to shudder and writhe, and she could not stop looking at him. All she could feel was her sore ass grinding against the bed, her fingers moving over her clit, and his eyes holding hers.

"Come for me," he demanded.

She quickened the pace of her hand, and began to moan, slightly. She closed her eyes.

"Keep your eyes on me," Liam said.

She opened her eyes, and moved her fingers faster. Liam's eyes were dark and wolfish. When she started to come, she closed her eyes again, but again, he commanded, "Look at me."

She fixed her eyes back on his as the spasms of her orgasm shook her. When the last shudders had gone through her, Liam began undressing.

"What now?"

"Now I'm going to fuck you properly."

He was naked in a flash and entered her in the quick, rude way that was becoming familiar. She hadn't thought she was capable of another orgasm, but as he thrust hard and steady inside her, she could feel the waves of arousal building again. Each thrust was a reminder of her sore ass, but she liked how it felt.

When she finally came again, he was right with her, groaning as she stifled a scream against his shoulder. Then he held her, and ran his hand over her hip.

"How do you feel?" he asked.

She grinned. "Properly fucked."

24

Jane surveyed the crowded, cheerful waiting area of the Thai restaurant near Liam's apartment. They'd ordered takeout, and had sat down to wait on a long, low-backed bench set against the blue-curtained front window of the restaurant. The bench was packed with people, and their legs were pressed close together. Liam had taken Jane's hand.

Every time the door opened, a tinkling bell rang out, and every time the bell rang, Jane looked up, expecting someone to approach Liam for an autograph, or a selfie.

The anticipation put her on edge. They were no longer at a sparsely populated resort on the Washington coast during the winter. They were in Seattle, a city where watching PBS and BBC broadcasts was mandatory for a certain segment of the population. Someone had surely recognized Liam by now. It was only a matter of time before an outgoing fan approached him.

He spoke near her ear. "Relax."

"Sorry. It's super crowded in here," she hedged. "It's getting to me."

"Want to take a walk down the street?"

"No. It shouldn't be much longer. I'll be fine."

"I don't think anyone's going to bother me here," Liam said, in a low voice. "If that's what you're worried about."

She turned her head to him. "Maybe. I'm just not used to it."

"Neither am I."

She lifted her eyebrows. He had to be used to it by now. If he wasn't, he wouldn't be able to handle the attention gracefully, and she'd witnessed him doing just that, more than once.

"It's a part of the job," he amended.

She cleared her throat, and matched his quiet tone. "I watched a few of your films last night. Or one film. And *Lear*."

"Had you ever watched anything I've done?" he asked.

"No." Her tone was blunt. "Sorry."

His eyes glittered with amusement. "It's all right. I love it." Then, with an abrupt change of demeanor, he asked, "What did you think?"

Jane sensed vulnerability in him. She considered making a joke, one he would have to be a good sport about. It would be an opportunity to drive a subtle wedge between them, and she was considering doing just that. Finding ways to put the brakes on emotional intimacy was her panic button, and she reserved the right to push it whenever she thought it was necessary. But instead, she answered honestly. "I thought you were amazing. I was actually kind of blown away."

Then she blushed. She wasn't in the habit of giving direct compliments. Sarcastic banter was more her style.

"Thank you." Liam's tone was circumspect, but full of some other emotion, just beneath the surface.

Then she did try to make a joke. "Of course, I haven't seen *everything* you've done."

"Right." He grinned ruefully. "I try to choose well, but a small portion of it is, unfortunately, shit. Bills to pay."

"Jane?" said a familiar voice. "Is that you?"

She looked up, and was bit shocked when she realized it was Mike. He stared pointedly at her and Liam's clasped hands. She felt an urge to pull her hand away, as if she'd been caught doing something wrong. But she resisted it.

"Hey Mike," she said.

"Dinner with the *boss?*" Mike asked, using a tone as sarcastic as he could muster. It was mild, at best. Mike was so good natured that sarcasm didn't come naturally to him. Jane felt a stab of guilt, but squelched that, too. She'd never promised Mike fidelity or permanence. She hadn't cheated on him. She snuggled a little closer to Liam.

"Good to see you again, Mike," Liam said pleasantly. He made no effort to disguise his voice to sound like Jane's fictional American boss, John Burns. Liam dropped Jane's hand and extended his hand to Mike, who gave it a perfunctory shake.

Jane decided the situation would be handled best with small talk. "We're waiting for our order. Are you here for dinner?"

"Yeah." Mike took a step back. "Me and some buddies were jamming and we got hungry. Guess I'll let you two get back to *work.*"

"Appreciate it," Liam said gravely. "Take care."

A strange look crossed Mike's face, as if he'd just figured out what had been going on all along. "See you around, Jane," he said. His features were a strange mix of under-stated sadness and anger. He went back to the main room of the restaurant and disappeared from view. Jane sighed with relief, as Liam took her hand again.

"Are you all right?" he asked.

"I'm fine. Although that was a bit awkward."

He looked like he wanted to ask more questions, but their order was called then. *Just in time*, she thought.

However, when they were seated at the bar in Liam's stainless steel and red-toned kitchen, he pressed the issue again.

"Are you sure you're okay?" he asked. "You seemed a bit rattled after Mike showed up."

She shrugged. "I just feel bad about lying to him. You know, that night at The Mix?"

He dipped his head. "That was my fault. I'm the one who pretended to be your boss that night. You didn't have anything to do with it."

"But I played along. Mike knew something was up, and I kept lying to him. Mike's a good guy. He didn't deserve that."

Liam took a sip from the large beer bottle they'd been sharing. "It's none of my business," he said. "But was there ever anything serious between you and Mike? Because he seemed a bit—put out—back there."

"No." Jane sighed. "Not on my end, anyway. But that night at The Mix, he sort of let me know that he wanted more."

"Ah. I see." Liam kept his tone casual. "So how did that land with you?"

Jane looked him in the eye. "I'm not into Mike. I took *you* home with me that night. If you remember?"

Liam smiled into her eyes. "I do remember. It was a very pleasant evening."

She smiled back, but all at once the moment felt too

intimate, and she had a sudden urge to press that panic button. Liam, maybe sensing her discomfort, changed the subject.

"I talked to Ingrid. After our dinner out? She likes you."

Jane thought back to her short conversation with Ingrid, and frowned. "She doesn't know me well enough to like me."

"She told me what *you* said," Liam continued, "about not being obligated to like you? She said that made her more inclined to like you, but she would 'need more time to know for sure.'"

Jane grinned. "Now that sounds like where we left things. I don't know much about kids, but for what it's worth, I like Ingrid, too. She kind of terrifies me, but I like her."

"She terrifies me too, sometimes," he admitted. "I feel like she understands more than she should."

"Maybe she does," Jane suggested. "She seems like an insightful kid."

Liam was smiling at her with real warmth. All at once, her earlier feelings of apprehension returned in a rush. Sex had temporarily chased those feelings away. But now, she began to dread what he might say next.

"How's the job?" she asked, hoping to get him talking about something more egocentric. "Any news?"

"Yes," he said. "In fact, I wanted to talk to you about that." He hesitated, like he wasn't sure if he should go on. She could see his internal fight on his face. Then he reached for her hand, and looked her in the eye. "We're starting the new project rather soon. The cast is meeting up and we begin pre-production next week. So I'll be in Vancouver for the rest of the month."

Jane sat up straighter and smiled at him. She felt oddly relieved. "So that's good, right? No waiting around."

"In terms of the work, it's ideal. But the timing is a bit...off."

"Timing?" Jane asked.

He squeezed her hand and looked directly at her. "I know we've only known each other a month. But I like you."

"Umm. I like you too." Her heart was beating fast.

"I wish I could pursue things with you in a more gradual way," he went on. "But this job—I'll be wrapped up in it for long stretches of time. My work can kill relationships that are already established, and we've only just started to get to know each other. So I feel I have to be more —rushed—about this than I'd prefer."

"Rushed?" she repeated. She hoped if she kept parroting his words as questions, it would prevent him from saying something that would make her want to run for the door.

"How do *you* feel?" he countered, catching her off guard.

Unexpected warmth spread through her, sexual, but more than that. It touched behind her heart, in the same place she'd felt during her first night with Liam. It was a good feeling. But it also scared her to death. In short, she was confused.

"Because I suppose," Liam added quickly, "I'm making assumptions, outright talking about 'pursuing things with you.' As if it's a given that you want that."

Feeling very fluid and fragile, Jane repeated, "I like you, too."

He studied her face, then prodded, gently, "But?"

"It takes a long time to get to know someone," she said. "It takes me a long time to trust people."

"Trust can be built," he ventured. "That's why I'm

telling you how I feel now. Before I get absorbed in work. While I'm working it's easy to forget about other people in my life. Not forget, exactly, but I do tend to take people for granted. It's a breeding ground for misunderstandings."

"I imagine it could be," she said, her voice faint.

Liam gave her an apologetic smile. "I'm sorry. I didn't want to upset you. But I did want to tell you how I feel."

Jane looked at him. "I'm not upset, exactly. I *do* have feelings for you. I just—I—I don't know what I think about them yet."

He tugged on her hand. "So don't think about them right now. Let me show you the rest of the flat."

Liam gave her a quick tour. The large living area at the end of the hallway was sunken by a couple of steps, a retro design. It spanned most of one side of the apartment. Large sectioned picture windows provided a panoramic view of the marina.

To the left of the entryway was a small bedroom and a detached bathroom. For Ingrid, Liam said. There was already a bed, nightstand, and lamp in Ingrid's room. The room was otherwise bare, with nothing to indicate it belonged to a little girl, except for a small purple plush toy on the pillow.

"That's Zachary the Dragon," Liam chuckled. "Ingrid's very upset that she left him behind. I told her I'd keep him safe for her, but I think I'll have to ship him back to L.A. on Monday."

"What if he gets lost in transit, though?" Jane reached out and picked up the dragon, and turned it over in her hands. It was mostly new, but the plush purple fur was worn on one side, like it had been well-loved.

"Good one," he laughed. "I'll tell her it's best if she retrieves him next time she visits. We can't have Zachary getting lost! That might just make sense to her. *And* it will save me some time."

Jane looked up. "No, I'm serious. To her, this little purple guy is real. I mean, probably. She'll be devastated if she loses him in the mail."

Liam's eyes softened. "All right. I'll convince her it's best for Zachary to stay here for now." Then he grinned. "Although if I did send him, I'd ship him in style. Only the best and most comfortable box."

She put the plush toy back on the pillow. "Well, I hope they'll be reunited soon."

Back at the kitchen bar, Jane peered inside one of the takeout containers. "This was delicious, but I can't eat another bite."

Liam got up. "I'll put it away."

She watched while he closed up the boxes and transferred them to the refrigerator. When he was done, he came over and leaned against the counter, across from her, and smiled. "You had a strong reaction to Zachary the Dragon."

"Did I?" she asked.

"Is there something you're keeping from me?" he teased. "Did you have a bad experience with a plush toy as a child?"

"No," she laughed. "I just think it's sad to lose things you love, you know? I mean, especially if you don't have to lose them."

"Well, of course," he agreed. "It's better not to lose those things."

She could sense he wanted to press her further on the subject, so she decided to throw him a bone. If he was going to keep probing into her emotional life, it was better if she decided what she wanted tell him.

"I need to set something straight," she said. "There *is* something I told you that wasn't quite honest. When we were at the coast."

He raised his eyebrows, but seemed unconcerned. "I can't even think of what that might be?"

"It's nothing huge," she assured him. "It was just something I didn't want to get into. I told you my dad died, and that's not true. Well, honestly, I have no idea if it's true or not. He left when I was a kid, and I never heard from him again. So he could be dead, but the truth is I don't know if he's alive, or dead."

Liam reached for her hand again. *He's so kind*, Jane thought. He was the sort of man you wanted in your life. Not because he was famous, but because he was a good person. And also, of course, because he was really, really hot. That helped too.

"I not asking for sympathy or anything," Jane hastened to add. "I just don't like lying, so. I didn't want to lie to you."

"It's not the same thing as lying," he said. "You simply made a decision on how much to share about yourself."

An intimate vibe had begun to hum between them. Again. Jane both hated and loved it. How could she be so drawn to him one moment, then want to run away the next? It was confusing. Exhausting. And then she remembered that maybe, he had his own secrets.

"Can you tell me something?" she asked.

Sure," he smiled. "What's on your mind?"

"Why did you really move here? Because it seems like you had this place locked up *before* you knew you had the job in Vancouver."

He didn't answer right away. "It was a gamble, I suppose," he acknowledged, finally. "I really wanted the job. Renting this place seemed like an act of faith that I'd get it."

"But why leave L.A.?" she asked. "I mean, your daughter lives there."

He grimaced. "I suppose that seems odd, doesn't it? Ingrid's mother and I've discussed the possibility of her living here during the school year, and in L.A. for the summer. We're both ambivalent about her growing up in L.A. There are advantages, but also quite a few pitfalls. Nothing has been for sure decided yet."

"So you moved here because of Ingrid?" Jane asked.

He gave her a knowing look. "If I'm being completely honest, I wanted a break from L.A. When I came here for the Foundation benefit, I was already looking for a new place to live. I need to put some distance between my life before the divorce, and my life now."

"Wait, so how long ago was it?" she asked, suddenly. "The divorce, I mean?"

"It's been over a year." He paused. "Are you worried it's too soon for me?"

"Not exactly..." she trailed off.

"It's not," he said, earnestly. "Too soon, I mean. My marriage was over long before it was over, if that makes sense. I've been processing the end of it for much longer than a year, really."

Jane took a deep breath. "So—what would 'pursuing things with me' look like? What exactly do you have in mind?"

He smiled broadly. "Seeing you again. And again. And again after that."

"Exclusively?" she asked.

His eyes gleamed. "I suppose it's a bit soon to ask for a commitment."

"But that's what you want?" she ventured.

"If I'm honest, yes," he said, surprising her. "An exclusive relationship is exactly what I want with you. But I understand if you feel it's too sudden." He flashed a quick, disarming grin, and she couldn't help but smile back at him. "Don't think about it right now," he said. "Let's enjoy the rest of the evening."

25

Jane woke in the early morning hours, feeling anxious. And, as she lay awake in the dark, a sense of knowing and dread overwhelmed her. She couldn't commit to pursuing a relationship with Liam. Not now, not six months from now, not even a year from now. And definitely not in the way it seemed he wanted.

She wished he hadn't told her how he felt. Hadn't confessed that he wanted an exclusive relationship with her. If they could have just enjoyed the weekend, with no talk of exclusivity or commitment, she would have been fine.

Liam, however, was someone who knew what he wanted. He knew what kind of jobs he preferred to take. He knew where he wanted to live. And now, he seemed to know that he wanted her. But she couldn't reciprocate, because all *she* wanted was to feel safe, and maybe happy. The idea of being exclusive with Liam—or with anyone—did not make her feel safe. It made her feel trapped. For her, that killed any chance of being happy, too.

She felt sad and certain in her knowledge of her own

limitations. She watched Liam as he slept, wishing she could cry without waking him up. Then, mercifully, she fell back into sleep herself.

Later, she found him in the kitchen, making an omelette. She slid on to one of the barstools and said, "Hey."

He turned around. When he saw she was already dressed, he smiled. "Going out?" he asked.

"No," she said. "I just—I just got dressed."

"You're right on time for breakfast." He cut the omelette in half, slid the halves onto two plates, and pushed a plate in front of Jane.

"Thank you." She smiled at him. It was easy to smile at him. He'd taken a shower and his hair was still damp. He smelled good.

Liam sat down next to her, then said, "Oh, coffee, I forgot." He leapt up to pour coffee from a silver colored machine with a digital display, then re-joined her with two full mugs.

As they ate, Jane began to doubt her decision. Liam was humming with pleasant energy. She liked him. She liked being near him. He understood her sexually, and he made fantastic omelettes. Did she really want to give him up?

"How's the omelette?" Liam asked.

"Good," she said.

After a few moments, he added, "And how are you?"

She turned to him, unhappy, and saw understanding dawn on his face.

"Not very good, I see," he said, quietly.

"I need to talk to you," she blurted.

He gave her a sad, somewhat cynical smile. "I can guess what about. But go ahead. Say what you need to say."

His visible shift from being a cheerful, omelette-making guy to a jaded guy expecting bad news made her feel terrible. Her stomach hurt.

"I can't do what you were talking about last night," Jane said. "I can't ever be your—whatever you were proposing."

"It's the exclusivity bit," he guessed.

"I can't do it," she repeated.

"I brought it up too soon."

"No." She shook her head. "You could've waited a year and I'd still feel the same."

He looked as if she'd hit him for a split second, but then his face became an unreadable mask. "Well I'm an idiot, aren't I? Although, you did say you had feelings for me last night, didn't you? Did I misinterpret that?"

"I have feelings for you. I absolutely have feelings for you. This isn't about feelings," she told him. "It's about the fact that *I can't do this*. I haven't done this in a really long time."

"I see. How long is a long time?"

"Nine years."

Her words hung in the air between them. Jane stared down at the omelette on her plate. It still looked delicious, but she was no longer hungry.

"Nine years," Liam repeated, finally. "So, are you saying —you haven't been in a committed relationship since the abusive boyfriend?"

"Right," she nodded. "There hasn't been anyone serious since Carl."

"Jane," he said, softly, "I don't want to pry, but what did he do to you?"

"Nothing unusual." She was fighting hard to keep from crying. "I told you. He was abusive. He hit me. It happens to people all the time."

"But it happened to you," Liam said, gently. "You're not a statistic."

One tear escaped her eye, and she wiped it away with a furious swipe of her hand. "It happens to people all the time," she repeated. "Anyway, it changes you. It changes how you think. It changes how you function in the world. I *couldn't* function. At least, not until I met Bert. He helped me a lot."

"He sounds like an amazing friend."

"He's everything to me."

Liam reached out, as if he wanted to cover her hand with his. Then he hesitated and stopped. "I'm glad you have such a good friend," he ventured. "But don't you want more in your life?"

"Like what? A boyfriend?"

"A partner?"

Her voice grew fierce. "I don't want a partner if a partner is going to hurt me. That's why Bert means so much to me. I know he won't hurt me. He's—stable. Also, he knows me really, really, well. He cares what happens to me, and I need that. I've never had that as someone's girlfriend, or exclusive person. Or—whatever."

Liam's dark eyes softened. "Jane...."

She gestured between them. "Part of me wants to see if this would work. But when you brought it up last night, I just knew. I can't do it."

Liam reached for her hands. "I don't know if this will help. But you don't have to be afraid of me. I wouldn't hurt you like that."

"I want to believe you," she said, "but I can't. That's why I said it takes time for me to trust someone. No matter how much I want to believe people, I *don't* believe them. I can't, not until they prove themselves to me, over and over again."

Liam squeezed her hands. "So give me a chance to prove it to you."

"You don't want to live that way." She was desperate to make him understand. "Do you want someone in your life who fundamentally doesn't trust you? Who might not trust you for a year, or two, or maybe longer?"

"Give me a chance," he repeated.

She shook her head. "I'm too fucked up."

He sounded mildly annoyed. "You're no more fucked up than anyone else."

She looked in his eyes and saw he believed it. For a moment, she could see it herself, as if she were looking in a mirror. She wanted to believe him. To give in to him. But she knew herself. She was incapable of giving him what he wanted.

"Is there any way we could compromise?" she suggested, feeling desperate.

He frowned. "Compromise how?"

"We could see each other," she said. "When you're around. When you're staying here, at your apartment. But we—we wouldn't make it formal. No exclusivity. No titles."

He squeezed her hands one more time, then let them go. "No. I'm sorry. That doesn't work for me."

"It's your way or nothing?" she challenged.

He turned his attention back to his plate, took a bite of omelette, chewed, and swallowed. "I brought this up too soon," he said, finally. "I thought I had good reasons. I know how I'll be once I start this job. I'll be wrapped up in work, and forgetful, and often, I'll seem unavailable. I didn't want you to be confused. I wanted you to be sure of where you stand with me before I go to Vancouver." He sighed. "But it was still too soon to bring up exclusivity and commitment."

She looked away from him, upset.

"Maybe it doesn't seem fair?" he suggested. A note of hope crept into his voice. "Is that it? Does it seem unfair for me to want a commitment when I'm the one who's about to leave town for a month? Because we can talk about that, if that's what's bothering you."

Jane cut a bite of her omelette, but couldn't eat it. "Doesn't commitment scare you at all?" she asked.

"Scare me?"

"I mean, after your divorce? Doesn't it freak you out to get more serious with me? Or with anyone?"

"Sure it does." Liam flashed a quick, cautious smile. "But I really like you. So my attitude was 'Well, fuck it.'"

Her voice was just above a whisper. "I really like you too."

He watched her face, and brushed his hand gently across her cheek. "I'm glad." Then he turned away from her, and picked up his coffee cup. "But you're still going to bail on me, aren't you?"

She wanted to tell him he was wrong, if for no other reason than to be contrarian. But he was not wrong. "Yeah," she said, as her body hummed with misery. "But it's not because of what you said. It doesn't feel unfair. It's being exclusive itself. In any circumstance. With you, or with anyone else. I can't do it."

"Well that's it then, isn't it?" he sighed. "Just don't expect me to be waiting around for you to change your mind, especially since you've made it clear you won't ever change your mind."

Jane could hear the hurt in his voice. "Should I leave now?" she asked, quietly.

"Don't be silly. Finish your breakfast."

She looked down at the omelette again. "I'm not hungry. I think I'll just go." She slid off the barstool, then went in the bedroom for her shoes and overnight bag. When she entered the hallway, Liam was waiting with her coat.

"I didn't see a purse," he said. "Did you bring one?"

She had a sudden memory of getting out of her car, locking it, and leaving her purse on the front seat. "I left it in the car."

"I hope it hasn't been stolen. Come back and let me know if you need money or help or anything."

He shook the coat out and held it open for her. She turned around and let him help her put it on. His hands lingered for a split second on her shoulders, then he let go. She buttoned the coat, and turned to face him. They stared at each other as strong undercurrents of emotion moved between them.

"I'm sorry," she said, her voice breaking.

"No need to apologize," he said gently. "It's just not going to work out."

Then he broke the moment, went to the door, and held it wide for her. She walked forward.

"Take care of yourself," Liam said.

"You too."

She stepped through the door, and he closed it behind her. The sound of it shutting was something she felt in her gut. Then she straightened up and walked down the hall to the elevator. When she got to her car, she found her purse still sitting on the passenger seat, intact. Relief flooded through her.

But finding the purse was confirmation she was doing the right thing. She wouldn't have ever left it in the car if she hadn't been feeling so stressed about her relationship with Liam, and she didn't need that kind of stress in her life. As bad as it felt to walk away from him, it was for the best. She exited the garage, and drove out into the grey light of the day.

26

Once she was home, Jane nursed a bottle of wine while watching cable news. Then she yelled at the screen, the way Uncle Chuck used to do. Drunk on wine and bad news, she was able to avoid crying for the rest of the day.

Monday morning, she saw she'd missed a text from Bert.

How was your weekend with Mr. Masterpiece? Call me.

She ignored it, and got in the shower.

Even though it was a Monday, she was surprised by how good it felt be at work. All the little things about the office that usually infuriated her kept her mind occupied. The day flew by.

It wasn't until she returned to her car in the parking garage that the urge to cry hit her. That morning, her car had reminded her of her daily commute. But now that she was about to go home, the car reminded her of Liam.

"No crying on the road," she told herself. "Bad for visibility."

On the way home, she smoked without bothering to

ration her cigarettes. Once she was inside the condo, she poured a glass of wine and let the tears flow. It was healthy to cry, she thought. She would cry Liam out of her system. Eventually, she'd get to the end of the tears, and then, she'd be able to move on.

As she was getting ready for bed, she saw several texts from Bert on her phone. Again, she ignored them. Bert would know immediately that something was wrong, then ask her probing questions, and she didn't feel up to one of his well-meaning interrogations.

The next couple days played out exactly the same. It was a relief to be at work. She chain-smoked on the drive home. Then she cried until she fell asleep. She continued to ignore Bert's texts.

Thursday afternoon at the Foundation, Sasha came up to the receptionist's station to vent. "I just had the most ener-vating meeting with Caleb," she groaned. "Forty-five minutes of wild hand gestures and rapid-fire speech. I need a drink."

Jane smirked. "You mean you don't carry a flask?"

"Like I would tell you," Sasha grinned. Then she looked at Jane and did a double take.

"What?" Jane said.

"Are you okay?" Sasha asked. "Please don't think—I'm not doing that bitchy 'are you okay' thing to insinuate you look like shit but—you kind of look like shit."

Jane guessed her eyes were getting irritated and swollen from her nighttime crying sessions. Smoking more than usual probably wasn't helping her appearance, either. But she was trying to purge Liam from her system. It had to work. Eventually.

"You don't have the flu, do you?" Sasha took a step back. "I know Caleb lays a guilt trip on you when you fail to show up as the cheerful face of the Foundation, but use your sick time if you're sick. Please."

"No, I'm not sick. It's allergies. Dust allergies," Jane amended, because it was still too soon for pollen. "I haven't been doing enough dusting and vacuuming, you know, at home? I need to get on that."

Sasha narrowed her eyes. "You don't strike me as the kind of person who has household dust problems, but all right."

"So there's a type?" Jane asked. She tried for a punchy tone, but failed. She was truly not feeling her best.

Sasha came close again, and said, in a quieter voice, "You know, if anything's going on, if you need to talk, not in an employee to HR way, but in a person to person way? I'm just down the hall." She pointed in the direction of her office.

Jane forced a smile. "I'm fine. But thanks, Sasha."

"Okay," she said, moving away from the reception counter. "But in case you change your mind?" She pointed toward her office one more time, then turned and started down the hall.

Jane watched Sasha retreat with a sense of frustration. It would be nice, maybe, to talk to her. But how could she confide in Sasha, when Sasha had also been interested in Liam? Given that she'd written him off, she might be more than happy to trash-talk him. But Jane didn't want to trash-talk Liam. She just wanted to forget about him.

As she drove home, she realized she hadn't listened to her mix cds all week. She had no desire to play them. Was she growing out of them? Was there still a frozen mac and cheese meal in her freezer? She hoped so.

Back at the condo, she rummaged through her assortment of frozen boxed meals, trying to find the package of mac and cheese. Tears were already streaming down her face. Then her phone rang. It was the ring for a video call, and it was loud.

"I thought I turned off the ringer," she muttered. She went to the phone, which she'd left on the kitchen counter, and saw that it was Bert. She hesitated. Bert still hated video calls. Jane sighed and picked up.

"What?" she asked, feeling pissed.

"What?" Bert mimicked her tone. "What the fuck is going on, Jane?" he yelled. "We don't ignore each other. That's not something we do. I was worried Mr. Masterpiece turned out to be a serial killer or something. I HAVEN'T HEARD FROM YOU SINCE LAST THURSDAY." Bert's defined facial features were especially animated on the small phone screen.

"I'm sorry," Jane said, dully. "I didn't feel like talking."

"You're supposed to at least tell me when you don't feel like talking," he said. "Even 'fuck off, Bert' would be better than nothing."

"I'm sorry," she repeated.

"What happened?" Bert asked. "What happened with Mr. Masterpiece? Did that fucker dump you?"

"No." She shook her head, feeling exhausted.

"So what the fuck happened?"

"I don't feel like talking."

"Tell me the short version. Starting with dinner. Last Friday."

Suddenly standing up felt like too much effort. Jane slid down to the kitchen floor, still holding the phone.

"Jane?" Bert said.

"I'm here."

"Short version," he insisted.

"Ok," she sighed. "We had dinner on Friday. He wanted me to meet his daughter. So I met her. She's nine. And precocious."

"Okay, so you met the daughter. Then what?" Bert prompted.

"So then the next night, I went to see Liam's place in Ballard."

"Liam lives in Ballard?" Bert sounded confused. "I thought he lived in L.A."

She forced the words out. "New job he got. Films in Vancouver. He just moved here. Easier to travel."

"Okay, sorry. So Liam has a new place in Ballard, and you went there."

"Saturday night," Jane affirmed. "His daughter was back with her mom. So I went to see him, we had sex, he told me he wants to be exclusive, and *I* dumped *him*. So you can stop asking me," her voice broke as she choked on a sob, "about fucking Mr. Fucking Masterpiece."

Bert's face on the screen of her phone looked troubled and stormy. Then he said: "I'm coming out there. Now."

"What? No, you're coming out in March. You said February was too busy."

"I'll be on a flight tomorrow. I'll see you tomorrow night."

"Bert," she protested. "Don't be nuts."

"We need to talk. I'll see you tomorrow." He ended the call.

Jane stayed on the floor, staring at the phone.

. . .

Bert sent a text Friday morning to say that he was on his way. Then, while Jane was driving to work, he sent another one.

Be there late afternoon or early evening. Will text when land.

While she was at a red light, she sent him a return text, asking if he would need a ride from the airport.

She had to concentrate on driving then, and didn't have another chance to stop until she parked her car. While she rode the parking garage elevator up to the street, she read Bert's reply.

No. Will take a car to you. Text me your address.

As soon as she was seated at the receptionist's station, she sent her address to Bert. He replied that his plane was about to take off, and that he'd be in contact again when he landed.

Like the rest of the week, Friday went by quickly. In the afternoon, Jane felt a presence at the reception counter, and looked up. It was Nancy, Caleb's assistant.

"Oh, hey Nancy," Jane said. "Does Caleb need something?"

"No. At least, not right this second," Nancy amended. "I wanted to talk to you."

"*Moi?*" Jane said, pointing to herself in an incredulous fashion. It had the desired effect. Nancy laughed.

"No, seriously, what's up?" Jane asked.

"I never got to talk to you after the benefit," Nancy said. "But I wanted to tell you, that playlist you put together was *awesome*. I had so much fun dancing that night. Lots of people did. You didn't stay long enough, but it turned into a massive dance party."

"Well, thanks. Sorry I missed the dance party, but I was

super tired. I stayed up most of the night making that playlist."

"Well if you ever do it again, I'll be certain Caleb asks you ahead of time." Then Nancy's face shifted to a look of mild horror, and she held up her hands. "I can also try to be sure Caleb *never* asks you to do it again.

"No," Jane reassured Nancy, "it turned out okay. It might be all right to do it again. With advance notice. Lots and *lots* of advance notice."

"Okay," Nancy said, grinning, "So are we good?"

"Yes. Of course. I know none of that was your fault. Caleb's a bit...unpredictable?"

Nancy's face went solemn. She let out a heavy sigh and said, "Don't I know it."

27

When Jane left work, she still hadn't heard from Bert. She wondered if he'd miscalculated his flight time, because if he'd taken a nonstop flight, he should have landed already. She did a quick neurotic search of the news on her phone, looking for any reports of plane crashes. Thankfully, there was nothing. Maybe he'd taken a flight with a layover, and his second flight had been delayed.

On the way home, she stopped at the grocery store to pick up wine and extra food. She carried her two grocery sacks around to the front of the building, and saw Bert sitting on the front step. He was wearing jeans and a leather jacket, and he looked pissed.

"Bert!" Jane cried out, surprised. "I didn't think you'd be here yet."

"I only sent fifty-thousand texts," he said, irritably. "Didn't you get them?"

"No. Dammit. My cell phone carrier sucks. The messages will show up later, I bet. I'm sorry," she apologized. "How long were you out here?"

"Oh, just about forty-five freeze-my-ass minutes."

"Let's go in." Jane set the groceries on the ground so she could retrieve her keys. Bert sighed, then picked up the grocery sacks. He followed her inside and up the stairs to her condo. While he was waiting for her to open the door, he rustled the bags. "There'd better be alcohol in these."

"Of course," she assured him, pushing the door open.

Bert handed off the groceries. Jane took them to the kitchen, and he followed her through the door. She set the bags on the counter and turned around.

"I'm so sorry you were stuck out there," she said. Then she burst out laughing.

Bert held his arms open and she stepped into his hug.

"Good to see you, Janey."

"It's so good to see *you*."

He patted her back. "Now make me some hot-spiced wine before I get pneumonia."

She stepped out of the hug and raised an eyebrow at him.

"You still know how to make that, don't you?" Bert asked, beaming. "I have such fond memories of it."

"I haven't made it in forever. But it actually sounds good," she relented. She rummaged through one of the bags and pulled out a bottle of wine. Bert took off his jacket and hung it on a chair in the dining room.

"Did you eat dinner?" she asked, rummaging through her kitchen drawers for the corkscrew.

"I ate on the plane," he said, as he returned to the kitchen. "I'm not super hungry."

As Jane got out a saucepan and spices for making the mulled wine, Bert went to the other grocery sacks and began unloading them.

He held up a package of aged Gouda cheese. "You remembered."

"Yup," she said. "And Bosc pears, too."

"I'll cut them up." He began unloading the fruit. "And the cheese. That will be enough for me. Do you need more? Protein?"

"Cheese and pears sound great right now," she affirmed. "I can always eat more later."

"Get me a cutting board. I don't know where you keep anything in here. Nice place, by the way."

Jane handed Bert a knife and a cutting board, and they fell into an old rhythm, working around each other in the kitchen. They'd often cooked together when they'd been roommates. She'd eaten much healthier when she lived with Bert. He liked cooking, and he'd always taken the lead, so it had been easy to help him. Especially since he'd never insisted on perfection.

She slowly spiced and heated the wine. It was the one thing she could do well in the kitchen—if mulled wine counted as cooking. While she stirred the wine, Bert sliced the pears and the cheese on to a plate, making a decorative arrangement.

"Who's taking care of Felix?" Jane asked. "Were you able to get a cat sitter?"

"Joaquin is taking care of Felix," Bert said.

"Oh." She grinned. "*Joaquin* is taking care of Felix. Of course."

He looked over at her. "Have I told you about Joaquin?"

"I don't think so. Would Joaquin be the 'guest' who was over when I called you from the coast?"

"Yeah." Bert cast a sidelong glance at Jane. "That would have been him."

"Are you living together?"

"Not yet," he said. "But we're at the stage where he's at my place four or five nights a week."

She smiled at him. "So, it sounds good."

He smiled back. "It's too soon to say for sure, but yeah, so far, so good."

Once the mulled wine was ready they took two large mugs, the plate with the cheese and pears, and two smaller plates to the dining room table.

"I never eat here," Jane confessed. "I eat on the couch."

"Well, you should eat here," Bert said. "It's civilized."

She surveyed his handiwork. The slices of cheese and pear were arranged in alternating swirls. "That looks too perfect to disturb."

"Not to me!" He picked up the serving utensil and began putting slices of pear and cheese on his plate.

"You killed it!" she cried, horrified.

"Everything dies," he intoned, then gestured to the plate. "Eat, snowflake."

She served herself, then gave Bert a pointed look. "So. You said you wanted to talk to me?"

"Yeah." His handsome face looked immediately troubled, the way it had during their last video call. "But can we eat first? Then we can sit down and talk?"

"Oh right. I forgot. No intense conversations while eating."

He grinned broadly. "It *is* one of my rules."

"How does Joaquin like your rules?" she asked.

He raised a lascivious eyebrow. "He hates most of them, and likes enough of them."

"Does he like cats? Does he like Felix?"

"He loves Felix. Felix loves Joaquin. Felix loves Joaquin so much I'm actually a little jealous."

After they had finished the pears and cheese, Jane refilled each of their mugs. They took the wine to the living room, and sat on the couch.

"Okay," she said. "What do you want to talk about?"

Bert spoke slowly, as if he were having to push the words out. "Can I ask you some questions about the Mr. Masterpiece thing?"

"Why?" She felt sulky. "I don't want to talk about him."

"Why'd you break it off?" he asked, abruptly. "I know you were into him."

"Why are you assuming I need or want a boyfriend?" she countered. "Maybe I don't."

"I'm not talking about needing or wanting a boyfriend," he said. "I'm talking about *this* guy. You liked him a lot. He wanted to get closer, and you pushed him away. Why?"

"I don't know why. Really. I don't."

"Really?" Bert asked. He took a long drink of his spiced wine. "This is so good." He fixed her with a look over the top of his mug. He was not accepting her answer.

"It was too much," she sighed.

"Too much good?" he guessed.

She felt tears threaten, but didn't answer.

"I worry sometimes..." Bert hesitated, as if he were not sure how much to say. "I worry that you count on me too much."

"I thought we counted on *each other*," she retorted, her voice sharp.

"We do. Let's start over. I'm worried you're avoiding people who could make you happy. And I'm worried I'm enabling you."

Though Bert's facial expression was neutral, Jane saw the concern in his eyes, and she put her hand on his arm. "No," she said. "It doesn't have anything to do with you."

"It's been nine years," he said, quietly. "Is this how you want to live?"

She didn't answer. She knew her misery was visible on

her face.

Bert shifted on the couch, putting one leg over the other. He turned toward Jane so he could address her more directly. "Tell me something. How does Mr. Masterpiece—how does Liam make you feel?"

"I don't know." She shifted her own seating position, and folded her arms over her chest. "Okay, fine. He makes me feel alive. But he also makes me feel like I'm going to fall apart. I can't live like that. Maybe I'm weak, but I know I can't deal with it."

"Relationships are scary..." Bert started.

Jane interrupted him. "I know. For me this is beyond 'relationships are scary.' I was able to handle it for a couple weeks, when I could tell myself it had a known end-date, or that maybe it'd be an on again, off again sort of thing. But if he wants it to be serious, and it lasts a long time? I can't do that."

Bert had been cradling his mug of spiced wine in his hands. Now he took a long sip from it, keeping his eyes on Jane.

"Maybe I need counseling," she sighed. "Or EMDR. Or something."

"Maybe," he agreed. "It could take the edge off your anxiety. There are probably lots of different things you could try. You should do anything that helps you. But nothing will take the risk out of life itself."

"Right," she said, looking at him. "That's the real problem."

"Did you tell Masterpiece how you're feeling?" he asked.

"I told him..." she thought for a moment. "I told him I didn't know how soon I'd be able to trust him, or if I ever would."

"What did he say to that?"

Jane let out a shaky sigh. "He said he could handle it."

"So maybe you should believe him?" Bert suggested.

"Maybe he's just saying that, so he can have what he wants right now."

"Maybe. But maybe not. He is a grown man. He might actually have attained some level of self-knowledge and maturity."

Jane made a face at Bert, then said, "Anyway. It's too late. He told me he won't wait around for me."

Bert nodded. "Saving his pride. You may have to grovel if you go back to him. But don't grovel too much. It's never good to grovel too much."

She groaned. "Stop trying to make it sound like this is something that can happen. It's not going to."

"I just want you to be happy, idiot."

"I don't believe in happy," she reminded him.

Bert let out a dramatic sigh. "Fine. You don't believe in happy. How about the feeling alive part? Isn't it worth it just to feel alive? Maybe that's your happy."

"I know what you mean," Jane said. "I like feeling the way he makes me feel. I like it a lot. But I don't want drama or you know, I don't want it to be—really bad."

They exchanged glances. As always, it was a relief to know that when she said "really bad" Bert knew exactly what she meant. He had been there in the aftermath of "really bad."Now, he took her hand and held onto it. "You know," he said. "If you start a relationship, you'll need a game plan for what to do if 'really bad' happens. How you can get out. I hate that you need to do that, but you need to do it. And it's not just so you can get to safety. It's also to give you the psychological ability to stay put if it *doesn't* happen." He squeezed her hand. "A counselor probably could help you with that. It might be a good idea to see one."

"You're right," she sighed. "But sometimes, even if women have a plan, even if they know all the right things to do, they get stuck anyway."

Bert went quiet. The refrigerator hummed in the background.

"He's not safe because he's famous, you know," Jane went on. "In fact, that would make it worse if he turned out to be...not the good person he seems to be. It would make it even more difficult to get out. It really scares me, Bert."

"How you feel makes sense," he said, finally. "I wish I could give you a perfect situation that would make you not feel that way."

She leaned her head against his shoulder. "So do I."

They sat like that for awhile, her head leaned against him, their hands clasped together.

"You're a good friend," she told him.

"Well, duh," he said.

Bert was booked on a flight back to the East Coast the next afternoon. Jane drove him to the airport. Since she didn't want to say a rushed goodbye at the drop-off point, she parked and walked with him to his terminal.

When they stopped outside the terminal doors, she said, "I'm really glad you found someone. Joaquin, I mean."

Bert smiled. "So am I."

"I hope you're still coming out in March?"

"Trip's still booked," he confirmed. "You should come out to New York, too. Maybe for the holidays, if traveling isn't a pain in the ass. With or without Mr. Masterpiece."

"Probably without. But it sounds like fun."

Bert gave her a knowing look. "If you decide to give him a chance, remember to make a plan. Be honest. Tell him what's okay with you and what isn't. And tell him if he hurts you there's a team of vicious thugs who will hunt him down, so he'd better treat you well."

"A team?" she asked.

"Me. Joaquin. Felix."

She laughed. "Felix?"

"Felix is one tough motherfucker." Then, dropping his voice low, he said, "Just think about it. I'll support you, whatever you decide. But I doubt you're going to meet a guy like Liam every time you log on to a dating app."

Feeling tears threatening again, she went for bravado. "Well, first, I don't use dating apps, and second, you just want me to be with Liam so you can say Mr. Masterpiece came to Thanksgiving at your place this year."

"And what's wrong with that?" Bert asked, deadpan. Then he held out his free arm and they hugged goodbye.

"Are you going to set up an appointment with a counselor?" he asked, as he released her.

"Umm," she faltered. "Yeah. I mean, sure."

He sighed. "I can't tell you what to do. But do it anyway. Please?"

"I'll make an appointment soon," she told him.

"Promise?"

It was Jane's turn to sigh. "I promise."

He smiled. "Thank you. Call me anytime."

She let him go, and he went toward the airport doors. Then he turned around and waved. She waved back, then went to her car.

Driving home from the airport reminded her of the drive back from the coast with Liam. She wondered how long it would be until she stopped thinking about him.

28

Jane decided to limit her cathartic nighttime crying. No more than a half hour, and no more crying herself to sleep. She put de-puffing cream on her eyes before she went to bed. She also quit smoking. Completely. Valentines Day came, and went, and she survived it.

At work, Sasha told her she looked better. Jane made sure to check in with Bert, to let him know she was all right. Everything was progressing normally, she reasoned. She was coping with a natural, emotional reaction to an attractive and magnetic human being. Even if she and Liam hadn't known each other long, she'd definitely been in his thrall. Now that she was outside his orbit, she felt disoriented. And that made sense.

A week after Valentine's Day, Sasha came up to reception wearing a look of genuine concern. "Are you feeling better?"

Jane shrugged, and tried to grin. "More or less."

"Well good. I'm glad." Sasha started to walk away, then turned around. "Oh my God! I almost forgot why I came over here. I was wondering if you wanted to do happy hour. Tonight, after work?'

"On a Monday?" Jane asked.

"Monday's perfect. Not too many people. Just a quick drink and some greasy appetizers. C'mon Jane. If you hang out with us, you'll miss rush hour. That's good, right?"

"Who's 'us?'" Jane asked.

"Whoever I can get. I mean, it's Monday. It won't be a ton of people."

Jane sighed inwardly. It probably would be good to go out. Definitely better than moping at home and obsessing about Liam Burns. "Sure," she said. "Count me in."

In the end, it was just Sasha, Jane, and Nancy who met for happy hour. They went to The Mix. As they sat at a table nibbling on appetizers and sipping their drinks, Jane wondered if Sasha was thinking about her "date" with Liam Burns.

Every time Jane glanced over at the bar, she recalled her own time with him at The Mix. How he'd faked being her boss. The feeling of a growing attraction between them. Connecting with him on the dance floor.

From everything she'd observed so far, she had to admit that Liam seemed like a "good person." He'd been kind to her. And his daughter obviously adored him.

But I still don't know him well enough to trust him, she reminded herself.

Sasha was waving someone over to their table. A scruffy looking thirties-ish guy with a lopsided grin came over to them. Sasha stood up, and she and the guy shared a long hug.

"Sit down and join us, Sean," she told him. He pulled up

the empty chair at the table, and aimed his crooked grin first at Nancy, then Jane.

"This is Sean," Sasha explained. "He's part-owner of The Mix. Sean, this is Nancy—she's our boss's right-hand person. And this is Jane, our receptionist, face of the organization, and jack of many trades."

Sean's face burst into a full grin as he turned to Jane. "So you're the one with the DJ skills!"

"DJ skills?" Jane repeated, confused.

"Sasha's been telling me stories," he confided.

"What kind of stories?'

Sasha smiled wide. "I was just telling him how you deejayed our last benefit, and what a good job you did."

"I didn't deejay that benefit," Jane protested. "I made a playlist. That's all."

"And it was an awesome playlist," Nancy chipped in. "It turned the benefit into a dance party."

"So you've never deejayed professionally?" Sean asked.

"Nope, never." Jane shook her head, and reached for her drink.

"Would you ever want to learn?" he pressed.

Jane's reaction was automatic. "No."

Sasha leaned over to Sean. "We'll work on her," she assured him.

"What is this?" Jane asked, laughing. "I feel like I'm being set up for—something?"

"We're thinking of starting an '80s dance night on Mondays," Sean explained. "It's the slowest night of the week. We've been trying to brainstorm ways to get more people in here."

"Well yeah," Jane allowed. "That sounds like a cool idea. I'm not a DJ though. So, you know, good luck finding one."

"I think you could do it, Jane," Nancy urged. "I bet you'd kick ass."

"Because of the playlist I made for the benefit?" Jane scoffed.

"No," Nancy frowned. "Because I think you'd actually be good at it."

Jane immediately put her hand on Nancy's arm. "I'm sorry. I didn't mean to be rude."

"We don't necessarily want a professional DJ," Sean told Jane, earnestly. "We actually *want* it to be more like a playlist. That's how it usually is here, anyway, just tons of good songs. You've been dancing here before, right?"

"I come here fairly often," Jane agreed.

"We want someone who knows a lot of music, and who also has a sense of what songs will get people out on the floor. Sounds like you already know how to do that." Sean gave her a quick but respectful once over. "Plus you'd look amazing behind a DJ console."

Jane flushed. Sean stood up, and shook her hand. "Nice meeting you Jane. Think about it. It's just one night a week and a little extra cash. Complimentary meal every time you work." He tossed his lopsided smile in Nancy's direction, then in Sasha's. "I won't take up any more of your time. Enjoy your evening, ladies."

As he walked away, Sasha smirked and looked over at Jane. "So what do you think of him?"

"He seems like a nice person," Jane evaded.

"I think he's hot," Nancy declared, then looked around as if she were worried Sean might have overheard her.

"He's both." Sasha's face broke into a full grin. Then she gave Jane a pointed look. "And he's single."

"Why are you telling *me* that?" Jane asked, as both Sasha and Nancy laughed.

"You've been a little down lately," Sasha said. "I've known Sean since college. He's a super fun guy."

"We don't want to pry," Nancy added. "But we figured maybe you had some uh, man trouble? A breakup or something like that?"

"Something like that," Jane admitted.

"Even if you're not into Sean, you should think about the DJ job," Sasha urged. "I bet it would be a lot of fun."

Jane gave an amused laugh. "I don't really see myself standing behind a DJ console, bopping along to the smash hits of the '80s."

"I do!" Nancy gushed. "Sean was right. You'd totally look the part."

She laughed harder. "Of a DJ? From the '80s? Don't I need a different haircut?"

"Stop putting yourself down," Sasha cut in. "Just open your mind and consider it."

"Okay fine." Jane drained her drink. "I'll consider it." She picked at the remnants of the mixed fry basket they'd ordered to share.

"I think I want one of those mini-plates of mac & cheese," Nancy said. "Does anyone want to join me?"

They stayed for dinner and didn't leave The Mix until after eight. As Jane drove home, she had to admit she felt better. It had been good to get her mind off her problems for a few hours. It had also been nice of Sasha and Nancy to take her out. However, she wondered how Sasha would feel if she knew Liam Burns was the man Jane was having "trouble" with.

She tried to push her thoughts of Liam aside, and hit "play" on the car's cd player. One of her mixes began blaring through the speakers. She adjusted the volume, and listened.

"I *am* good at this," she said aloud. "I mean, for someone who's not a real DJ."

She laughed. The idea of her as *any* kind of DJ, either a real DJ, or a glorified playlist maker, was absurd. Still, she couldn't help but wonder if it might be fun. She had a strange urge to text Liam and ask him what he thought about it.

It was a bad time to text. She was driving. Plus, she and Liam were over. She squashed down the desire to talk to him, and began singing along with the song coming out of the car speakers.

"Oh shit!" She'd forgotten to call a counselor, like she'd promised Bert. She didn't like to break promises, ever, but she especially didn't like to break promises she'd made to Bert.

Bert had been her center of gravity for a long time. Even when he'd moved to the East Coast, nothing about their friendship had fundamentally changed. He was her rock.

But now, for the first time, she wondered if Bert needed a break. Maybe he didn't want to spend the rest of his life being the person who kept her together. Maybe it wasn't fair of her to lay that burden on him indefinitely. She resolved to call and make an appointment with a counselor the next morning. For real, this time.

Jane sat in a downtown counseling office, taking in her surroundings. The counselor, a woman named Maggie Price, was somewhere else in the office suite, getting them both a cup of tea. A total of four counselors worked in the suite. They shared a waiting area, and also, apparently, some sort of kitchen or kitchenette where one could make tea.

Maggie Price's office was small, but she'd managed to cram a sofa, a mini coffee table, a chair, a small desk, and an end table with a lamp into the tiny space. There was a potted plant on the desk. Jane wondered if it was real or fake. She was just about to get up and examine the plant when the counselor returned with two full tea mugs.

"There you are," Maggie said, setting Jane's tea in front of her. "I hope it's still hot enough."

"Thanks for squeezing me in at the last minute."

"Of course!" the counselor replied. She settled in her chair and gave Jane a friendly smile. "So what can I help you with?"

Jane cast her eyes around the small office again, as if the answer to the counselor's question might be found there. Maggie Price had light brown hair that framed her face. She didn't look much older than Jane, but she seemed old enough to impart some sort of valuable wisdom. At least, Jane hoped so. She was in need of a fuckton of valuable wisdom.

"There's no right or wrong answer," Maggie encouraged.

Jane sighed. "I guess, in general, I'm just messed up," she said. "I don't trust myself to pick the right people to be in my life. So I keep them at arms' length." Then she thought of Bert. "Or with some people, I maybe rely on them too much." She looked the counselor in the eye. "I think I need to change that."

Maggie smiled at her again. "Well, that sounds like a productive place to start."

"Great," Jane said. She hoped the counselor was right.

29

"Thanks for showing me the DJ setup," Jane told Sean. He was behind the bar at The Mix, fixing her a complimentary drink.

"It was my pleasure." Sean treated her to his lopsided smile.

Sasha and Nancy had hounded Jane all week, and finally convinced her to talk to Sean about the DJ job. So Jane had driven down to Seattle late Saturday morning to meet with Sean before The Mix opened.

With a flourish, he placed a coffee mug in front of her. It was topped with a dollop of whipped cream. "One Irish coffee. Do you need anything else?"

"No," Jane assured him. "This looks super good."

Sean winked. "Wait until you taste it."

She took a sip of the coffee, and swooned. "It's wonderful."

"Told you," he grinned. "So. I have to ask. Do you think you want the job?"

"I'm not sure," Jane admitted. "It sounds simple

enough. Just make the playlist, then play it, and adjust the levels if I need to?"

"It's mostly that simple," Sean assured her. "Most of the work is assembling the songs ahead of time."

"I don't know," she mused. "I just can't see myself acting like Ms. Fun Times behind the console. I'd probably just stand there like a lump. That can't be a good look for a DJ."

Sean grinned. "Even if you're a lump, you'll still look incredible." He had a direct way of giving compliments that was somehow so wholesome, it couldn't feel offensive.

She smirked. "So would you be hiring me for my playlist-making skills, or for how I look behind the DJ console?"

"Both," Sean said frankly. "But the most important thing really is coming up with a set that gets people out on the floor."

Jane took another sip of her coffee, and pointed to the mug. "Seriously, this is the best Irish coffee I've ever had in my life."

Sean leaned against the bar. "Why don't you try out the DJ gig this Monday night?" When he saw the horrified look on Jane's face, he amended, "Or next Monday, if you need more time. You could do a trial run next Monday, and see how it goes. If it's awful, no hard feelings. We'll still comp you a drink and a meal. But if it works out, you might want the job."

"I could do that," Jane acquiesced. She supposed that deep down, she wanted to see if she could do it. She wouldn't have let Sasha and Nancy talk her into a meeting with Sean if she hadn't actually wanted to give it a try.

The club owner's face stretched into a full grin.

Jane held up her hand. "But if I suck, or if I hate it, then that's it. I'm never doing it again."

"It's a deal." Sean put his hand across the bar. Jane shook it, and an unexpected feeling of excitement fluttered in her stomach.

During the next week, she grew alternately eager and nervous about her upcoming trial run as an 80s DJ. Sasha and Nancy stoked the fire of her anticipation, constantly bringing it up at work. They were both planning to come out to The Mix to support her.

On Wednesday, Jane had another appointment with Maggie Price. She managed to tell the counselor she'd been seeing someone she really liked, but it hadn't worked out because she'd had a hard time trusting him. She left out the fact that it was Liam Burns who she'd been seeing. Still, Maggie made her feel like breaking things off with him was not the end of the world. She'd taken a risk, and then she'd pulled back, and that was all right. There would be other risks to take in the future. She could try again, if she wanted to. She had options.

Jane had no doubt Liam was doing just fine. He had his new job, and his new apartment. And he had Ingrid. Eventually, or even immediately, he would find another potential partner. She was sure that a month, three months, or one year from now, she'd come across a gossipy news piece about his latest love interest.

And that was her frame of mind when she returned home Thursday night. She was beginning to see herself as re-grouping, and preparing to take more risks. Risks that didn't involve Liam Burns.

But then, she got the letter. It was waiting in her

mailbox with a couple bills and some weekly grocery store ads. The envelope was heavy and cream-colored, and her address was written on the front in spiky black script. The return address was a town she'd never heard of in British Columbia, Canada. Instead of a name, above the return address was written simply: "LB."

Jane's heart began to pound. Liam wouldn't have written her a letter. People didn't write letters in the twenty-first century, did they? In fact, had anyone ever sent her a letter in an envelope, other than a Christmas or a birthday card?

She climbed the stairs to her condo in an adrenaline-fueled rush, and pulled out her keys. Her hands shook as she attempted to unlock the door, and she dropped the mail on the ground. She retrieved it, then pushed the door open.

After depositing the mail on the kitchen counter, Jane fished out Liam's letter, taking it with her to the couch. She sat down and stared at its cream-colored surface, as if she could discern what was in it by holding it in her hands. What if he was angry with her? What if the letter itself made *her* angry? Or upset?

She considered throwing it away without reading it. A part of her wanted to. But another part of her was curious, and that part won. She slit the envelope open, tearing it, and pulled out four handwritten sheets on heavy paper. The handwriting was the same spiky black script from the front of the envelope.

Dear Jane,

I'm sitting here in a hotel room in a small town some distance from Vancouver. We've been filming here all week. It's beautiful but very cold. This project is so far everything I'd hoped it would be. Possibly more. So, in that sense, I could not be more happy.

However, I'm troubled by how you and I left things. Maybe you aren't; maybe you said everything you wanted and needed to say. I, however, did not, so I hope you will forgive the imposition of this letter.

(Please also forgive the formal language. It's this over-extravagant paper, as well as the pen I'm using. It doesn't dip in ink but it writes as if it had been dipped in ink. It seems to change the way I use words.)

First, I want to correct something I said. I told you I would not "wait around" for you. That was unfair of me. We haven't known each other more than a month. I had no business giving you any sort of ultimatum. I do know how I feel about you, and I know my schedule. I thought by telling you my feelings, I was being practical. However, I didn't consider your feelings or your comfort level and that was wrong of me. I'm sorry.

You asked if I was frightened to try again after my divorce. Yes, I have been. Believe it or not, I've been cautious ever since. However, the day I met you at the Foundation, I was intrigued. Intrigued, and a bit overcome by lust. The night of the benefit my intrigue (and lust) increased.

You left the benefit early, and I thought: well, that's that. But then, we crossed paths again. And it seemed if there is, in fact, an overarching plan to the universe, then that plan was nudging me in your direction. I loved spending time with you. Fucking, talking, not talking, not fucking. All of it.

I can't begin to understand how your less than fair experiences in life affect you day to day. Last time we spoke, you made it clear you don't want to burden me with your pain or your problems. But I wish you would burden me. No one gets through life without some damage. I have my own damage and my own burdens.

By this time I hope I've learnt a bit about judging character. I've seen you interact with your co-workers, I've seen you stand up for a friend, and I've seen you relate to my daughter. Give me some credit for liking what I see.

So. That's what I wanted to say, and also to tell you that I will leave the door open. I can't close it, because you said you have feelings for me. I can't forget you saying that.

I don't want to crowd you, or harass you if you've decided you have no such feelings, so I'll leave the decision of making contact up to you. I may, however, send a text next time I'm in town. Reply STOP if you want the texts to stop. (That was a joke. But please do reply STOP if that's what you want.)

I told you I wouldn't "wait around" for you because my pride was hurt. But life is too short for face-saving ultimatums.

Regardless of whether we speak again, please take care of yourself, Jane.

Liam

Jane wondered if she would ever stop feeling the need to sob uncontrollably. She put the letter aside, and tried to calm down. Then she picked it up and read it again. Finally, she left the letter on the coffee table, and went to bed.

At five a.m. Friday morning, she decided to call in sick. She sent an email to the General Office Manager and Sasha. Then she went back to sleep. When she got up again a couple hours later, she had a return email from Sasha, telling her to take care of herself.

She made coffee, then left for a walk at the beach. It was a chilly grey day and the wind was blowing. The unpleasant weather meant there were fewer people out walking on the beach path. The relative solitude allowed Jane to be alone with her thoughts. Phrases from Liam's letter kept repeating in her head. *But I wish you would burden me. Give me some credit for liking what I see. Life is too short for face-saving ultimatums.*

At the end of the beach walk, Jane stopped. The water was choppy and grey. In contrast to the turbulence in front of her, her thoughts were strangely clear and calm.

She'd found a way to live that worked: her job, her friendship with Bert, her pleasures—music, coffee, cigarettes, and no-strings sex with Mike. Her life, post-Carl, was something she'd worked hard to build. If it was nothing impressive, it was better than falling apart.

But Liam had burst in and gently dismantled the structure of her carefully constructed life. She was not sure she could put it back exactly the way it had been. She was not sure she wanted to. She was not sure what she wanted, period.

All the damage from the past was simply there. She could feel it, a dark, sore place inside. There was no magic formula for making it disappear. It was a part of her.

But what she saw clearly, as she stared out at the choppy grey water, was that if she did want Liam, she simply needed to tell him.

She spent the rest of the afternoon reading on the couch. When she'd finished her book, she called Bert.

"I feel weird," she said.

"Weird? Why?"

"Liam sent me a letter from BC."

"A letter?" Bert asked.

"A handwritten letter," she confirmed.

"Was it a good letter?"

She closed her eyes. "It was really—nice. Better than nice."

"Spit it out, Jane."

"If I were to try this," she ventured, "with Liam, I can't imagine how—how would I handle all the actor crap? You know. He gets recognized. And all the publicity? That's not my thing."

"For what it's worth," Bert said, "I don't think publicity is *his* thing."

"How do you know that?" she scoffed.

"Because I *looked* for it. I searched all over the damn internet. All I found was a handful of two-minute interviews. Just him talking about a few of his roles. Hardly any tabloid press."

"But what if he gets more famous or something? Like if he does an American movie that makes a lot of money and wins an Oscar...."

Bert's tone was firm. "Then you'll deal with it. Stop making up dumb reasons to keep pushing him away. What's actually bugging you? Get it all out."

Jane stretched out on the couch. "What if he just wants someone convenient? He moved here, and I was available. What if he's into me because it fits his current schedule, or his lifestyle, or whatever? I mean, I'm a receptionist. I'm not even on his level."

"I doubt he needs to settle for the first person who shows interest in him," Bert said. "And give yourself some credit. Yes, you're a receptionist, but there's so much more to you than that. I know that. Maybe he sees that, too."

"Maybe." She was unconvinced.

"Do you need to ruminate on the convenience point some more, or can we move on to the next thing?"

Jane made a face at Bert, even though he couldn't see her. "Okay. The next thing is that he has an ex-wife."

"Yeah I read about that. Where does she live now?"

"She's in L.A."

"And he just moved to Seattle, right?" he pointed out. "Doesn't sound like she'd be in your face much. Look, I understand not wanting to deal with an ex-wife, but most men his age will probably have an ex-somebody. Or even two. What else?"

She sighed. "He doesn't know anything about my family crap. I told him about some of it. But not much."

"Do you know everything about *his* family crap?" Bert asked.

"No. He just told me about his divorce. I figured he doesn't have any family crap."

"Everyone has family crap," he laughed. "Stop thinking you're so special."

"Bert."

"Jane."

"All right," she sighed. She knew Bert was trying to nudge her back toward taking risks. To being the kind of person she'd been before she met Carl. But she feared she'd changed for good.

"Did you set up an appointment with a counselor yet?" Bert asked.

"I did. I've seen her twice, now."

"Is it going well? Sometimes you have to try a few before you find one that fits."

"No, I like her. So far, anyway. I mean, maybe she'll really piss me off next week, but she hasn't yet."

"I'm proud of you, Janey," he said.

She let out a surprised laugh. "Why?"

"Because you're trying to figure shit out. It's a good thing to do."

"Well," she laughed again, but her voice was a little shaky. "Thanks."

30

On the night of her trial run as an '80s DJ, Jane changed her clothes in the bathroom at the Foundation. She'd debated wearing something to work that could double as her DJ outfit. But she'd finally decided she'd rather start the evening with a fresh change of clothes. She'd chosen a sleeveless color block dress with black on the bottom, and dark red on top.

When she met Sasha and Nancy in the lobby, Sasha wolf-whistled. "That is some dress," she marveled. "Another one of your thrift store finds?"

"What else?" Jane asked, as the elevator opened. The three of them got on, and waited as the elevator car dropped down to street level.

"I can't wait to dance," Nancy bubbled. She was brimming with genuine excitement.

"It's a Monday night," Sasha cautioned. "There probably won't be many people out on the floor."

"I don't care," Nancy retorted. "I'm going to dance even if I'm the only person on the floor."

They drove in Jane's car, and after circling The Mix, they

found a place to park on the street. Both Sasha and Nancy lived in the city, so they could get transit or a car home later.

The pace at The Mix was decidedly slow, and Jane was relieved. She didn't relish the idea of making her DJ debut in front of a large crowd.

Sean came over to them right after they'd chosen a table. He reminded Jane about her complimentary meal, and they all ordered dinner. When their food arrived, however, Jane could barely eat. She was nervous, even though she didn't think there'd be many people around to witness her set.

Just after seven-thirty, Sean came to collect her. They'd agreed her set would start at eight and end at eleven, but Sean wanted to give her a quick refresher on using the equipment at the DJ console.

"Good luck Jane!" Nancy cried.

"You're gonna kill it," Sasha promised.

After Sean had finished reacquainting Jane with the DJ equipment, he grinned at her. "You ready?"

She raised her eyebrows high. "As I'll ever be, I suppose." She threw him a shit-eating grin. "I mean, I just have to hit the right buttons. Right? And there aren't *that* many."

Sean gave her a warm, appraising smile. "You'll do great." He inclined his head in the direction of a doorway just behind the DJ area. "I'm going for a quick smoke," he said. "I'll be back by the time you start."

"Can I join you?" Jane asked.

"Sure." Sean held the door open for her, and then they were alone together in the alley behind the building. She asked if she could bum a cigarette. He produced one from his pack, then lit it for her.

"I'm trying to quit," she said, ruefully.

Sean gave a short laugh. "Me too."

While they smoked, he made small talk about the other businesses that opened onto the alley, and some of the weird happenings he'd observed in and around the venue. He was a good storyteller, and he was funny. By the time they went back inside, she was relaxed from the nicotine, but also from laughing with Sean.

Jane glanced out over the empty dance floor, and took her place at the console. Sean nudged her arm with his own, then winked. "Break a leg."

"Thanks." When the clock hit eight, she started her playlist.

Two songs in, she felt completely ridiculous. Not one person was on the floor. From where she was situated, she could see the door to The Mix, so she knew people were entering the venue. But so far, they were staying in the bar and restaurant area.

And where were Sasha and Nancy? They were supposed to be supporting her. She frowned, and folded her arms over her chest. Then, she heard a sound of loud whooping, and Nancy exploded into the room, dragging Sasha with her.

Nancy immediately began getting down to David Bowie's "Modern Love." Jane had hoped that by the time "Modern Love" came around, there would be at least a handful of people on the floor, and that the song itself would draw even more dancers to the room. But there was only Nancy, dancing her heart out, and Sasha, looking a bit self-conscious, but doing her duty as the person who'd pushed Jane to take the DJ gig in the first place.

About halfway through "Modern Love," a few more people ventured in to the room. Slowly, through the next several songs, patrons began to trickle inside, until there were about thirty people on the floor dancing.

When Roxy Music's "More Than This" came up, Jane worried the small crowd would struggle with the transition from previous high energy tracks to Bryan Ferry's more mellow vibe. But it was as if everyone in the room felt what Jane had intended, and they shifted to fit the song's dreamy, mid-tempo energy.

She looked up toward the entrance to the dance space, and saw Sean standing there, watching her. She realized she'd been swaying along to the song, doing her own understated dancing behind the console without knowing it. Sean had a glass in his hand, and he raised it to her in a quick salute. Then he moved away from the doorway, as a few more people paid the cover charge and entered the room.

Sean and his crooked smile were on Jane's mind as she drove home that night. Even though there had never been more than thirty people dancing at the same time, he'd been pleased. He'd said he thought the '80s dance nights had a good chance of taking off, and she'd agreed to take the Monday night DJ job.

She was looking forward to spending more time with Sean. Jane had a hunch he was the kind of person who, like Mike, would be open to a no-strings sex arrangement. He was attractive. Plus, he seemed like a decent guy. Like someone she didn't need to be afraid of. She'd just have to spend more time around him to be sure.

Since he would technically be her boss, one way to know whether he was a decent person would be if he kept a respectful distance, until and unless she signaled that he could cross the line. Her gut feeling was that he would pass the test.

Then she felt like a coward, considering starting something casual with Sean, when Liam's letter was sitting in the top drawer of her dresser. She'd been taking it out and reading it a couple times a week. She missed him, and she still wanted him.

She missed fucking him, of course. But she also missed his dry humor, and the way his eyes lit up whenever he looked at her. She missed the energy he brought to a room, and the way she felt when she was in his presence. She could admit to all that. But she still couldn't bring herself to contact him.

31

February turned into March, and still, Jane did not contact Liam. She continued to read through his letter, and every time she did, she could see the choice in front of her. But she felt paralyzed. She couldn't make a decision. Deciding meant either stepping into the danger of a relationship, or letting Liam go for good, and she didn't feel ready to make either choice.

In mid-March, Bert showed up for his scheduled visit. He and Jane spent time in the San Juan Islands, and Bert took tons of pictures to show Joaquin. They also spent a lot of time cooking together. He only brought up the subject of Liam Burns once, to ask her if she'd responded to his letter yet. She told him she wanted to, but she wasn't ready.

"Do you miss him?" Bert asked, as he stirred a pot of marinara sauce on the stove. The whole kitchen was fragrant with the aroma of it.

Jane was drinking tea, and she set her mug down on the kitchen counter. "Yeah. I miss him. Although it seems kind of nuts to miss somebody I've only known for a month."

"I was pretty sure about Joaquin after three months," Bert offered.

"That's still two whole more months," she pointed out.

He turned away from the stove and faced her. "I've got this theory: you have to take what life gives you before it's over."

"Right," she said. "You told me about that theory before. You developed it when you were overseas, right?"

Bert nodded. "Life goes faster than you think."

"I know you're right," Jane sighed. "But *I* have a theory, too, based on my experience with Carl? My theory is it's a waste of time tying your life to someone like that. Because it takes time to get out. It takes time to get over it. It just eats up all your time. I don't want that."

When Bert didn't answer right away, she added, "I'm talking to my counselor about it."

"Look," he said. "You don't have to have a happy ending for my sake. But if you decide to try things out with Mr. Masterpiece, and it doesn't work, I've got your back. And I'll kick his ass if he hurts you." Bert smiled warmly and spread his hands wide. "But what if it could be good? Then if you don't give it a try, you're keeping yourself from something good. You're letting that motherfucker Carl keep you from something good."

Jane felt tears threatening, and gave Bert a tremulous smile. "I know you're right. But could we stop talking about this now?"

"Of course." He turned back to the marinara sauce, and gave it another stir.

. . .

The day Bert was scheduled to fly back to New York, Jane went to work and left him alone at her place. He was going to get a car to the airport in the early afternoon.

When she returned home that night, she saw Bert had filled her refrigerator with prepped raw vegetables, cubed cooked chicken, and cubed tofu. A large note was taped to one of the refrigerator shelves. "EAT REAL FOOD!"

Jane chuckled. Then, because the food was already prepped, she took the time to make a quick stir fry with the chicken and the vegetables.

While she was eating, her phone alerted her to a text message. She figured it was probably Bert checking in, to see if she'd cooked up the "real" food. Grinning, she reached for the phone. Then her eyes went wide. The text was from Liam.

Hello Jane. Liam here. How are you?

Why was he texting her? She wanted to respond, but hadn't he said he was going to wait for *her* to make contact? She picked up the phone and typed, slowly. She told Liam she was fine, and that she hoped he was doing well, too. He responded:

Good to hear. Are you available for a (very) quick phone call?

She sighed. If he wanted to talk to her, *maybe* he had a good reason. She agreed to the phone call. Seconds later, she saw his number come through, and answered.

He was immediately apologetic. "I don't want to take up your time." Then he hesitated. "Did you receive my letter?"

"Umm." Her heart began to beat faster. "Yes. Yes, I got it. And I uh, I read it."

"Okay, good. You don't need to say anything about it. Like I said in the letter, I'm leaving everything up to you.

That hasn't changed. I'm not calling to badger you. But I did want to tell you I just had a meeting with Caleb, and I've committed to helping out with the salmon benefit in June."

"Oh, all right," Jane's voice softened. "I'm sure Caleb was ecstatic."

"I just wanted to let you know. So it wouldn't catch you by surprise."

"Thanks for telling me."

Liam's tone became abrupt. "Truly, that was all I wanted to say. I'm glad to hear you're well. I'll let you go."

Jane stopped him. "No, wait. How are you, actually? How's the job?"

"I'm still enjoying it immensely."

"And how's Ingrid?"

"She's fantastic. She asked about you." He paused. "I hope you don't mind, but I told her we're good friends who aren't able to see each other too often, because of our schedules. I figured that was the easiest way to explain things to her."

"No, it's all right," Jane said, softly. "Tell her I said 'hello.' I mean, as long as that won't make things too confusing for her."

"I'll tell her," Liam promised. "So is there anything—new—in your life?"

She shifted on the couch. "This might sound weird, but, yeah. I um, started working as a DJ at that bar, The Mix?"

"I remember The Mix." He cleared his throat. "So did you quit working at the Foundation?"

"No," she laughed. "The DJ thing is just on Monday nights. I do a three-hour set of '80s music. It makes it hard to get up on Tuesday morning, but it's a lot of fun. So it's worth it."

"Well that's wonderful. I'm happy for you," Liam said. "Listen, if you ever want to crash at my place on Monday nights when I'm not there, I mean—you're welcome to stay there."

When Jane was quiet, he amended, "I'm sorry. I'm sure that would make you uncomfortable, actually. Forget I mentioned it."

"No, it's okay," she assured him. "I guess I'd need to think about it?"

"All right," Liam sounded relieved. "Just send me a text if you ever want to use the apartment."

"Okay. I'll let you know."

"I'll let you go now," he said. "Thanks for talking to me."

"It was good to hear from you," Jane told him. And she meant it.

"So I'll see you in June. At the salmon benefit?"

"Oh right," she agreed. "Yeah, I guess so. See you then."

As they hung up the phone, she realized that for weeks, she'd been assuming she would never see Liam again. But now, she was going to see him in June, and she couldn't deny that she was looking forward to it.

32

By early April, Jane had been deejaying at The Mix for a month. She loved it, but the late Monday nights and early Tuesday mornings were beginning to wear on her. Finally, she broke down and accepted Liam's offer to use his apartment on Mondays.

He had a key and a parking pass hand-delivered to her at work. When the envelope arrived, she opened it at the receptionist's station. The parking pass was the kind you hung behind your rearview mirror, and the key was electronic. It wasn't a card key, but a strange key shape that was coded to unlock his door.

Ever since their phone conversation, she and Liam had been texting occasionally. They'd been speaking more on the phone, too. It took the sting out of their earlier separation by making it seem less melodramatic. She was fine with that; she figured she'd had enough melodrama in her life already.

. . .

"So," Maggie Price said. "Last session, I suggested checking out a domestic violence support group. Have you had a chance to do that, yet?"

Jane shook her head. "No. Not yet. I'll do it eventually though. It sounds like a great idea." She felt bad, because she had no intention of ever checking out a domestic violence support group. She didn't feel like she had the bandwidth for it. But she wasn't going to admit that to her counselor.

"All right," Maggie said. "Whenever you're ready. Is there anything else you need or want to talk about today? Anything that's on your mind?"

"Maybe," Jane grinned. "I had a kind of breakthrough. Or epiphany, or whatever?"

"Great! Let's hear it."

"I've been wondering why the relationship part of romantic relationships is always so hard for me. And why sex—isn't. And I'm not sure if this is why, but before I left Carl—sex was the one thing he didn't ruin."

"He didn't ruin it," Maggie repeated. "What do you mean?"

"He never hit me during sex. He kept sex separate. Or at least, I got out before he could ruin it."

"I see. So sex with him wasn't violent."

"No. But outside of sex, it got pretty violent."

"That definitely sounds like an important insight," the counselor agreed. "What do you think it means?"

"Maybe that I compartmentalize sex?" Jane guessed.

Maggie made a few notes on her notepad, then looked up. "Even if you compartmentalize sex, if there's violence in the relationship, it's still a violent relationship. Even if the violence isn't technically in the bedroom."

"I know," Jane said. "It's just something weird my brain is doing. It's convinced me sex is safe, and everything else isn't."

The counselor shifted position in her chair, and smiled at Jane. "How's your relationship with Liam going? Are you still exchanging texts? Talking on the phone?"

Jane had recently told the counselor Liam's first name, but she still hadn't divulged that he was Liam Burns, the actor. "We talk on the phone sometimes," she confirmed. "It's not every day, or anything."

"But it's more or less consistent?" the counselor guessed.

"Right," Jane agreed. "I feel like we're finally getting comfortable with each other. Before that, it was just sex. I mean, I was fine with that. He's the one who wanted to make it more." She sighed. "But that goes back to, you know. Me having problems with relationships outside of the sex part."

"Because you're afraid things might get violent outside the bedroom?"

"Well, yeah. Yeah, that's exactly what I'm afraid of."

"How do you feel about getting to know Liam as a person now?" Maggie probed.

Jane thought for a moment. "It's interesting. It makes him feel more familiar to me. I guess that's a good thing. But I also feel like it gives him something to use against me. I know that's messed up."

"What would he use against you?"

Jane looked up. "I don't know if he would *actually* use anything against me. But what I'm *afraid* he'll do is use something I tell him to hurt me, later. Or, I'm afraid he'll use something he tells me about himself to justify his own behavior. I think that's one of the reasons I prefer to keep relationships at the sexual level. Less danger of being manipulated, you know?"

The counselor kept her face blank, but her manner was solicitous. "Given what you've told me about your home life, and your relationship with Carl, I can understand why you'd have that fear. But how about Liam, specifically? Can you think of a way he's manipulated you since you've known him?"

Jane let out a combination laugh and loud sigh. "I don't think I've let him get close enough to manipulate me."

"What about in your sexual relationship? If you feel comfortable discussing it, of course."

She was puzzled. "Are you asking if there was any manipulation going on in our sexual relationship?"

Maggie nodded. "If you're comfortable discussing it. Manipulation can also exist at that level."

Jane was quiet as she considered the question. There was something that had bothered her about sex with Liam, something she'd hardly been able to admit to herself. She looked up at the counselor, and laughed. "If we're talking about sex, I have a kind of embarrassing question to ask you. I'm not sure if it's about manipulation or not, but it's been bugging me."

Maggie Price leaned back in her chair, and opened her arms wide. "Go ahead. I'm listening. I'm not here to judge you. Just tell me whatever you're comfortable telling me."

Jane took a deep breath. "So when me and Liam were together, we did a lot of, you know. Spanking stuff? As in he would spank me. And I know that's a super common sexual kink, but I keep thinking that maybe, for me, there's something fucked up about it?"

"What would be fucked up about it?"

"I'm just wondering, since Carl hit me, and since I like being spanked—does it mean—some part of me likes being abused?" Jane's cheeks burned deep red. Now that the thought was out in the open, she *was* afraid of being judged.

"Okay," said the counselor. "First of all, there's a difference between abuse and a sexual kink. The line might get fuzzy sometimes for certain people, but in essence, sexual kinks and abuse are two fundamentally different things. If you're comfortable, can I ask you a couple questions about your sexual relationship with Liam?"

Jane nodded. "Yes."

"Okay, first, were you aware of your spanking kink before you met Liam? Or is it something you discovered in your relationship with him?"

"I was aware of it before that," she said, slowly. "I didn't always know how to ask, you know, my partners to do it? But I would fantasize about it, so yeah. I was aware of it before I met him."

"Then my next question is, when Liam was spanking you, how did you feel?"

"How did I feel?" Jane repeated.

"Were you scared?"

"No."

"Did you want to get away from him?"

"No."

"So how did you feel?

"Turned on," Jane said, finally. "Excited. And um, really happy that he figured out what I wanted."

"I have another question for you. How did you feel the first time Carl hit you?"

Jane spoke deliberately. "Shocked. And scared. And...ashamed."

"And did you want to get away from him? From Carl, I mean."

"Yes," she said. "I was scared to leave. I felt frozen, but I wanted to run away and never come back."

"So when Carl hit you, you felt fear, shame, and a desire to flee. Is that right?"

Jane nodded.

"And when Liam fulfilled a spanking fantasy you already had, you felt turned on, excited, and happy. Do I have that right?"

"Yes," she affirmed.

"So can you see the difference between the two?"

Jane felt tears fill her eyes. "Yeah, I see the difference."

Maggie Price leaned forward. "How *you* feel is what matters. And you know what? You can change your mind. Anytime. If Liam is spanking you and suddenly you think, 'Hey, this is scary, I don't like this.' You can change your mind. You can tell him to stop. And if he doesn't stop when you ask him to, that's abuse."

"Right," Jane said. "It's the whole 'respecting limits' thing."

"Respecting limits, and the whole respect thing, period," the counselor said. "Your limits, your needs, your desires, your boundaries—all of them are worthy of respect." She leaned back in her chair and gave Jane a friendly smile. "We're almost out of time. Are you going to try to find a domestic violence support group?"

"I'm not sure," she admitted. "I just feel like—it's too much of a time commitment."

"I understand," Maggie nodded, sympathetically. "But sometimes you have to invest some time to get your life back. Tell you what. I'll email you a list of three or four groups, with a little description of each. No pressure to go to any them. But I know it can be hard to figure out where to start."

Jane shrugged one shoulder. "Okay sure. I'll take a look at the list."

33

B ut she didn't look at the list. She meant to, but then one busy week ran into the next, and she never seemed to have time. All at once, it was June. The Foundation's salmon benefit at the end of the month was approaching fast. Work got busy, as the entire staff began to prepare for the benefit.

Jane was feeling excited, but also nervous, about seeing Liam again. They were still texting, and sometimes talking on the phone. Communicating with Liam had somehow become a comfortable part of her daily life. But she knew once she saw him in person, everything would feel different.

When she told Bert about Liam's return, he was annoyingly irreverent.

"Someone's going to get laid," he laughed.

"Not necessarily," she contradicted. "Nothing's been decided about whether we're—if we're even—on that level."

"C'mon Jane. You stay at his place every week. You're

talking to him on the phone. You text each other constantly. It's foreplay."

"Not everything has to be sexual, you know," she said, primly.

Bert laughed. "No, it doesn't have to be, but with you and him, it is. So, when the two of you finally do it again, I expect a text. Something like, 'You were right' or 'You're always right, Bert.' Either one is fine with me."

"Shut up, Bert!"

"Foreplay," he repeated.

It was the third week of June when Liam finally walked into reception at the Foundation. Ingrid was with him. He came over to the receptionist's counter and stopped in front of Jane. He'd had his hair cut in a close cropped style that tamed his dark curls.

Jane hadn't seen him in person since the morning she'd left him at his apartment. Being face to face with him was a definite shock to her system. He looked good, he smelled good, and she knew immediately that she wanted him. At least in the carnal sense.

"Hello Jane." He gave her a wary, yet devastating smile. "You look well."

"Hi Liam. Did I see Ingrid come in with you?"

"Yes, I'm here!" Ingrid called out. She was standing on tiptoe, because she wasn't quite tall enough to see over the receptionist's counter.

"We're just popping in to say a quick hello to Caleb," Liam explained. "I'm coming back for a longer meeting tomorrow."

"On Saturday!" Jane exclaimed. "Typical Caleb, I guess."

"Isn't it?" Liam laughed. He kept his eyes on her.

She remembered her job. "Do you need me to page him for you?"

"He's expecting us. We'll wait."

"Do you need anything to drink? Soda? Coffee? Water?"

"I'd like a diet soda!" Ingrid piped up. Then she added, "Please?"

Jane stood and started for the kitchenette. "Do you want anything?" she asked Liam, as he and Ingrid moved toward the couches in the waiting area.

His eyes gleamed at her. "Just bottled water."

As Jane went for the drinks, she sensed that he was watching her. It made her hips feel fluid as she walked down the hall. When she returned and set the soda in front of Ingrid, the little girl said, "Thank you. I like your dress."

"Thanks Ingrid," Jane smiled at her. "It's good to see you again."

Liam grinned. "I like your dress, too."

She grinned back. "Well, thanks."

Caleb entered the room with his usual aplomb. "Liam! It's so good to see you! We so appreciate you doing this for us, and for the second time! Above and beyond. I truly can't thank you enough."

Liam stood up, tapped Ingrid on the shoulder, and she stood too. "Caleb, this is my daughter, Ingrid."

"Well hello Ingrid! Are you ready to learn about saving our Pacific Northwest salmon?"

"Yes. I'm a vegetarian, by the way."

"Fantastic!" Caleb exclaimed. He made a sweeping gesture with his arm. "Follow me, and we'll get acquainted. Or re-acquainted, in Liam's case. Jane!" Caleb yelled across the room.

"Yes?" she asked.

"Hold all my calls until we're done talking. Straight to voicemail, no exceptions."

Liam turned and flashed Jane a mirthful grin. Then he, Ingrid, and Caleb disappeared down the hall to Caleb's office.

Once they were gone, Jane felt shaky. She'd thought she'd prepared herself to see Liam again. She'd discussed it with Bert, and with her counselor. She'd given herself a few pep talks. But apparently, she still hadn't prepared enough.

When Liam emerged from Caleb's office over an hour later, he came straight over to her.

"Where's Ingrid?" she asked.

"Sasha took her to the ladies' room. Listen Jane, I have a favor to ask. You can absolutely say no."

"Okay?"

He looked apologetic. "When I meet with Caleb tomorrow, I need someone to spend time with Ingrid. Most likely for the whole day. She can't come with me. It would be too long and boring for her. I can hire someone, but I was wondering if you'd be willing to be Ingrid's companion for the day? I'd pay you too, of course."

"You know I don't exactly have a ton of kid experience, right?" she asked.

"I know," he smiled. "But I trust you. Plus, she specifically asked for you."

Jane smirked. "She must have finally decided that she likes me."

"Will you do it?" Liam asked.

She considered for a moment. It was gratifying to know Liam trusted her, even though she was truly out of her element with kids. "I'll do it," she said, finally. "And you don't have to pay me."

"You will? Are you sure? It'll be all day, from morning

until late at night. Caleb wants to go to dinner with a few of the big donors."

Jane waved off his concern. "I'll take Ingrid to the beach in Ballard. And I'll show her the fish ladder. I think I can fill up most of the day."

Ingrid called out, then, from the other side of the room. "Dad!"

Liam turned. "Ready to go, sweetheart?"

"I'm ready. Dad, did you ask her?"

Liam looked quickly at Jane, then back to Ingrid. "Yes. You'll be spending the day with Jane tomorrow."

Jane stood up behind the reception desk. "I'll see you tomorrow Ingrid. Do you have good shoes for walking?"

"I'm sure your mum packed you some walking shoes, right?" Liam said.

Ingrid frowned. "I have sneakers."

"Good enough," Jane assured her.

"I'll text you tonight," Liam said. Then he ushered Ingrid out the door.

Jane showed up to Liam's at nine on Saturday morning. She'd dressed in jeans and a sweater. Even though she had a key, she rang his doorbell. He opened the door with a smile, and stood aside to let her in.

"Good to see you," he said. "Ingrid's massively excited. She's been trying on different pairs of shoes."

"What?" Jane laughed.

He waved her into the living room, where Ingrid had lined up three pairs of shoes on the floor: a pair of rain boots, a pair of Mary Janes, and a pair of sneakers.

"Hi Jane." Ingrid pointed to her shoes. "Which ones do you think I should wear?"

"Hmm." Jane pretended to consider. "Those boots look sturdy."

"Mum said I should pack 'em in case it rains," Ingrid explained.

"I don't think it's going to rain today," Jane said. "So you probably won't need the boots. I'm sure your sneakers are sturdy, too, right?"

Ingrid picked up the red sneakers. She brought them over to Jane, who made a show of inspecting them.

"Oh yeah." She grinned at Ingrid. "These are perfect. And cute, too."

The kid beamed and held the shoes aloft in triumph.

"Why don't you go put your other shoes away, sweetheart," Liam suggested.

As Ingrid gathered up her shoes, Liam ushered Jane in to the kitchen. He reached in his pocket and pulled out his wallet. "I'm going to give you some cash," he said. "Please don't argue. I'm not paying you, but you might need to spend money to keep her entertained, and I don't want it coming out of your own pocket."

Jane accepted a small wad of twenties from Liam and put it in her purse. "Is there anything else I need to know?"

"Just give me a call if anything goes wrong. But I'm sure you'll both be fine. I might be as late as midnight, is that all right?"

Jane shrugged, then grinned. "It's not like I'm going to church in the morning."

"Ingrid goes to bed at nine. And you're going *straight* to bed at nine?" Liam raised his voice, as Ingrid re-entered the room. "You're not going to give Jane any trouble?"

"Yeah Dad." Ingrid looked annoyed. "I'll go to bed on time."

He went over and gave his daughter a quick hug. "I'll see you tomorrow morning sweetheart. Be good for Jane."

Liam gave Jane's shoulder a quick squeeze on his way out the door. She tried to ignore the lingering sensation of his hand. Then she smiled brightly at Ingrid. "Why don't you go get your sneakers on? We have a lot to do today."

It was after ten before they made it out the door. Jane took Ingrid to the Ballard Locks, first. They watched as boats waited their turn to pass through the canal between Puget Sound and Lake Washington. Then, they took the footbridge over the canal to see the fish ladder.

Ingrid had been marginally interested in the boats, but she was enamored with the fish ladder. They stood in the darkened viewing room, where they were below the water's surface, and could watch the fish swimming past a large glass window. From inside, the water had a greenish cast. The fish floated by, wiggling their bodies to maintain their forward momentum.

"Where are they going?" Ingrid asked. Her nose was pressed against the glass of the fish viewing window.

"I think they're going upstream to spawn," Jane replied. "You know, lay their eggs?"

"To make more fish?"

"Right, to make more fish."

"They look very wise," Ingrid said, solemnly.

Jane stifled a laugh, but then, as she watched the salmon moving with watery determination, she could see what Ingrid meant. There did seem to be something wise and even majestic about the fish.

She pointed at the glass. "That's what the benefit is about. That's why your dad is here. For these guys."

"Are they in danger?" Ingrid asked.

"The places where they live are always in danger."

"Their habitat?"

"Right," Jane agreed. She didn't know whether it was impressive for a kid Ingrid's age to know the word "habitat," but regardless, she was impressed.

Ingrid turned away from the fish to look at Jane. "My dad was really excited to come here."

Jane smiled. "Well, he must care about the fish."

"I think he was excited to see you."

"Oh," she faltered. "Well that's, uh, that's...."

"Can we get something to eat now?" Ingrid interrupted. "I'm starving."

Jane drove them to the pizza restaurant where she'd met Liam and Ingrid for dinner so many months earlier. They stuffed themselves on pizza. Then they took a long walk at the beach. They finished the evening by watching the first Harry Potter movie, which Ingrid said she'd already seen "dozens of times."

"Dad's sick of it, but I was hoping you wouldn't mind?" The girl's tone was hopeful. Jane was simply relieved she hadn't had an accident with Liam's kid in her car, and that Ingrid had been so well behaved.

"Sure," Jane told her. "I haven't seen it in a long time. It'll be like new for me."

Ingrid knew the movie well, and repeated most of the lines aloud, acting out the different characters. Jane knew Ingrid wanted to be a writer, but she suspected the kid had also inherited Liam's acting talent. By the end of the movie, she also understood how he could get weary of hearing Harry Potter re-enacted "dozens of times."

At nine, Ingrid did push to stay up late, but when Jane reminded her she'd promised her dad she'd go to bed on time, the kid caved and went to brush her teeth. When Ingrid had settled in bed, Jane went to say goodnight to her.

She stood just outside her bedroom door. "Thanks for hanging out with me today," she said.

Ingrid yawned. "Thanks for showing me the fish ladder."

"Do you want your door open or closed?" Jane asked.

"Could you leave it a little bit open, please?"

"You've got it."

Jane settled in the living room to wait for Liam. She turned off the television, then retrieved a book from her purse.

She was still on the couch, reading, when Liam walked in the door, just after eleven. She turned her head and gave him a brief smile. He came over and stood near the couch.

"Is she asleep?" he asked.

"For the last couple of hours," Jane confirmed.

"Did she give you any trouble?"

"No trouble at all. She was a delightful companion all day."

Liam smirked. "She's not always like that. But I'm glad she was on her best behavior. She really wanted to spend the day with you." He started to sit down next to Jane. Then he stopped himself. "You probably need to get right home."

"No, it's okay," she said. "I can stay for a couple minutes."

Liam sank down on the couch, putting not quite a foot of space between them. She could feel the heat of his body, and a ripple of arousal moved through her. He looked over at her and sighed, then grinned, wearily.

"Did Caleb wear you out?" she guessed.

"In a good way, I suppose. Dinner was lovely, the donors were lovely, but I think I'm already weary of salmon."

"Uh oh," Jane grinned. "The fish ladder was Ingrid's

favorite thing we did today. So you'll probably hear about salmon again first thing tomorrow morning."

Liam put his head in his hands, pantomiming an over-dramatic reaction. Then he shrugged and grinned at Jane. "I'll live."

"Hey," she ventured. "I wanted to say thanks for letting me stay here on Mondays. It helps so much with the DJ job. It's way easier to commute from here Tuesday mornings."

"It's no trouble," Liam assured her. "It's good to know someone's using the place while I'm away." He smiled at her, and something in his eyes made her cheeks flush. "Listen," he said. "Could we call ourselves friends, now? We've been texting for months, you're crashing at my place, my daughter really likes you...."

"Sure." She cut him off, and returned his smile. "We're friends."

"Well, good. I'm glad that's settled."

"Me too." She couldn't look away from him. Suddenly, he reached over, and gently turned her face toward him. Then he kissed her cheek, near her mouth. She felt the scratchiness of his stubble against her skin. Sweet, aching sensations traveled through her body.

He pulled back, and looked her in the eye. "I'm not going to push you."

"Right," Jane managed.

"But I want you to know—I'm still waiting."

"Okay," she said. She hated how paralyzed she felt.

"Is that all right?" he asked.

"It's okay. But, um, I should probably get back home. It's late."

"It is late. Do you want to stay?" he suggested. Then he held up his hands. "As a friend. On the couch. Or with me on the couch."

She shook her head slightly. "I'd actually like to wake up in my own bed tomorrow morning."

"Of course." Liam stood up. "I'll walk you to your car."

In the garage, he thanked her for watching Ingrid. "Could you text me when you get home?" he asked. "Just to say you're all right."

"Yeah," she assured him. "I'll do that."

She got in her car and slammed the door shut. As she started to drive out of the garage, she saw Liam entering the elevator back up to the lobby. He turned around and waved at her as she drove past.

So Liam was still waiting for her. It made her happy to know that he wanted her. But if knowing that made her happy, why couldn't she just be with him? It was like she was trapped in a place where she was unable to go backwards, but also unable to go forwards. She wondered if she would ever break away from that place, or if she would be stuck there for the rest of her life.

34

Jane woke up to her phone ringing. It was Sunday morning, and relatively late, ten a.m., but she was sleepy and groggy. So she was grumpy when she picked up the call.

"Hello?"

"Hey, hello, Jane? It's Carl."

Suddenly, she was wide awake. She pulled herself to a sitting position on the bed, and leaned her back against the wall.

"Hello?" Carl repeated, sounding nervous. "Are you there?"

"Yeah. I'm here."

"I'm sorry to bother you, but I never heard back from you after I—I left you this voicemail a long time ago—and I never heard back. I was wondering if you got it?"

"I got it." She felt like someone else was inhabiting her body and speaking to Carl. She was merely the observer. It was exactly how she'd felt for a long time after leaving him, until Bert's friendship had slowly helped her feel more like herself again. She hated that she was experiencing the same awful, disconnected feeling now. She'd thought that feeling was something she'd left behind her. For good.

"Listen," Carl went on, "I'm sorry, I'm not trying to be pushy, but I just wondered—I wondered if you're okay?"

"I'm fine," she said.

It was silent on both ends of the line for a few moments.

"What do you want?" Jane asked, finally. Her voice was weary, and more afraid than she wanted it to sound.

"I don't want anything."

She waited.

Carl let out a sigh. "I guess—I guess I just wanted to tell you, I mean I wanted you to know that I've changed. I know what I did to you was wrong, and I'm sorry. I'm not the same person I was back then. I'm trying to be a better person."

Listening to his voice, Jane felt a deep heaviness. Like she was being sucked back into the past against her will. But then, from somewhere inside the heaviness, an equally deep feeling of calm began to emerge.

So he was sorry. So, according to him, he'd changed. Even if it was all true, she didn't owe him a thing. She could congratulate him. Or she could hang up on him. She could call the cops. Whatever course of action she decided to take in this moment had nothing to do with Carl. It had to do with her, alone. His behavior did not have to dictate her decisions. For the first time since she'd picked up the phone, she felt present, instead of detached.

She spoke slowly. "I accept your apology."

"Oh Jane. Thank you. That means—that means so much to me. I can't even tell you how much...."

She interrupted. "I'm happy for you if you've changed. I really hope that's true, for your sake. But as far as I'm concerned, I don't want you to ever call me again. And if you do, I'm calling the cops. In fact, if you argue with me right now, I'm calling the cops. Do you understand me?"

There was a short silence on the other end, then Carl took a deep breath. "Yeah. I get it."

"I'm hanging up now. And don't call me again. Ever." She pushed the "end" button on her phone, and rolled over in bed. Then, she began to shake. Next, the sobs came, from deep in her gut. She sobbed until she couldn't wring any more of them out of her body. When she was finally spent, she lay on her back and stared at the ceiling, doing nothing but breathing.

Presently, however, she grew hungry. Not just hungry, but ravenous. And she wanted a cup of coffee in the worst way. So she got up and went in the kitchen to find something for breakfast.

Later that afternoon, Jane stood outside the door of a meeting room at a strip mall. After Carl's call that morning, she'd looked up the domestic violence support groups Maggie Price had sent to her. One of them met on Sunday afternoons. So she'd driven to the meeting.

However, now that she was at the door, she wanted to turn around and leave. But she stopped, and reminded herself why she'd come here. After Carl's call that morning, she'd known she did need to try a support group. At least once. She'd promised herself she would do it. So, she took a deep breath and opened the door.

She was late. The group members were already seated in a circle on folding chairs. There was a coffee pot and a plate of stale-looking cookies set out at the room's entrance, and Jane stopped to help herself.

Maybe this *was* a mistake. She'd only chosen this particular group because it met tonight, and she'd wanted to do this while her urge to go through with it was still strong. But what if this wasn't the right group for her? Besides, the whole thing seemed so cliche. The spare, ugly room. The stale refreshments. The circle of women. It was like a bad movie.

She was about to escape out the door with her paper coffee cup and napkin of cookies when someone from the circle called out to her. "Hello! Are you here for the domestic violence meeting?"

"Yeah," Jane sighed. She walked toward the circle, and saw a couple of empty chairs.

"Go ahead and have a seat," said one of the women. She had long brown hair streaked with grey.

Jane sat in one of the empty chairs, and balanced her cookies on her lap.

"We've already started," the woman apologized. "But if you feel comfortable, maybe you could tell us who you are and why you're here?"

"Sure," she said. "Umm...." She looked around at the circle of faces. Some of them were younger than she was. Some were older. They were all waiting for her to speak. "Umm," she repeated. "I'm Jane and, uh, I guess I'm a domestic violence survivor. And uh—I'm here to get my life back."

"Welcome Jane," chorused all the women. And suddenly, even though she hadn't shared any of her darkest stories, she had a flash of insight. What she'd told the other women was absolutely true. She wanted her life back.

That evening, after the meeting, she pulled Liam's letter out of her dresser drawer and re-read it several times. One line kept hitting her hard: *Life's too short for face-saving ultimatums.*

Since the first time she'd read his letter, she'd known on a gut level that if she wanted him, all she had to do was tell him. He'd confirmed it the night before, at his place, when he'd said he was still waiting for her. She still hadn't been able to give him the green light, though, because she hadn't felt strong enough to allow herself to want him.

Liam was a gamble. There was no way to know for sure if he would be trustworthy for the next several months, the next year, or even longer. But that was going to be true of anyone else she might meet. At some point, she needed to learn to trust herself to handle whatever life situations she chose. And as much as the thing with Carl had sucked, she *had* handled it.

Life was short. Too short for face-saving ultimatums, and too short for cowering in fear. She was still scared, but now she could admit the truth to herself. She wanted Liam. And for the first time, it seemed more dangerous to push him away than to let him in. In fact, she felt that if she didn't give in to the part of herself that wanted him, something vital in her would die.

She didn't want that part of her to die. So she had to tell him how she felt. Soon. Before he had a chance to leave town. Maybe the night of the benefit. Possibly even before. But she *was* going to tell him, face to face, as soon as she could get him alone. She was tired of putting the rest her life on hold.

35

On the night of the salmon benefit, the Foundation closed at noon so everyone could get dressed and prepare for the party. This time, instead of a DJ or a playlist, there was going to be a swing band, and swing dancing for anyone who was brave enough to try. The fundraiser was at an older, stately hotel in downtown Seattle. Some of the Foundation employees and donors had taken rooms at the hotel for the night, but Jane went home to get ready.

Once there, she tore her closet apart. She'd wanted to find a dress that would twirl and swirl if she attempted to swing dance. But the only dress that fit the bill was the cream-white fit and flare she'd worn the night she'd met Mike at The Mix. The same night she'd taken Liam home with her, instead.

She'd also hoped to wear an outfit no one had ever seen her in before. But every dress she had that fit that description was too restrictive for dancing. So in the end, she decided on the fit and flare. She wondered if Liam would remember it.

Tonight, she was going to tell him how she felt about

him. That she wanted him. Her whole body was thrumming with nervousness, but she knew she had to do it. She'd tried to get him alone earlier in the week, but he'd been so busy, it had been impossible.

She'd stayed at his place as usual after her Monday night DJ shift, this time on the couch, since Ingrid was still visiting. Liam had been asleep by the time Jane returned from The Mix, and she left for the Foundation in the morning before he got up, so she hadn't been able to talk to him. The rest of the week hadn't been any better. He'd come over to her receptionist's counter to chat a couple times, but it had never seemed like the right time or place for telling him something so personal. And she didn't want to do it over the phone. Or in a text.

So. It had to be tonight. Before she lost her nerve.

It was a warm summer evening, so she hadn't worn her signature garter belt and stockings. Her legs felt naked as she walked out to her car. She threw a light cardigan in the passenger seat, then got on the road to go back to Seattle. At the hotel, after leaving her car with the valet, she went inside and followed the signs to the ballroom.

This time, the attendees had dressed up for the occasion. Most of the men were in tuxes, or at least suits, and all the women were wearing party dresses. No one was sporting business casual attire, and there were no jeans in sight tonight. Jane found Sasha and Nancy at the bar, and joined them.

"Oh my God, Jane, that dress is so perfect!" Nancy exclaimed.

"You look like you walked out of a time warp," Sasha added. She was wearing a black cocktail dress, and her sleek blond hair framed her face in soft waves.

"Well, you both look glamorous," Jane said magnanimously.

Nancy dropped her voice low. "You're lucky you were late. Caleb was looking for you. I think he wanted you to stand at the door and greet people on their way in."

"It took me a super long time to decide what to wear," Jane explained. It was true, but she was tickled she'd managed to dodge one of Caleb's schemes.

A dark-haired, bearded man joined them and put an arm around Sasha. With her heels on, she was slightly taller than him. She melted into him as he kissed her. Then she turned to Jane.

"Jane, this is my friend, David."

David smiled, and put out his hand for Jane to shake. He had warm eyes and a sweet smile. "Nice to meet you."

"You too," she smiled back. She could tell Sasha was completely taken with him. That was a relief, because she'd worried Sasha might still be secretly carrying a torch for Liam.

A hush came over the room as Caleb made his way to a podium that had been set up in one corner. He welcomed everyone, then began to go through his usual corny spiel. Nancy leaned over and spoke in Jane's ear. "Have you seen Liam yet?"

Jane shook her head, and felt a nervous flutter in her stomach at the same time. *I have to tell him tonight.*

"He looks absolutely delicious," Nancy informed her.

Just then, the room began applauding Caleb's speech, and he stepped away from the podium to welcome Liam. As Liam shook Caleb's hand and took his place in front of the podium, Jane had to agree with Nancy's assessment: he did look delicious. He was wearing a tux, and the formal attire enhanced his dark features. When the welcoming applause had died down, he began to speak.

"I want to thank you all for being here tonight, and I especially want to thank Caleb Williams for inviting me to take part in yet another event with the Hope Project Foundation.

"As you all know, we're here to raise money to restore habitat for a variety of Northwest salmon species, many of whom are listed as endangered species.

"Back in January of this year, I was here to lend my support to a Foundation event that benefitted research for Multiple Sclerosis. It's a cause that's near to my heart, as a dear friend of mine suffers from MS. It was second nature for me to throw my wholehearted support behind that particular cause.

"However, when Caleb first asked me to help with tonight's fundraiser, I will admit I wasn't feeling the plight of the salmon in my bones. I initially agreed to appear based on the strength of the Foundation itself, my previous experience working with Caleb, and all the other wonderful people here at the Hope Project. Recently, however, I've had two experiences that have helped me understand the cause we're all here to support.

"I've been spending the past several months on set in Vancouver B.C., and it was actually there that I first began to gain an understanding of the complex ecosystem that sustains Pacific salmon.

"On my days off, I often explore Vancouver. On one of those days, I took a trip to the Capilano Salmon Hatchery in B.C. It wasn't spawning season, so I didn't see many migrating fish, but I did learn about the salmon and how interwoven they are with myriad other species in the region, including the iconic Orca whale.

"As many of you here know, salmon are an essential part of the food chain, but beyond that, I began to gain a sense of their spiritual significance, especially to the indigenous tribes that have relied on them for centuries. It's not a spirituality I can claim to understand, but I've gained an immense respect for it.

"That was my first experience getting acquainted with the salmon. The second experience is quite recent, and involves my daughter. Recently, a good friend took her to see the fish ladder at your local Hiram N. Chittenden Locks. My daughter was able to view some of the salmon species on their journey back to their spawning grounds. She was absolutely captivated by them.

"She couldn't stop talking about the salmon. But it went beyond the excited chatter of a young person discovering something new. It affected her at the soul level, I think. She's a little different since she witnessed the migrating salmon, and that affects me too. She has an emotional stake in their survival now, and by extension, so do I. I want these miraculous creatures to be here generations from now, when all of us are long gone. Hopefully, our legacy will be that we helped make the survival of the Pacific Northwest salmon a reality.

"So, in closing, I want to say thank you to all of our guests for spending a ridiculous amount of money to be here tonight. It's for a truly worthwhile cause. Please enjoy the buffet, and the swing band, and thank you for indulging me this evening."

Liam stepped away from the podium as the room burst into applause.

Sasha looked over at Jane and raised an eyebrow. "I wonder who took Liam's kid to see the fish ladder?"

Jane shrugged. "That was actually a great speech."

"You should go tell him!" Nancy urged.

"I think I will," Jane said. "Want to come with me?"

Nancy shook her head. "I might talk to him later."

"You should go. You talked to him last time," Sasha said, mildly.

"So did you," Nancy retorted.

Sasha looped her arm through David's. "I don't have anything to say to him tonight."

Jane let out a dramatic sigh. "Well, I'm going to tell him we *all* loved his speech." She left Sasha, David, and Nancy at the bar, and began making her way through the crowd to Liam.

It took her longer than she'd planned. As she made her way to where he appeared to be holding court, she ended up making small talk with other Foundation employees. She wondered why Liam wasn't mingling with the crowd, the way he had at the benefit in January.

When she finally got to him, he raised his eyebrows at her, and held up a discreet finger. He was talking to a balding man who looked as if he'd been stuffed inside his tuxedo. Nevertheless, the man carried himself with supreme confidence. Jane wondered if he was one of the donors.

She hovered near Liam, waiting for him to finish his conversation. Wondering if now would be a good time to tell him how she felt, or if she should wait. Probably, she should wait. Choose a more appropriate time, when they weren't surrounded by so many people. But she was starting to feel like she would burst if she didn't finally say it out loud. *I want you. Let's give this a try. I'm ready.*

After the balding man moved on with a hearty laugh and a handshake, Liam turned his attention to her. "Hello Jane," he said. "You look lovely this evening."

"Thanks." She flushed a little. "So do you. Or I mean, whatever the equivalent is in uh, man terms."

"'Lovely' is fine," he beamed. "Are you enjoying the evening so far?"

"Sure," she said. "Listen, I wanted to tell you how much I loved your speech. We all did. It was—heartfelt."

A woman who was standing near Liam, with her back to him, turned around and took his arm. "It was an amazing speech, wasn't it?" she purred. Her dress, made of a silvery colored silk, clung to her lithe curves. She gave Jane a once over, then looked up at Liam with a possessive smile. "We were all very proud of you, darling."

Jane tried to keep her features composed. It appeared Liam Burns was attending tonight's benefit with a date.

36

"Jane," Liam said, "this is Claudia Castor. Claudia, this is Jane Daniel. She works for the Foundation."

"Oh, how lovely!" Claudia exclaimed. Her voice resonated with money and privilege as she gave Jane a hollow smile. "And what's your role at the Hope Project?"

Jane kept her voice matter-of-fact. "I'm the receptionist." She could hear the live swing band tuning their instruments in the background, and she wished they would start playing.

"Jane also moonlights as a DJ," Liam added.

"How interesting. Jane, that dress you're wearing is so —unique. I have to ask you, where did you get it? And what's that exquisite fabric?"

Jane moved her eyes from Claudia, to Liam, then back to Claudia. Smiling sweetly, she said, "Thank you so much. It's a polyester blend. I got it from Cheap Dresses Are Us? It's my favorite online thrift store."

After a beat of awkward silence, the band began to play. Jane held up her hand. "Sounds like the swing band's swinging. Think I'll go dance. Nice meeting you Claudia!"

She swept herself away from Liam and Claudia and went out to the floor, where she realized most people were dancing in pairs. She didn't have a partner, and she felt lost for a moment. Then Nancy bumped into her.

"How's Liam?" Nancy bubbled. "Did you talk to him?"

Jane rolled her eyes. "Yeah, I talked to him. He's busy with his date."

"Oh!" Nancy's eyes went wide. "Who's his date?"

"Some rich—person."

Nancy cast a furtive glance in Liam's direction, then lowered her voice. "I saw him come in with her."

"Oh, really?" Jane said.

"Don't get mad," Nancy pleaded, "but is something going on?"

"Going on?"

"Yeah. Sasha said she saw you talking to Liam at work, and that it was really—intense. She said she could have sworn something was going on between the two of you."

Jane was about to deny it. To protest it was ridiculous to even think such a thing could be possible. Then she gave a resigned sigh. "Sasha's not wrong."

"Oh my God," Nancy said, staring at Jane. "Oh my *God*."

"Obviously," Jane pointed out, "It's not working."

"Are you okay?" Nancy asked.

"I don't know. Right now I just want to forget about it. And dance, or something."

"I'm always up for that." Nancy surveyed the dancers on the floor. "Everyone's in twos."

Jane gave a short laugh. "We could dance together. You and me, I mean."

"Sure!" Nancy enthused, then warned, "I don't know anything about this kind of dancing."

"Neither do I." Jane laughed again. "We'll make it up as we go!"

They took a few more steps out on the floor, then stood and observed the moves of the dancers around them.

"I'll be the man?" Jane offered.

"I'll be the not man!" Nancy cried out.

They began twirling across the floor together, mimicking the movements of the other dancers. They kept at it until they were both laughing hysterically, and making everyone else around them laugh, too.

When Jane finally excused herself from the dance floor, Nancy picked up a new partner. Jane had a feeling she could have found a new dance partner for herself. She and Nancy had attracted a fair amount of delighted attention. But she wanted a drink.

She found Sasha and David at the bar, whispering to each other while they watched the swing dancers on the floor.

"Good job out there," David smiled, as Jane joined them. "You and Nancy were spectacular."

"I can't keep up with her!" she laughed. She gave her drink order to the bartender.

Sasha slid her eyes in Jane's direction. "What's Liam Burns up to?"

She looked across the room, where Liam was talking with a small group of people. Claudia was still by his side. "Entertaining his guest, I suppose."

Sasha raised an eyebrow. "Yeah, I saw them together. She was hanging on his arm so hard, it looked like he was wearing her. Like an accessory made of skin and silk."

Jane accepted her drink from the bartender and thanked him. "Well," she said, trying to sound jovial. "He's an actor, and he's famous. I'm sure he feels a lot of pressure to—accessorize."

"I'm sure," Sasha echoed. She looked hard at Jane. Jane ignored her, and sipped her drink. If Liam Burns was inclined to "accessorize" with rich socialites, then it was good she'd found out tonight. It was also good she'd found out *before* she did something stupid, like tell him she wanted him.

But, seriously, what the hell was he doing? Why had he told her he was still waiting for her, just days ago, when he was clearly not waiting at all? And how could she have fallen for his bullshit? *I must have wanted to*, she thought to herself. *On some level, maybe I* am *actually ready to move on with my life.*

She tried to tell herself that was the important part. She was ready to move on. That was still true, even if Liam was not who she'd come to believe he was. Her own state of mind and her own health was what she needed to focus on.

But she'd wanted to believe in Liam. He'd won her over, little by little. By seeming to care for her. By not being afraid to declare how he felt about her. And finally, by backing off and not pushing her, by giving her time to come to her own conclusions.

Now though, it seemed it had all been an act. Maybe he'd truly been fond of her. But at the same time, he'd also been carrying on with women like Claudia Castor and God knows who else. She felt stupid for not seeing through him sooner.

"Idiot," she muttered under her breath. She took a large swallow of her drink.

· · ·

Near midnight, she went to the ladies' room to freshen up before she drove home. Many of the guests had already cleared out of the hotel, but there were still people swing dancing on the floor downstairs. Liam had stayed glued to Claudia for most of the night.

As Jane reapplied her makeup in front of the lighted mirror, she tried to talk herself into a more optimistic frame of mind. So fine. Liam was out of the picture. But maybe she would meet someone else. Someone better. And whenever she did meet that person, she'd be prepared. She was actively building a support system, and she wouldn't be alone. She tried to smile confidently at her reflection, but it came out more like a grimace.

The truth was, the situation sucked. After all the work she'd done on herself, and after finally making a decision to take a chance on Liam, to find him here with some other woman *hurt*. No matter how hard she tried, she couldn't happy-talk herself out of her feelings.

Deflated, she left the ladies' room and started down the wide, dramatic stairway to the main level. Just before she reached the bottom of the stairs, she spotted Liam. He was off to the side of the stairway, and his back was to her.

Her heart began to pound. She was flooded with conflicting emotions: desire, anger, and disappointment. She thought about slipping away. He might not even see her. But then, her anger pushed through to the surface, overriding all the other emotions she was feeling. She wasn't going to slink away in defeat. She was going to confront him.

She descended the last few stairs, and went to stand in front of Liam.

His eyebrows went up. "Jane." His voice was low, but the sound of it thundered through her.

"Where's your date?" she asked, trying to ignore her physical reaction to him. "Where's Claudia?"

"In the ballroom. Talking to one of the donors." He spoke casually, as if they were two acquaintances. As if they'd never been together. As if he hadn't, just one week ago, said he was "still waiting for her."

His nonchalance pushed her over the edge.

"You must really think I'm stupid," she hissed, in a low voice. "And maybe I am, because I fell for your entire act." She let out a sarcastic laugh. "I actually believed you. I believed your damn letter. I believed you when you said you were waiting for me. God, I *am* stupid." Her voice began to rise. "I'm so fucking stupid!"

Liam started to speak, but she ignored him and kept talking.

"All this time," she went on, "I thought I was making you put your life on hold because I couldn't make a decision. But I wasn't holding up your life at all, was I? There's Claudia, and who knows who else? Right?

"Jane," Liam said, with urgency.

She lowered her tone, and her voice shook as she spoke. "I was going to tell you I wanted you tonight. Can you believe that? I finally fucking trusted you, and I was going to take this big, stupid risk. Then you show up here with your society girl and her silk dress and her snobby attitude and introduce me to her like it's no big deal." She stared at him. Then repeated, in a bleak voice, "I am so stupid."

Out of nowhere, Claudia appeared at Liam's side. She attached herself to his arm, and gave a tight smile. "What's going on here? A little catch-up session?" She looked up at Liam. "Are we almost ready to leave?"

"Jane," Liam said, ignoring Claudia. "If you would just let me speak for one minute. Even thirty seconds...."

Claudia arranged her face in a bored expression. "It's late, darling. Let her go if she wants to go."

Jane looked from Claudia to Liam with disgust. "I don't need to hear anything he has to say. Have a great night. You two—you *enhance* each other." She turned on her heel and began walking away from them, quickly. She was dimly aware that a small crowd had gathered near the stairwell, and that they'd been watching her little drama with Liam and Claudia.

Well. Fine. Let them watch. Let them judge. She just needed to get the fuck out of here, turn the music up LOUD in her car, and smoke as many cigarettes as she could manage between the hotel and home. She had to forget Liam again. Only this time, it would be for good.

And then, all at once, he was behind her. He took hold of her arm. "Jane, you need to listen to me."

She yanked her arm away and whirled around to face him. "Leave me alone. I don't want to hear it."

"Oh for fuck's sake," he said, exasperated. "You little idiot. Claudia and I aren't seeing each other. I'm not with her. I want you."

She looked up at him, bewildered. "You...what?"

He took her face in his hands, and smiled at her. Not the quick flash smile, but the deep warm smile that made her insides turn to mush. "I'm not with her," he repeated. "I want you."

"Oh," she smiled, weakly. "Well then, I uh. I uh kind of just made an ass of myself, didn't I?"

"A completely glorious ass of yourself," he agreed. Then he pulled in closer, and kissed her.

Right there. In front of the crowd that had gathered to watch. In front of Claudia. Jane melted into him.

When they finally broke apart, the little crowd began to clap. Liam ignored them.

"Did you mean what you said back there?" he asked. "When you were angry? Did you mean it when you said you wanted me?"

Jane smiled at him, feeling almost shy, but also happy and sure of herself. "Yeah," she told him. "Yeah, I meant it."

Liam reached out his hand, and brushed a finger over her cheek. "I'm really glad. I think I might even be ecstatic."

"WELL DON'T MIND ME!" Claudia barged past them. "I'll be fine. I'll get my driver to take me home. He's on the way."

"Have a lovely evening!" Liam called after her. But she was already halfway to the door of the hotel. He turned back to Jane, and they both burst out laughing.

When they'd calmed down, Liam asked, "Did you really think I was serious about Claudia?"

Jane nodded. "Yeah. I mean, she sure seemed pretty serious about you."

Liam made a frustrated noise. "She's just someone Caleb set me up with," he explained. "It was his idea. I couldn't turn him down, because I couldn't ask you to be my date, because I was trying to...."

"You were trying to give me space," Jane finished for him.

"Exactly."

She frowned. "Still. You should have told me you had a date. I mean, after what you said to me at your apartment last week? When you said you were still waiting for me? Seeing you with Claudia was super confusing."

"I should have told you," he agreed. "And I'm truly sorry. But if I'm honest, I was hoping maybe, just maybe— you'd be a tiny bit jealous?"

"Mission accomplished," she admitted, finally. Then she fixed him with a stern look. "But don't do that again."

"I won't," he promised. Then a slow smile began to spread across his face. "So. What now?"

"Do you need a ride home?" she ventured.

His smile seemed to grow wider and deeper. "Only if you come home with me."

She laughed, feeling a sudden, intense happiness.

"Does that reaction mean 'yes?'" he asked.

"Yes," Jane grinned wide. "That's a yes."

37

Liam kept his hand on Jane's waist as they rode the elevator up to his apartment. He was radiating heat, and waves of sensation coursed over her skin. They all but stumbled out of the elevator and in to the hall.

"I feel drunk," she said, as he put his key in the lock.

"That is not how I would describe it," Liam said. The door opened, and he ushered her inside. Jane took her purse off her shoulder and set it down, slowly, on the floor.

In the next moment, they were pressed together, their bodies straining to get closer. Liam ran his hands down the middle of her spine and unzipped her dress. She helped him push it off her shoulders, and it fell to the floor. Then he backed her up against the wall in the hallway, and began kissing her neck, running his hands over her curves. She sighed with happiness.

"I just want to fuck you here," he breathed.

"So do it," she urged.

"No." Then he took her hand and led her to his bedroom.

Once they were there, Jane's confidence faltered.

"You all right?" he asked.

"I'm scared."

"That's okay. What are you thinking?"

"Lots of things." *You're too good to be true. Life is full of people who get a shitty deal. Why should I get something I want?* She felt a shudder go down her spine. Then she stepped as close to him as possible, and put her hands on his chest. "I'm good," she told him. "I'm glad I'm here."

Liam kissed her, a long, sweet kiss that left her knees weak. He reached for the hook at the front of her bra, and unfastened it. Then he slid the straps down her shoulders, and let the garment fall away. He drew her close to him, so her bare breasts flattened against the fabric of his shirt.

"It's a day by day thing," he said, near her ear. "Moment by moment. Yeah?"

She pressed her palms against him, took a step back, and looked up into his eyes. Then she began undoing the buttons on his shirt. Her fingers trembled a little, but she kept at it, until all the buttons were undone. He had gone almost completely still, but his breathing was deep and excited.

Jane slid her hands inside his shirt, and pushed it off his shoulders. He helped her remove it. As she looked back up, she felt a smile spread across her face.

Suddenly Liam grasped her hands, and began waltzing her around the room with exaggerated dance steps, making her laugh.

"We never got to dance tonight," he explained. "I really wanted to dance with you." He took her for a few more turns around the room, then finally danced her over to the bed, where he stopped, and looked at her.

"What do you want?" he asked.

"You mean, umm, sexually?"

His eyes glittered in the dim light. "That's what I mean. Tell me."

Her voice was a bit breathless. "Spank me. Then fuck me."

He backed her all the way to the edge of the bed, and her knees trembled at the look in his eyes. When she felt the mattress pressing against the back of her legs, she sat down.

Liam dropped down on the bed and flipped her over on her stomach. Then he pulled down her underwear and leveled a life-giving slap on her ass. She moaned into the mattress.

"Do you want more?" he asked.

She turned her head so he could hear her. "Yes."

He smacked her ass nine more times, each slap stinging more than the last, each one making her more wet, more desperate to have him inside her. Then she heard him shedding the rest of his clothes. She shook with anticipation.

Liam turned her back over, and she reached for him. He lowered himself on her and kissed her roughly, then slowed down, tasting the inside of her mouth with his tongue.

When he pulled back and looked down at her, she pleaded, "Please just fuck me now."

"So impatient," he teased. But he reached over to the nightstand, and took a condom from inside it. He held her eyes while he unwrapped it and rolled it over his erection. Then he grasped her hips and pushed inside her.

He fucked her with hard, slow strokes, the way she'd learned to like it with him. She felt a new kind of euphoria as she came, something reckless and alive and free. When Liam came, she clung to him, but with a sense of victory, not desperation.

He fell asleep soon after. But Jane was wide awake. She

crept out from underneath the covers and saw there was a new wooden bench at the end of the bed. She knelt and opened it, slowly, hoping it would not make noise and wake Liam. She found a couple blankets inside, and took one. Then she wrapped herself in the blanket and went out to the living room.

She snuggled on the couch and stared through the picture windows at the understated marina lights shining through the dark. A deep, peaceful feeling began to come over her, starting in her chest and spreading through her limbs. She simply felt good, and happy to be here with Liam. Suddenly she grinned, and said, aloud, "You were right, Bert." She would text him in the morning.

"There you are," Liam said.

She turned her head and saw him standing behind her, just above the living room. He was wearing a robe belted at the waist.

"I couldn't sleep," she told him. "Want to join me?"

He took a seat beside her. "Gorgeous view, isn't it?"

"I like it better than a view of downtown," she agreed. "There's something kind of cheerful about boats."

"I like them too," he said. "They're not immovable, like buildings."

"Right. They can go places. Then come back home—if they feel like it."

He reached over and touched her cheek. "You're not trapped, you know. We get to decide how this thing is going to work."

"I'll get you my draft of our relationship bylaws in the next couple of days," Jane quipped.

"Smart-ass."

"That's not going to change," she warned.

He laughed. "I wouldn't change it."

They sat quietly together, watching the winking lights at the marina. Presently, Liam reached for her hand, and held onto it.

Jane took a snapshot of the moment in her mind: her hand interlaced with Liam's while they watched the twinkling marina lights. Just touching him turned her on. She was going to want him again, soon.

Moment by moment. In this moment, she was happy. She could feel the happiness settling in the strange new space behind her heart. She felt alive, and it was enough. For now.

END

ACKNOWLEDGMENTS

Very briefly, I would like to thank Matt Cory for the awesome book cover, and Michelle Meade for the insightful editing assistance. A big hug to my friends who were willing to sign up for my fledgling mailing list, who provide their support on social media, and who encourage me in a million little ways that make all the difference. Finally, a heartfelt thank you to all the writers who have generously shared their own writing journeys on Clubhouse. Your stories have made *doing* this seem actually possible.

ABOUT THE AUTHOR

Ruthie Rayburn writes steamy romance stories with quirky characters. She likes hot ginger drinks, invigorating strolls on the beach, and novels with great dialogue. When she isn't writing, she's probably catching up on General Hospital, or experimenting with new ways to make mac & cheese.

www.ingramcontent.com/pod-product-compliance
Lightning Source LLC
Chambersburg PA
CBHW052033240626
47153CB00006B/2060